A Vicar, Crucified

Also by Simon Parke
Pippa's Progress: A Pilgrim's Journey to Heaven

A Vicar, Crucified

An Abbot Peter Mystery

Simon Parke

DARTON·LONGMAN+TODD

First published in 2013 by
Darton, Longman and Todd Ltd
1 Spencer Court
140 – 142 Wandsworth High Street
London SW18 4JJ

ISBN 978-0-232-52997-5

A catalogue record for this book is available from the British Library

Phototypeset by Kerrypress Ltd, Luton, Bedfordshire.
Printed and bound by Bell & Bain, Glasgow.

To Rowena and Andy,
For so many years now,
always there.

My profound thanks to Elizabeth Spradbery, Clive Williams, Eryl O'Day, Shellie Wright, Anthoulla Kyprianou, Joy Parke and David Moloney – the kind and insightful readers who read the manuscript in various degrees of completion. Sadly, none of you agreed about what needed changing – unanimity always helps the writer; but you all observed and you all made a difference.

My thanks also to the team at DLT …

The murder mystery genre is one I've always longed to explore; and DLT, against all the odds, have given me that opportunity.

Enough.

*'Murder is always a mistake.
One should never do anything that one
cannot talk about after dinner.'*

Oscar Wilde

Act One

'The thing is, Sergeant, I know all people well in a manner. It's a gift I have.'

One

'Crucified?' said the hesitant man in the dressing gown.

'That's the nub of it, Sir.'

'I'm still in my pyjamas, you see.'

At the other end of the telephone line, the police sergeant struggled for a link.

'I mean I've just woken. A rather long night, I'm afraid.'

'On the razz, eh? Tell me about it.'

'A church meeting.'

All thoughts of razz died in the sergeant's mind as old ladies and hard pews came to mind. But he wasn't happy. He wanted to get away and this hesitant man was an irritation.

It should be said that Sergeant Reiss was easily irritated, a man who allowed a wide variety of people to get on his nerves. In this instance, it was the silences at the other end of the phone. Why the silences? Given the news he'd just delivered, Reiss wanted reaction, some hysteria he could then calm with his 'man-of-the-world, seen-it-all-and-then-some' manner. He craved that sense of superiority. Instead, he was offered unnerving pause.

*

For the one in pyjamas, fit for his sixty years on earth, it was early for crucifixion. He'd had no coffee, enjoyed no quiet breathing in rhythm with the waves, been given no time to recover his soul from a restless

3

sleep invaded prematurely by the persistent dring-dring-dring of the phone. At the other end was the flat voice of the local constabulary.

'A vicar has been crucified, Abbot. That's what I'm saying.'

'And you've said it most clearly, my friend. It's just not something you hear every day.' He said this partly out of concern for the sergeant. After all, it was probably his first crucifixion; they can't be common on the south coast. So he was being kind, allowing for some normal human shock. But Reiss didn't want kindness; he wanted man-of-the world superiority over this irritating cleric.

'Some days it's a burglary, other days it's crucifixion, get over it, we have to,' he said.

The Abbot noted the irritation as he noted everything. He'd known within thirty seconds of conversing with Reiss that this unfortunate sergeant suffered low-grade depression and had issues around unacknowledged rage and a poor sense self-worth. Here sadly was someone too brutalised to receive goodness. But now his mind moved on as he wondered whether he knew the victim. It was possible though hardly a given.

'Are you still there?' asked the sergeant.

'Yes, I'm still here, thank you,' came the reply. 'As is the tide.'

For Sergeant Reiss, this was going way too slow. He'd been up all night and was weary to the bone. Admittedly, he'd spent much of the shift eating Jaffa Cakes and reading fishing magazines, but still had room for self-pity. He was the self-pitying sort, born to it, always hard done by, always moaning, always grasping, but never quite given enough in an unfair world. And now he wanted to go home. It was time for a bath and a beer and in such circumstances – and not wishing to sound uncaring because the police are a public service as the inspector often reminded them – a freshly crucified vicar is the last thing you need. Especially when you're then instructed to ring an idiot who imagines silence can somehow advance the conversation.

'You're no doubt familiar with the practice of crucifixion, Sir?' said the sergeant.

'I am,' replied Abbot Peter, who'd spent twenty five years of his life in the deserts of Middle Egypt, responsible for the monastery of St James-the-Less. He hadn't always lived by the sea. 'But permit me a little surprise, Sergeant .'

'The world's a bastard – Sir.' The 'Sir' was a late addition, too late to suggest any respect.

'So it can appear though crucifixion hasn't been much used since Roman times,' observed the Abbot.

'Then it seems to have made a come-back.'

'Where exactly?'

'Last night, in St Michael's Church.'

'St Michael's?'

The Abbot's focus sharpened.

'It's the church by the fish and chip shop.'

'Yes, I know St Michael's, I know it very well.'

*

St Michael's was the parish church of the ancient sea town of Storm-haven. It stood at the top of the cobbled high street with a newsagent, a mini-mart, the chippy, a down-at-heel estate agent and a shop that had opened and closed so many times, in so many guises and under so many owners that Abbot Peter was tired at the mere thought of it. It was currently called 'Hobby Horse' and sold children's toys, but no one anticipated a long stay. Suffice to say that Stormhaven, despite the seagulls and ice cream, was not a retail paradise. The Crown, the town's main hostelry, had been on the brink of extinction for years, returning every so often with a revamped interior, larger TV and a sign saying 'Under new Management'. But as Peter's launderette lady said to him, 'You have to do more than declare "Under New Management" in Stormhaven. You have to wake the dead.'

But no one, it seemed, would be waking this unfortunate vicar.

*

'A crucifixion by the sea,' pondered the Abbot, mainly to himself. 'And surely the first crucifixion ever on the south coast of England.'

He put things in perspective long before he felt them. His friends called him calm, insightful, lethal; his enemies called him distant, isolated and a fraud.

'An untimely death,' said Sergeant Reiss, remembering the phrase from somewhere.

'As all crucifixions are, Sergeant . There's really no good time for nailing a human on wood. I'm with Amnesty International there.'

Reiss wearily clocked another do-gooder, busy with other countries, critical of his own.

The do-gooder then had to ask the question. 'Do you know the identity of the deceased?'

'We do have a name.'

As the sergeant searched, with unnecessary and deliberate delay, Abbot Peter listened to the sea. The answer would make a difference to his day.

'Yes, here we are, the crucified vicar was ... a Reverend Anton Fontaine.'

Silence.

'You knew him well, we understand.'

Abbot Peter allowed the truth in, feeling a little.

'I knew him well in a manner, Sergeant.'

Past tense, knew, when he'd been speaking with Anton not twelve hours ago. Less than twelve hours ago they'd shared words, shared life. I am knowing, I did know, I once knew; time and tide could be most sudden.

'How did you know him?'

'A good question.' Sergeant Reiss dreamed of a straight answer.

'The thing is, Sergeant, I know all people well in a manner. It's a gift I have.'

'I'm sure it is, Sir.'

The new shift was arriving. If Reiss could wind up business with this idiot and effect a quick handover, he'd be home within the hour to his new home in Burgess Hill. He was mocked at the station for choosing a place most famous for its elderly population. But at least no one dropped used condoms in the street, urinated in his garden or smashed in the windows of his Ford Mondeo as they had done in Newhaven. Scum.

'I have very few gifts, of course,' added the Abbot, 'so I notice those I possess.'

Like a giant pretending to be small, a lion claiming to be a fly, it was sometimes best to disappear into the hedgerow of supposed incompetence from where his talents could be more gently revealed. He'd had the words of Emily Dickinson taped to his desk in the desert:

> 'As lightning to the children eased
> With explanation kind
> The truth must dazzle gradually
> Or every man be blind.'

He would play the fool if it helped the moment. But for Reiss, it was time to conclude things.

'The Detective Inspector will be along to see you at about ten, if that's convenient, Sir.' They'd be along at ten even if it wasn't, Reiss wanted to say that. I mean, what was an Abbot doing in Stormhaven anyway? Weren't Abbots child molesters or was that someone else?

'A Detective Inspector?' said the Abbot with genuine enthusiasm. 'I'll have some coffee ready. But why me?'

'You were apparently the last person to see the vicar alive.'

'Well, not quite the last. Someone else must have gazed on him as they banged in the nails. Crucifixion is rarely suicide.'

'We must I think keep an open mind, Sir.' The Abbot was aware there were few minds less open than that of Reiss but he played along.

'Of course, Sergeant, we must all bow to the god of open-mindedness.'

'You're in one of those small houses on the seafront?'

Small. It was the sergeant's passive revenge.

'That's right. The last one before the white cliffs rise up in all their English glory from the sea.'

'Each to their own.'

'It's called Sandy View.'

There was a pause as Abbot Peter surveyed the stony shore outside. It had crossed his mind that he must be one of the few people to retire to the seaside yet find himself surrounded by less sand than in his previous home.

'I'll pass that information on, Sir,' said the policeman.

'And this isn't a joke?'

'What d'you mean?'

'The crucified vicar thing.'

'A joke?'

Reiss nearly swore.

'I suddenly fear a comic outcome with Anton dancing into my front room overcome with the mirth and hilarity of it all. He does that sort of thing and it would make a very poor start to the day.'

'It's unlikely, Sir. His body still hangs in the vestry nailed to the cross on the wall.'

'A good punch line, Sergeant.'

'The Detective Inspector will be with you at ten, Abbot Peter.'

'I'll be waiting.'

'And just to confirm the news, because, well, you do seem to be struggling a little: the Reverend Anton Fontaine, vicar of St Michael's, Stormhaven, has been found in his vestry in a state of crucifixion.'

Two

○

Hell's Mouth, Afghanistan,
Late nineteenth century

They had finally stopped and the man was removing their blindfolds. Blinking in the dying sun, Gurdjieff and Soloviev took in the scene.

'Welcome to Hell's Mouth!' said their guide, happy at last to announce some truly bad news.

Before them was a rope bridge over a deep chasm. Their adventure had finally become dangerous, which was reassuring. For how can there be an adventure without danger?

*

Gurdjieff, the taller of the two travellers, reflected on their journey to this point. Bokhara had been a flea pit and one they were well rid of. Like all who passed through that trading town, the two young adventurers had wished themselves elsewhere.

The city had not always been so. For a brief and exhilarating moment in the tenth century, Bokhara had been the centre of all that was civilised and remarkable. Even the stupid were wise in Bokhara, wise by their geography, so clever and inspiring was the climate of the town. The famous doctor, Avicenna, lived there, author of the remarkable 'Canon of Medicine', which discerned more about the human body than western medicine could manage even 700 years later.

Yet all had been destroyed and all made stupid in 1219, when Genghis Khan's Golden Horde – an inaccurate name – left the lecture halls and art galleries full only of skulls. The bearers of enlightenment were dead and so was Bokhara. Ruled in turn by Iranians and Uzbeks, it was now a Russian toy, made drab and dirty with the neglect of strangers. It was a place to make money but not friends. This was the talk on the street.

Certainly they'd found few friends on arrival. Once their desired destination was known, every door slammed in their face. Two lepers would have been more warmly welcomed. Some told them that no such place existed. Others said the community they sought had moved from the region long ago. Others simply bid them 'Go! Go from my house, go from this city!'

Their most unnerving encounter, however, had been with the thin-fingered man. George Ivanovitch Gurdjieff and his friend Igor Soloviev had been sitting in the market, drinking bitter coffee and looking out for girls. Having been turned down by every guide in the city, they had nowhere to go and nothing to do. A large man had appeared at their table, paid their bill and suggested they go with him and that their search was over. They were intrigued and duly followed.

Leaving the donkeys, sewage and carpet sellers behind, they zig-zagged down alley ways and back streets until quite lost. Gurdjieff suspected they were walking in circles until the large man stopped and ushered them through a dirty door. Once inside, however, they stood in a light and spacious space. Offered a glass of cool lemon, they drank and talked together, joking nervously, the large man having disappeared. Gurdjieff saw the effete décor and loudly declared it to be a disreputable House of Pleasure.

'This is what they're like!' he said.

'You seem to know much about it,' said Soloviev.

They laughed about sex and then noticed the large mural depicting bees collecting honey. Soloviev said he'd like some honey in his lemon, a little tart for his taste. Tart! Then they were laughing about sex again.

It was only after a few minutes that they became aware of a figure sitting quite still in the far corner. He had been there all the time.

'Our travelling friends. Greetings!'

The two looked round to see a small wiry man, smoking an aromatic cigarette. He did not get up and neither did he invite them to sit.

'I have heard so much about you.'

'How?'

'The market place is not a good place for secrets I'm afraid. And you do have a secret?'

Gurdjieff was not intimidated by this polite charade. He stood almost a foot taller than his travelling companion, had led since their school days together and he would lead now.

'It's no secret. We merely seek a guide,' he said.

'A guide?' said the host. 'How intriguing! A guide to where?'

'Is it any of your business?'

'I'm a great believer in the unity of mankind; that we are all facets of the divine oneness. Perhaps I can help you.'

It was a possibility that Gurdjieff had to consider. They had come to the end of their own resources, after all.

'We seek the Sarmoun Brotherhood,' he said. *'We have business there.'*

'The Sarmoun Brotherhood?' came the reply. *'I do not know of them, I'm afraid. Describe them to me.'*

'We believe they have a secret knowledge.'

The thin-fingered man offered a melting smile. He had watery eyes of cold gentleness.

'A secret knowledge, you say? How we would all like a little secret knowledge. Then we could be gods and lord it over others.'

Gurdjieff said: *'Perhaps we seek the knowledge not for power over others but for power over ourselves. Perhaps it is only ourselves we seek to transform.'*

'A good answer, my friend but sadly, all else is bad. You are on a futile journey and a worthless adventure. I do so dislike worthless things.'

He swatted a fly and looked concerned.

'Then we'll try our luck elsewhere,' said Gurdjieff. *'We won't give up.'*

'My only fear is for your good selves,' said the host. *'I would not wish to see you wasting your time.'*

'We seek only the truth,' said Soloviev, surprising himself.

'Seek and you shall find,' said Gurdjieff in support.

'Find and you may be disturbed,' said the thin-fingered man.

'We're ready for that,' said Gurdjieff.

'And are you ready for that?' asked the host, looking directly at Soloviev. *'Are you ready to be disturbed? You would be unusual if you were.'*

Soloviev paused.

'You seem to make everything your business,' said Gurdjieff.

'Of course.'

'But we're a team.'

'Indeed, and much to be applauded – you cling together with admirable determination. But sometimes teams are not all they appear,' said the thin-fingered man. *'There is hidden dissonance in the chemistry, discerned quickly by those with eyes to see.'*

'I too am ready,' said Soloviev quickly.

'Ah, he speaks!' said the man. *'Marvellous. And believe me, I admire your courage despite its close acquaintance with stupidity. Goodbye, my friends. Go and seek the truth! It is an honourable pursuit. I suspect you will not be long in this city.'*

Three

'What strange and disturbing flotsam the tide of life brings to our shore lines,' thought Abbot Peter as he put down the phone.

As far as he knew, of all the world's nations, only Sudan currently employed crucifixion as a method of punishment. But his thoughts were only briefly with the people of Sudan, formerly his neighbours in the desert but never close. Instead of North African reflections, he dressed quickly and opened windows to let the eager sea breeze through. He would make fresh coffee for the Detective Inspector and open the packet of shortcake left over from his birthday tea. This was an unexpected adventure and not one to miss. But should he be feeling more devastated?

Clearly the death of Anton was tragic and shocking and awful and many other newspaper headline words. But tragic and shocking and awful passed through Peter almost unnoticed at times. Life only made sense in the moment which was a brief and unattached affair. To burden it with further significance, with the gradual coming of heaven, led only to hysteria or unhelpful feelings of self-importance.

But while these were his private thoughts, his public persona would play a different game. In public, he would stay with the tragic and shocking and awful as he shook his head in appropriate disbelief.

'A tragedy and a profound shock,' he would say.

He'd even pretend the surprise demanded in the face of murder. People may have been killing each other since the dawn of time yet still it demanded incredulity.

11

'You don't imagine it happening in a place like this!' they'd say.

'Why not?' Peter would wonder.

What sort of a place is it where you don't expect murder? Mars, perhaps, due to the absence of humans. But wherever there are humans, as on Planet Earth of late, murder remains a frequent guest and as surprising as a cloud in November.

'And I mean, of all the people it could happen to!' people would then add, wading deeper into stupidity.

As if one type of person is better suited than another to the random assault of the temporarily insane, which murder always turned out to be.

But what Abbot Peter presently noted was his excitement. He was more excited than shocked and more wondering than incredulous, for while he'd seen much death in his life, and some of it messy, he'd never as yet met a Detective Inspector. And suddenly, despite the seagull cries, he was back in the monastery library.

*

As an Abbot in the desert, it had been his idea for the monastery library to develop its own crime section. 'There's more to life than the theology of St Basil,' he'd say.

And so, east of Cairo, there was now no finer record of murder and deceit than in the monastery of St James-the-Less, even boasting Series 4 of *Columbo* on DVD, though without the requisite screen on which to view it.

'Perhaps you should have been a detective, Abbot,' they'd joke as they washed plates in the pantry after the evening meal.

'When my investigation into the murder of the human soul is over, I may be free for other cases,' he'd say.

It was possible he'd only ever wanted to be a detective and that the role of Abbot was a time-filler before the real thing. But the real thing is what we do, not what we dream of and they'd been good days in the desert wilderness. The desk and chair where he now sat in his small study were the only physical reminders of the place where he'd spent so many years of his life. But what was done was done. Others had made their decisions and he'd exchanged the Sinai Peninsula for a pebble beach on the south coast of England.

It hadn't been his choice, but the surprising gift of a relation he'd never known, in a will he never saw, communicated by a solicitor he never met. He was called Mr Tumbly, which suggested part-time work in children's TV.

'You've been left a house, Sir,' he'd said in a legal manner over the phone.

'A house ?'

'It's not a large house. And there's no garden to speak of.'

'Then I'll need to sell my racehorses.'

There was an awkward pause; it was a joke too early in the relationship.

'A two-up, two-down really, with an extension room at the back that until now has been used to house a remarkable collection of porcelain figurines, dancing.'

A small vision of hell passed through the Abbot's mind.

'And am I, er, expected to maintain the collection?' he asked. So much hung on the question.

'Oh no Sir, no, I'm afraid they've been left to another relation.'

Profound relief flooded his body.

'So without the figurines, now sadly departed, that room could become a study perhaps?' he asked.

'Its usage would be entirely up to you, Sir.'

'Well I can't pretend this isn't exquisite timing, Mr Tumbly. I'm standing in the Egyptian desert, bags packed and nowhere to go.'

'Then I can tell you that you have a home, Sir.'

'Wonderful. It's good to have a home.'

'Indeed, Sir.'

Mr Tumbly probably had a very nice home.

'And would you like to know the country where you'll be living?' asked the solicitor, with his habitual attention to detail.

'Oh yes, that might be helpful.'

'England, Sir.'

'England. Well, why not?'

'On the south coast.'

'The south coast? Tell me it's Brighton. I've always been drawn to that place. Or Lyme Regis, I'd – .'

'Stormhaven, Sir.'

'Stormhaven? Ah. Something of an unknown for me.'

'There are those who like it.'

It was the solicitor's final line that had stayed with him, one of those failed positives, which loudly said, 'But most people think it's the saddest place on earth.'

*

And so here he was: retired, alone and an alien figure in the high street throng in his monk's habit; yet on the bright side, fifty yards from the sea, a friend of the beachcombers and about to meet a real Detective Inspector. Each day had its glory.

Four

Chief Inspector Wonder, balding, ageing, widening, drifting, had heard all the jokes; or at least he hoped he had. There's only one thing worse than hearing a joke against you and that's not hearing a joke against you.

'Chief Inspector Wonder is not one of the Seven,' they'd say. 'In fact the only wonder is how he's got where he has!'

He was familiar with several variations on that theme.

And after one briefing he'd heard two PCs in the corridor.

'Are you all right, Mick? You look ill.'

'Just a bit full of wonder,' came the reply and then they started laughing.

The nickname 'Chinless' was cruel but probably inevitable, strengthened by both its physical and psychological accuracy.

He played the bluff, tough Chief Inspector but still feared knowing what people thought and feared even more the dark mutterings which never reached his ears, conversations hastily aborted on his arrival in the room. He sensed such things in the air and they left him unhelpfully cautious.

'So who will be handling this case, Chief Inspector?'

And now he had the Bishop on the phone demanding answers. A vicar in his area had been crucified, which was pretty damn weird but really, what had it to do with the Bishop? I mean pray about it, send flowers, do *Thought for the Day*, but why ring the Chief Inspector? A murder is a murder and a secular matter from start to finish. He had no time for an interfering cleric right now.

*

He'd be civil to the Bishop. After all, he'd shared council-funded sherry with him in the Town Hall, which didn't denote friendship or anything close but remained a bond of sorts. They'd met and they'd

14

spoken, exchanged pleasantries of one sort or another so politeness now, certainly. But this was still not any Bishop's territory.

'I hope you don't imagine I'm interfering, Richard,' said the Bishop.

Richard? Since when had the Bishop called him Richard?

'Not at all, Stephen, not at all.'

Stephen? He'd never called the Bishop of Lewes, Stephen.

'It's just a very sensitive case, obviously.'

'A complete nightmare for the church, I can see, Bishop. I mean, a naked vicar crucified in the vestry, no one wants that.'

'Naked?'

The Bishop hadn't heard anything about a lack of clothes.

'Oh, didn't I mention that? Yes, it's an image that's going to disturb a lot of church goers and probably titillate everyone else – sadly. I mean, what the *Sussex Silt* will make of it I don't know! '

The Chief Inspector hadn't wanted to mention the press, but knew the *Silt* – a local paper bucking the trend of declining circulations – would just love this story. He also enjoyed the fear he now heard in the Bishop's voice.

'Well, that's just the sort of thing I'm worried about, Richard. We both know what a despicable rag it is.'

'But popular.'

Another twist of the knife.

'It's probably a random killing perpetrated by some drifter,' said the Bishop.

'I doubt that.'

'Attacks on priests are regrettably common, Chief Inspector, usually by the mentally unwell, the homeless, those sorts of people.'

'That may be so, Bishop, and I've handled one or two in my time. But those killings tend to be stabbing or battering, not crucifixions. Crucifixion requires time, planning and supreme confidence. I'd be very surprised if the vicar wasn't killed by one of his flock.'

'A rather large assumption!'

'Common sense.'

'Well, all I ask is that the matter is investigated in an appropriate manner.'

'Oh, you can be sure it will be, Stephen.'

Sensing the battle well won, Wonder was happy to offer familiarity to the loser.

'Investigated by someone aware of the religious sensitivities involved.'

'Of course, Bishop.'

'I mean, there's a fine Christian Detective Inspector near us, a faithful worshipper at the cathedral who could be just the one for the job.'

What was this? The church trying to choose their own detective? He'd be firm:

'I've already appointed the investigating DI, Bishop. They've just arrived from West Sussex on secondment with us.'

'Oh, I see. Sympathetic to our cause, I trust?'

'Ruthless, certainly.'

Five

Age had crept up on Abbot Peter in surreptitious fashion, like a ballet dancer moving silently towards him while he looked the other way.

'You're much too young to be sixty!' people would say with kindness and perhaps truth. But even so, though the spirit is free to dance the body is tied to decay, and he cherished each season that came to his shore, spring time and summer, misty autumn and bleak midwinter when 'frosty wind made moan'. Though last night there must have been another moan on the wind, the cries of Anton to heaven as the nails were hammered home.

Abbot Peter pondered the policeman he'd be meeting. They were all university types these days with more experience of management courses than crime, weren't they? Or was that a cheap stereotype? And how would the banter go? Peter struggled with male banter. He knew a little about cars, particularly the four wheel drives of the desert but cared little for share prices, golf or pornography which could make extended conversation with any man difficult. But on the plus side, Peter listened, which usually sufficed. More than conversation, men seek someone interested in what they have to say, whatever the nonsense, someone to hear them out and sometimes to laugh. Peter could be that man.

And the surly sergeant had been right: Peter had known the vicar well. On arrival from the big sand, he'd been quick to introduce himself to the church and they in turn had taken to him warmly. An Abbot from the desert was something of a trophy for a community struggling amid the cold winds of secular indifference and economic slide. He sat on one or two committees, floated amiably through the Summer Fayre and walked out on sermons only when he could absolutely take no more.

But what did Peter really know of the freshly crucified Anton Fontaine? Well, he was the first black vicar of St Michael's, something of a landmark and had been in the parish for nearly two years.

Previously a curate in London, he'd spent his twenties trying to make it as a dancer or actor but neither had paid the rent. It was then, at the age of twenty-nine, that he felt his calling. As he told Peter:

'I was walking down the street one day when I suddenly thought, "*Why the hell not?*" '

'And that was your calling to the priesthood?' Peter had tried to sound calm.

'I saw this old priest tottering down the road, looking completely out of touch and I thought, "I could do a hell of a lot better than him!" '

Peter wondered if Anton still thought similar things as he walked down the street.

'It was the answer to my frustration,' continued Anton. 'No one was listening to my opinions as an out-of-work actor – but as a priest?'

'So you began to dream of a pulpit.'

'I knew I could sort out people's lives, they just needed some good ideas and I have loads of those. I have ten ideas a minute! So enter Me, stage right! Don't know why I didn't think of it before really.'

Peter had been unconvinced.

'There's a thin line between compulsion and calling,' he'd once said to a novice monk whose disdain for people was nudging him towards the hermit's way. 'They're easily mistaken.'

But then who was Peter to say what constituted a true calling? Thinking 'Why the hell not?' was hardly a Damascus Road experience of light and love but perhaps it's whatever gets you over the line and that did it for Anton. And then again, isn't all talk of a 'calling' rather pompous anyway? Did a priest need more of a calling than a florist, a carpet layer or a second hand car salesman? Isn't every job holy?

Anton had no doubt been helped in the church selection process by the colour of his skin. As a bastion of white middle-England the church needed a few different skin tones in the team photo to boost its fading credibility. So no one had asked any deep or challenging questions in the interviews. After all, deep and challenging questions would appear racist, the new unforgiveable sin. So no one, for instance, had asked Anton why he was terrified by all talk of pain? Peter might have raised that one – it seemed important somehow. Instead, however, the interview panel had all said 'Great!' and now here he was, early thirties, single, charming, shallow and cracking on in Stormhaven. He knew that he wouldn't stay long in this backwater, but while he was here, he'd have some fun. And he'd be listened to!

Anton's first year in the parish had seen a flood of new ventures, salvation by initiatives, but more of them started than completed. He loved a new idea until it became an old one and then he was bored. And if he was careless with people's feelings, then perhaps they should just 'get over it' as he liked to say. 'We'll change this world together!' he'd once said to the Abbot, playfully punching him in the abdomen. It hurt a great deal but what hurt more was the fact that the vicar had barely spoken to him since.

'We must have lunch!' Anton would sometimes declare. Peter would duly offer some dates and then hear nothing back.

Press him on the matter and Peter would tell you Anton was an idealist for the future because he was running from his past. A future fantasy was essential for him, a positive sense of things to come, of everyone moving forward to something better:

'We're moving into better times!' he would often say in church.

But few nodded in agreement.

Mrs Edwina Pipe was not slow to offer an opinion and she had one about the vicar. She was a bitter woman, but she sometimes stumbled upon the truth, and Abbot Peter enjoyed their encounters.

'That vicar's all piss and wind,' she'd once said while arranging the lilies.

Edwina Pipe, in her solid fifties but not beyond a few daring shots of colour in her hair, was a persistent flower arranger at St Michael's. Otherwise, however, she held the church, its members, its rules and probably its God, in deep disdain and was therefore a valuable source for the darker information, the sort that went beyond the acceptable spite of community gossip.

'You do know that Malcolm Flight is mad, don't you?' she once said. 'He stood watching me for an hour the other day without moving! Who knows what's going through that mind? Probably a pervert, I wouldn't be surprised. Nothing surprises me!'

'Nothing surprises me' was Mrs Pipe's hook line, her depressed, self-aggrandizing signature remark; but Abbot Peter reckoned a crucified vicar in her vestry might at least raise an eyebrow.

And if she was uncharitable about Anton, Peter struggled to be more positive, seeing little authentic about him except his fear. He talked about changing the world, as some vicars do. But in Peter's experience, those who insist on changing the world do so only because they can't change themselves.

'The more frustrated we are with ourselves, the more passionately we harass others,' he'd say.

Whatever the truth, things came to a head in the parish and it was only last night that Abbot Peter had chaired a Parish Meeting called by the Bishop to decide on the vicar's future.

It had not been a happy last night on earth for Anton, both trial and execution. It was Stephen, the Bishop of Lewes, who had forced the vote through, much against the Abbot's wishes. Peter had suggested time for reflection. But like one possessed, the Bishop would have none of it; he wanted blood, not reflection.

And this morning, he had it; all over the vestry, apparently.

Six

Like so many Christmas presents, it had simply been waiting for its moment.

So now the murderer took the virgin notebook from the shelf and started to write. The famous, the clever and the enlightened should always record what they do for posterity. This was their thought as they made their first entry in the murder diary.

'My first day as a fugitive from the law. What do we call it, Day One? Strange feeling and who would have thought it? I am now a murderer, one of "those people" and suddenly beyond the pale. It's comical in its way. Well, it is! Others look at me and neither know nor suspect. Why should they? I hardly suspect myself. I'm innocent! There's a sense in which that's true of course.

And really, I'm no different now. A lot of women wrote to the Yorkshire Ripper in prison and many sent him gifts. I read that somewhere. So it's not as if murder makes you suddenly bad in a way that others aren't. The women who sent presents to Peter Sutcliffe knew that, knew he wasn't suddenly bad. Murder is part of normality, I haven't stepped outside any circle.

I'll return here.

It should be all right anyway. I'm still in the circle. It will all blow over, storm in a tea cup.'

Seven

The day before the murder
Tuesday, 16 December

Jennifer Gold was one of those heads who liked to be on the school gate at both the beginning and the end of the day. Here she sensed the undercurrents that swirl beneath the waters in every school community; here she saw people coming in every way possible.

'My Gary says he's being picked on again, Mrs Gold.'

Jodie was a poor excuse for a mother who somehow imagined herself a saint.

'And you believe him?'

'Why wouldn't I believe him? He's a good boy. Not an angel – .'

' – not an angel, no.'

Other teachers referred to him as 'Wasteof' as in 'waste of space', but not all staffroom insight was for sharing.

'But he says he gets picked on,' continued his mother.

'By whom?'

'By, well, I dunno – that's for you to find out.'

'Really?'

'I'm just registering the complaint, that's what I'm doing, standing up for my boy.'

Jennifer drew Jodie Daniels away from the milling crowd. 'Mrs Daniels, Gary is very fortunate not to be excluded at present.'

'Now you're picking on him!'

'Is his father around at the moment?'

'What business is that of yours?'

'He's generally more settled when his dad is around.'

'What exactly are you allegating?'

22

'I want Gary to succeed as much as you do, Mrs Daniels. He has his SATs next year and I don't want him to be dragging the school averages down. But unless he gets his act together he won't make next year, do you understand me?'

'No need to go into one.'

'And it doesn't help – are you listening, Mrs Daniels? – it doesn't help him that you act as his unthinking, unquestioning mouthpiece.'

'I'm his mother for God's sake!'

'Precisely. So act like his mother rather than his teenage sister. I'm on Gary's side, believe me, but I won't be on his side forever. Do you understand? And you won't want to know me when I turn.'

'I can have a word with him, I suppose.'

'That would be a good idea, Mrs Daniels.'

Sadly however, this would not be the last confrontation of the day for Jennifer Gold. Tonight, there was an Extraordinary Parish Meeting that had 'difficult' written all over it. As one of the two church wardens of St Michael's, she'd always been Anton's greatest fan, but knew the forces ranged against him now. At the meeting tonight, the Bishop would be bringing his full armoury and aiming it at both her and the vicar.

*

Bishop Stephen liked his reputation of being firm but fair, even if it was one he'd bestowed upon himself. But the restless Reverend Stevie Wickham was certainly trying his patience.

'Believe me, Stevie, it's not a gender issue,' he said in response to the accusation as they sat together in his study.

'Really, Bishop? I simply don't believe that if I was a man, I'd be sitting here having this conversation.'

'Not true.'

'I can think of at least five local clergy who enjoy a whisky more than I do.'

'Let's not be personal.'

'Probably six.'

'Really!'

'But have any of them been reported for excessive drinking?'

'I can't of course comment on individual cases, Stevie. That would be most inappropriate.'

'I'll take that as a "No". It doesn't happen, you see. In male clergy, it's an endearing trait, in female clergy, it's a problem. Men are loveable rascals, women are sad old soaks.'

'It's my pastoral responsibility to follow up on these things,' countered Bishop Stephen, with an overlay of sincerity. 'The church has a reputation to maintain.'

'And so do you, Bishop, don't you? Of all the people to be lecturing me on alcohol, I'm not sure you're the best choice.'

'Meaning what?'

'Well, I think we all read the story in the *Sussex Silt*.'

'That rag!'

'But often surprisingly true. Like the story it ran after you'd attended an event at the Town Hall involving generous servings of sherry. You apparently staggered out into the night rather worse for wear and got into a confrontation with some teenagers on Brighton sea front.'

'Here we go again. Pure supposition!'

'Several eye witnesses looked on as you challenged them to a fight after they'd apparently laughed at your briefcase.'

'Shall we get back to you now, Stevie?'

'What was the story? Oh yes, you raised your fists like a boxer and were shouting abuse at them, when a member of the public intervened. You then spun round, tried to punch them instead, lost your balance and fell over at which point they saw your purple shirt and said, "Oh my God – it's a Bishop!"'

'I have absolutely no recall of such an incident.'

'Well you wouldn't would you? For so many reasons. But when they called an ambulance, you were sober enough to realise the danger of appearing in some health service records, and so you got up from the pavement and made your escape.'

'As I have said many times in response to these allegations, I have no recollection of the events you've described and if you think unsubstantiated gossip is going to help you –.'

'Three adult witnesses, one of them a solicitor as I recall from the *Silt*. Did you sue the paper?'

'You're low-life, Stevie, and overweight: alcohol and weight issues. What is it with you fat people? Look at yourself, really! Do you really think that's a good witness to Christ in the world?'

There was a tense silence in the room and a short while later the interview was terminated with various warnings. The Bishop hoped he'd made himself clear and it was good that he'd mentioned her weight. Someone needed to say it.

And with one nettle grasped he now anticipated another. The meeting tonight at St Michael's would finally bring an end to the absurd tenure of the attention-seeking Reverend Anton Fontaine. Bishop Stephen was well aware that a clear-out of clergy was necessary in the area and he'd start tonight, whatever obstacles the irritating Abbot Peter put in his way.

*

'So how's Clare today?'

The therapist always started in this way and sometimes she answered and sometimes she just sat and wondered. It wasn't an easy question to answer.

'I don't know.'

'That's OK.'

This was the third time she'd seen this therapist, who was called Jonathan and seemed pleasant enough. She'd never tried therapy before, never even thought about it. But she sat here now because there was a sense that life could be better in some indefinable way and a friend had said therapy was helping her. And it wasn't as if Clare couldn't afford it. The business left to her by her father, and which she had grown, meant that money was not on her particular worry list.

'You haven't asked about my childhood,' she said.

'Do you want to talk about it?'

'Isn't that what you do with therapists? Blame everyone but yourself?'

'If the client wishes to speak about their childhood it can be helpful.'

'Who'd want to talk about their childhood? I want to go forwards not back!'

'So you want to avoid your childhood?'

'I'm not avoiding it. I just don't see the point in going there and digging up old graves. I mean, who really benefits from that?'

'We all rationalise our evasion in different ways.'

Clare sat quietly, feeling dark forces arising then settling. She didn't need this, she wouldn't be back, though who could tell, maybe she would? It just seemed such a long and exhausting walk back to the past.

'I was offered a rather deficient form of parenting,' she said in a matter-of-fact sort of a way.

'How do you mean?'

How did she mean? She wanted to stay in control, no breaking down because what good would that do? She liked to prepare her lines for the therapist but she hadn't prepared these.

'My parents were no doubt fairly average human beings but seriously lacking in the parenting department.'

'OK.'

'And I'm still limping.'

'You feel you're limping?'

'I wouldn't be here if I could walk properly.'

'OK. Most people might look at your life and say that you walk very well.'

'I'm not interested in most people.'

'What are you interested in?'

It was then that Clare remembered the meeting that night. It had been the talk of the parish, of course, but Clare was choosy where she got her gossip from, quality above quantity every time. Anton was a little boy really and not someone Clare could relate to with anything but distance. Yes, he made her laugh sometimes. But was that enough in a vicar? Shouldn't a vicar be more than an entertainments officer? And the way he'd treated the curate, Sally, was hardly acceptable. Perhaps a worse idiot would replace him, but even so, she hoped he'd get the push tonight and she for one would not be sad to see the back of the Reverend Anton Fontaine.

'What are you thinking?' asked Jonathan.

*

'Not a bad day, thank you very much, not a good day but not a bad day,' said Betty as she led Sally, the parish curate, into the small front room of her sheltered housing flat.

'That's good,' said Sally, glad of the warmth on this cold December day.

Betty was one of those church stalwarts who was easy to overlook. In a desperate attempt to make contact with new people, it was tempting for the church to forget those whose resilience had kept the show on the road down the years. And few had been more resilient than Betty Dodd, now in her eighty-sixth year.

'You don't want to worry about Betty!' Anton had said to Sally in one of their weekly meetings. 'She'd keep coming through a plague of locusts! It's the new families we need to visit, the young professionals of Stormhaven. That's where the action is and let's be frank, where the money is. Whatever else the church is, it's a business which needs to wipe its own financial nose.'

But though from a comfortable home, steeped in the mock-Tudor security of the middle-classes, Sally had spent her working life where the money wasn't, with people who struggled to wipe their own financial nose.

'So will you become vicar of St Michael's after being the curate here?' asked Betty.

'It doesn't really work like that,' said Sally, evicting an unwanted crumb from her lap.

'A curacy is a training post after which you go elsewhere.'

'So you make all your mistakes with us and then leave?'

Sally blushed. She didn't see herself as someone who made mistakes. But Betty was neither attacking Sally nor joking. She was simply stating a fact which was how she spoke.

26

'I don't think much of the new vicar,' she said.

'I suppose he's finding his feet,' said Sally, trying to stay loyal.

'Perhaps you should find them before you start.'

It was a fair point.

'They're on the end of your legs, it's not that hard. I've seen seven vicars at St Michael's.'

'Seven?'

'You would have thought there'd be one good one.'

'You seem angry, Betty.'

'You'd be angry if you were me.'

There was something festering with Betty, but Sally decided to let it go. In ten minutes' time, she had to be in Boat Street for a funeral visit. It was not the time to encourage emotional spillage.

'Are you okay for the meeting tonight?' she asked.

But as she left, the bigger concern for Sally was not whether Betty was okay for the evening's gathering but whether she herself was. She knew that vicar/curate relationships were often difficult. Clergy friends were full of nightmare stories. As one curate, stuck with a particularly inadequate vicar, recently said to her, 'How can such a dysfunctional man train anyone? Basil Fawlty would be an improvement.'

But of course her disappointment with Anton went way beyond training. She didn't know what outcome she wished for from this evening; indeed it could be said she didn't know very much at all at present.

*

Malcolm Flight sat in the supermarket canteen, sipping his coffee and reading a biography of the painter Lucien Freud. He was irritated by the writer's style but, having spent all morning on the tills, he was glad to be away from the tense faces in the queue. He was a steady worker but not a fast one, and daily felt the resentment building as each item was passed through the scanner.

'Can you go a little quicker, mate?' they'd say, still two away from being served.

Comments such as that only made Malcolm slow down. Once a university graduate and IT expert, he was now a stubborn supermarket worker. If a customer at the till irritated him he'd put everything down, ring his bell and ask a colleague to find the price of an item, there was always something to query. This could all take a while and from Malcolm's perspective, brought everything to a satisfying standstill. You didn't have much power on the shop floor so moments like these had to be cherished.

Sometimes customers would throw down their shopping and storm out of the shop in frustration at the delay. The manager got angry but it was no skin off Malcolm's nose.

'Here, Malc, what's the capital of Italy?' asked one of his younger colleagues sharing the coffee break and doing a quiz.

'Rome.'

'Sweet!'

Malcolm was familiar with being a resource for quizzes and if it wasn't the Prime Minister of Sweden or the last man to walk on the moon it was his colleagues' problems with their computers.

'So what are you saying, Malcolm? Is my laptop knackered?' He didn't mind. It gave him both a role in the store and a way to relate to people he didn't really understand.

The coffee breaks were the highlight of his day, particularly so recently with things so tense at church. St Michael's had once been his oasis but recent developments had ended all that. Anton had provoked Malcolm into a conflict he genuinely hated. Hopefully after the meeting tonight, he'd no longer be vicar; though whether that would assuage Malcolm's rage was hard to tell.

*

'And now I discover we have a traitor in our midst!'

'I'd appreciate a knock.'

'And I'd appreciate some loyalty!'

The Reverend Anton Fontaine had poked his head round the office door of Ginger Micklewhite, the church youth worker, who swung round menacingly to face the intruder.

'I presume you're going to explain yourself?' said Ginger.

It was a challenge to combat.

Anton started: 'You're a member of the Third Order of Franciscans, I understand, a catholic organisation?'

He attempted a smile throughout the question.

'And?'

'So you don't deny it?'

'Why would I deny it? A catholic conscience is no longer treason in this country.'

'Well, you may not have noticed, Ginger, but this is an Anglican church!' said Anton airily. 'The Roman Catholics are five minutes down the road – and four centuries behind us, ruled by a mad pope!'

'It's a Christian church,' said Ginger. 'That's the only label I'm interested in. Now if you don't mind – .'

'It's just something we should consider.'

'What is?'

'Not everyone loves the Romans as much as you seem to.'

'I'll tell you this once and once only,' said Ginger moving towards him.

'Calm down, Ginger!' said Anton with a chummy squeal. 'We don't need to get heavy!'

Ginger was a large balding man in his forties, with staring eyes and a powerful physical frame. People could find him intimidating; even Mrs Pipe trod carefully around him.

'Just chill out, man!' said Anton, with an 'innocent little me' shrug of his shoulders, but Ginger was going to say his piece:

'Francis of Assisi saved the church in the thirteenth century, saved it single-handedly. He reminded the church what it was about.'

'So what is it about?' said Anton. 'So hard to know sometimes! Especially here at St Michael's – it's like trying to light a fire with wet wood!'

'Unlike the priests of this time, St Francis showed some humility.'

'Really? So what happened to yours?'

A look of intense hostility hit Anton.

'Only joking!' said the vicar, whose routine attacks were always well-sugared. 'Why do you take everything so seriously?'

'The Third Order or Tertiaries,' continued Ginger, 'follow the same Rule of Life as those in the enclosed order but work in the world – I do youth work.'

'For now.'

'What do you mean?'

'I mean you have a job for now – who knows about next week?'

'I think you'd better go. But if you have any problems, Vicar, I suggest you take them up with the Bishop who we'll all be seeing tonight.'

Fear briefly crossed Anton's face.

'Speaking of which, Ginger, I trust I can count on your support?'

'Get out.'

'As if I care anyway!' said Anton, before sweeping out the door.

Eight

Wednesday, 17 December

Abbot Peter walked by the sea, his feet crunching the salty shingle. He had time to kill before the inspector's arrival and liked this unclaimed space with its cormorant cries, brisk wind and early morning carpet of weed and crab. A late convert to the coast, the shore was now home, neither sea nor land, belonging to everyone and no one. The beach was an in-between place, a place of uncertain identity, which needed its own special by-laws. No dogs between May and October and people climbed on the groynes at their own risk. Rusting chains, set in concrete blocks, sat with overturned boats and discarded deck chairs.

The coast was never still, never yesterday, always today, a moving margin round this strange island, an adjustment of wave and stone, wind and rock. Always young and always old, the pebbles beneath his feet were freshly soaked yet 80 million years old, washed from the chalk, tough flinty survivors of this shifting and eroding landscape. He looked across to the beach huts, more recent arrivals on the scene. Peeling Edwardian sentinels of the crashing waves, all stood in line, doors locked for winter yet portents of summer sun. And rising above them all, above beach hut and briny, shingle and shore, the cream white cliffs, an erect expanse of chalk, which two miles on became the famous Beachy Head, the highest chalk sea cliff in Britain. From there, you could look out as far as Dungeness in the east and Selsey Bill in the west. Or you could end it all by jumping the 530 feet onto the rocks and wash below. Beachy Head was one of the most notorious suicide spots in the world and the cliffs of Storm-haven had their stories too. Not everyone who walked up them walked back down again.

But Peter's mind was with the matter in hand. He knew the deceased and knew him well. But more interesting was this: he also knew the killer. He did not yet know their identity but he'd be most surprised if it was not the work of one present at the meeting last night. The chemistry of relationship had been one of savage dissonance. And he'd heard the opening words of the phone call Anton received when everyone else had gone. He had clearly been talking to his killer; and his killer had clearly attended the meeting. The inspector might be interested to hear of that.

So what of last night? With four of the Parochial Council away on a pilgrimage in the Holy Land, including Roger Stills, the other church warden, there had been nine present in the parish room of St Michael's, including Anton and himself. This left seven possible suspects: Ginger Micklewhite, the youth worker; Jennifer Gold, head teacher and church warden; Sally Appleby, the curate; Betty Dodd, long-standing member of the congregation; Malcolm Flight, treasurer, supermarket worker and painter; Clare Magnussen, successful businesswoman and Bishop Stephen, the Bishop of Lewes. One of those had wanted Anton dead. Perhaps they'd all wanted Anton dead, but one had acted with hammer and nails. One of them had stepped beyond acceptable spite.

The Abbot slipped on wet seaweed. Suddenly he was falling, tumbling down a pebble ridge; an ankle turned and his face slammed against hard stone. How quickly things change. Standing then falling, fearless then frightened, living then crucified, so much can change in a day, an hour, a moment. He lay still for a while, gathering his breath. He'd be all right, it was just a fall. He looked with a crab's eye view at the beach huts where the gulls gathered for rest and preening. His lip was bleeding, fresh red blood stained his white handkerchief but not the quantities that this morning stained the vestry. It was time to haul himself up and get back to Sandy View.

An Inspector was coming to call.

Nine

○

This whole adventure had been an accidental affair and started quite by chance.

Digging last spring in the abandoned Armenian city of Ani, Gurdjieff and Soloviev had stumbled upon an exotic discovery. An underground passage led them down some broken steps to a cell of apparent monastic origin. Amid damp stone and torchlight, they discovered a niche in the wall stuffed with parchments of Armenian origin. Confusing numbers jostled with hieroglyphics and the two adventurers thought only of the price these might fetch in the market. Until Gurdjieff, skim reading one of the oldest sheets, noticed a clear reference to the Sarmoun Brotherhood and the city of Bokhara. All ideas of selling were forgotten.

Rumoured to have existed as far back as 2500BC in Babylonia, the Sarmoun Brotherhood was said to possess knowledge of the most secret human mysteries, expressed in a nine-point symbol. If the parchment revealed the whereabouts of this elusive sect, then was it not the most priceless object on earth? Over the following summer, Gurdjieff and Soloviev had travelled slowly across Central Asia to Bokhara, only to be met on arrival by silence or threat.

'I suspect you will not be long in this city,' the thin-fingered man had said as they drank his lemon.

*

After three more days of silence, they'd been on the point of returning west when an old man with no teeth and appalling breath approached them in the market. He made much of the need for discretion and privacy. Having withdrawn to an alleyway by the laundry, he said his name was Mussa and that he would take them to the Sarmouni but that as well as paying him, they must pay also for the services of his son.

'My son will be most helpful,' he said. 'He knows this land like no other.'

'So why cannot he take us instead of you?' asked Gurdjieff.

'He knows the land. But he does not know the donkeys.'

Eager to be on their way, the two young men paid in full and set off from Bokhara. With secrecy still demanded, they left at night to avoid public gaze.

'Where is your son?' Gurdjieff had asked, noticing only the one guide. He remembered the financial arrangements; he always remembered financial arrangements.

'He has gone on ahead to ensure all things are safe. Now hurry, hurry.'

For twelve days they had travelled with the old man who whistled all day long through his scattered teeth. Lying exhausted by brushwood fires beneath big night skies, sleep came easily despite their hunger. The old man said they had not paid for food; had they wanted food, they should have said and it would have been included in the fee. Out of the kindness of his heart, he offered the occasional bleak biscuit and chunk of well-dried fruit, and, in this manner, they travelled until they reached the bridge. For the final two days, he had demanded they wear blind-folds.

'Welcome to Hell's Mouth,' said Mussa, happy at last to announce truly bad news.

Before them was a rope bridge over a deep chasm. The adventure was suddenly dangerous as adventures should be. In his memoirs, Gurdjieff would call it the 'perilous bridge' and not far beyond, they were told, lay the Sarmouni settlement.

'I go no further,' said the old man.

'But you promised to take us to the settlement itself. You can't leave us here!'

'You are not far away. Truly.'

'Truly?'

'It is a short walk only.'

'You have made this walk yourself?'

'Not myself. But my son – he says it is a short walk beyond the chasm.'

'So you will not cross the bridge?'

'I am old and ugly but not yet a fool.'

'Yet you are you a liar.'

'A liar? You call me a liar? My son will defend my honour!'

'He'll have to appear before he does,' said Gurdjieff.

'He went ahead.'

'He blends in well with the scenery.'

'Years of training.'

'The invisible man. Who wouldn't pay well to have the invisible man on their side?'

There was a pause in the conversation by the perilous bridge.

'So you won't kill me?' asked the old man.

'Kill you?'

'You swear on the grave of your grandmother that you will not kill me?'

'We will not kill you.'

'Or hurt me?'

'Or hurt you.'

'This is good and honourable, you are good men and I am a liar. I do not have a son.'

And now laughter broke. Hungry, scared and swindled it was all they had the strength for.

'You laugh because you are better?' asked the old man, suddenly taking offence.

'What?'

'You laugh because you imagine yourselves better than me?'

'No!'

'You think I am the excrement and laugh at me like you are not?'

'You are excrement,' said Gurdjieff, regaining his seriousness quickly. 'You lie, cheat and swindle. You let people down. You're a large pile of it.'

'Laugh at others but weep for yourselves too,' said Mussa. 'You are my brothers in the brown stuff, I think so.'

Soloviev looked uncomfortable.

'We just seek the truth.'

'As once did I, my friend, as once did I.'

'So what happened?'

'You reach a certain age, yes? And then realise you doing big waste of time.'

On leaving, Mussa took his donkeys with him. As he pointed out, they would be no use on the rope bridge. Gurdjieff and Soloviev watched him disappear. His last words had perhaps possessed a kinder edge.

'I lie about many things. This I cannot help, learned from my mother. But I am not Mr Lie when I say the Sarmouni community is nearby.'

Gurdjieff felt the thrill again, the call again. It was time to see what they and this rope bridge were made of.

Ten

Anton had his critics but then everyone has their critics from the Buddha onwards.

*

Arch-critic Mrs Edwina Pipe, flower arranger and occasional hair-colourer, said he changed everything and did nothing.

'You watch, Abbot,' she'd say, as she polished the chalice. 'He only leaves his large vicarage for things which interest him – or for holidays abroad. And have you been inside? The Reverend Stone was here twenty years and couldn't even get his door painted but this one? You wouldn't recognise the place now and all done with the church's money. He has a new power-shower in the old scullery. All that soaping of his body when he should be out visiting. Imagine it!'

Mrs Pipe appeared to be following her own instructions.

*

Everyone agreed, however, that Anton Fontaine had sorted out the parish finances. His first month in the job had been spent neither in the pulpit nor in pastoral care. Rather, he had settled down at his computer and had the time of his life, sorting out the figures. The change was instant, like dark clouds giving way to sun. For the first time in many years at St Michael's, people knew how much money there was in the parish account. This was a particular revelation to the Treasurer. Malcolm Flight had been appointed to the role whilst absent from a meeting and much against his wishes. He was a man who so disliked banks that he refused to have a personal account. He seemed the obvious choice to Anton.

And almost everyone liked Anton on their first encounter. He wasn't stuffy and he made them laugh with his impressions in the pub and his ability to burp at will. He loved hilarity and naughtiness and made jokes about body odour in sermons – which had its own delight after twenty-three years of the depressed Reverend Stone.

Yet like seeping oil on cardboard, unease stained the fabric of parish life. Anton got bored of you very quickly. He now wanted someone new to meet.

*

'Well of course Ginger and the vicar don't get on and never will,' said Mrs Pipe to Abbot Peter one day. (He remembered her hair as being blue that week.)

Ginger Micklewhite, the middle-aged youth worker, had just stormed out of the church in deep fury, after reading a note left by Anton.

'He won't have a boss, that one! Ginger does his own thing and God help you if you get in the way. With him, you start as his enemy and make your careful way from there. But the vicar isn't careful, you see. He isn't careful at all.'

Ginger had been a youth worker in the parish longer than most could remember. Funded by the Local Authority in an arrangement he handled himself, he ran his own show, free of the church's prying eyes. No one knew exactly what he did. By the time Ginger was at his desk, most of the parish were in front of the TV or asleep.

Everyone said he was doing a wonderful work with the young people of the area, but no one knew exactly what it was.

'The vicar wants to flush him out,' said Mrs Pipe. 'I heard them talking in the vestry. Ginger said they must be upfront with each other; he likes to see all your cards on the table.'

'And how did Anton reply?'

'He says: "I don't think you want me snooping around your little empire, Ginger. You might find I close it down!" Well! They weren't the best of words, Abbot!'

*

At a meeting of the Parochial Church Council when Ginger was absent, it was Anton who'd asked the unspoken question:

'Does anyone here actually know what Ginger does? I mean, really?'

Betty Dodd had said that he was very good with the young people but Betty was eighty-six and the fact remained that no one had seen anything of these young people in church, which was where they were meant to be surely?

'They need their own space, their own culture in which to grow,' said Ginger. 'They won't want to sing your songs and you wouldn't want to sing theirs.' And no one argued because they liked their songs and frankly, there was enough conflict in the world and Ginger could be so aggressive.

Certainly Betty Dodd didn't argue. At her age, perhaps she was past arguing. She'd seen off six vicars in her time in Stormhaven, Anton was her seventh, and each had been equally disappointing; seven different disappointments. She was one of life's servants, tucking in behind the leader, there to open up, close up, clear away and wash the toilets. Jennifer said she was loyal to a fault; that she should stand up for herself more. And then came what Edwina Pipe called the 'Bogbrush' affair.

'He called her "Betty Bogbrush",' would you believe? Anton called her "Betty Bogbrush"!'

'To her face?' asked the Abbot.

'Oh no. She'd left the room to go to the toilet but she heard him from the corridor. She was mortified.'

'And Anton? How did he react?'

'Oh, he thought it was all a great laugh.'

'He does like a laugh.'

'Well, she may have lived through two wars but something died in her that day. She never said anything, of course, but then you don't, do you? You just wait.'

'You know a lot,' said Abbot Peter appreciatively as Mrs Pipe continued with the arrangement of dahlias.

'Now of course she reckons that's what everyone quietly thinks. Like the vicar, they smile to her face and laugh at her behind her back. Betty Bogbrush!'

Eleven

○

The Sarkar returned to his cave and washed his bearded face. His physical body was tired but his spiritual body alive to the events of the evening. As their leader, he had today presided over the Ceremony of the Key, an annual enactment of great significance in the Sarmoun community. It was a moving event and one that defined their strange calling in the world.

The community of monks and lay members would wait until the setting of the sun. Under the darkening sky of the Hindu Kush, a procession of men and women holding candles then led the community, intoning a dirge. The Sarkar would greet them and the procession would halt. The ritual then required a dervish to approach him. Arms crossed, and hands on his shoulders, he would kneel before the Sarkar. Upon being handed a large key, the dervish would then make his way to a carved door, set in a large square wooden box. The box itself was a strange and slightly ugly affair, angular, awkward and festooned with flags, swords and maces – the imagery of war, power, coercion and authority. The dervish then placed the key in the ornate lock and slowly turned it.

There was tension in the air. The dirge continued in deep and haunting mantra but the flickering light revealed nervous eyes. Could the key create beauty? Would the miracle happen this year? And then slow change, as the box began to slide apart. Through the guile of clever engineers, pieces of the box rearranged themselves, turning on pivots, mysterious in movement but transforming the scene. What had once been a locked and rectangular structure now became something quite other: a picture of orchards, sailing ships, gardens and birds in flight made from wood and cloth.

For those familiar with the ceremony, it was the visual confirmation of their chosen path. Newcomers, however, needed the allegory explained and the Sarkar's words rarely changed: 'It is based on the idea that all teaching, however good and true, curdles into something unnatural, institutionalised, like the box. It becomes locked in structures that deprive it of air. The key of deep truth wisely spoken transforms the situation. The key of the one we call True Human opens up the real joy and meaning of life.'

It was the purpose of the Sarmoun community to be True Human and store this truth, like bees stored honey. Indeed their name, 'The Sarmouni' meant 'The bees'. And as the bees gathered their nectar from many different flowers, so the Sarmoun community gathered their knowledge from many different sources. It was a truth stored carefully, quietly and with little interest in labels, religious or otherwise. Some accused them of being Christians in disguise or Buddhists or Muslim sectarians; others claimed they harboured even more ancient beliefs from Babylonia. Such gossip was of no interest to the Sarkar, however. Let people say what they wished; it was truth rather than label which mattered. His only responsibility was to ensure the continuing quality of knowledge.

And this knowledge was not to be kept entirely secret. At certain points in history, an emissary would be sent into the world and the truth, like a white dove, released to fly. Had that time now come? The Sarkar would make that decision soon. If truth was unused by those with earthly power, it began to leak away and be lost to the world. Imbalance and disharmony followed. Perhaps the visitor was the man to restore balance and harmony. It was the young man's passion that had impressed him; his refusal to be pushed away by doubting words.

Would he now make it to the settlement? There had apparently been problems with the journey but that was as it should be. Nothing good is gained cheaply. He knew the one called Gurdjieff had at least reached the chasm and the rope bridge but nothing had been heard of him since.

A moth landed on his thin fingers and climbed with difficulty onto his ring. He smiled at the success of the creature's struggle. The omens were good.

Twelve

In preparation for the Detective Inspector's visit, Abbot Peter wiped a small stain from his monk's habit. On leaving the monastery, he'd had no other clothes. The desert doesn't demand a large wardrobe and he'd found it simplest to continue with the same. The alternative was the outrageous choice of the clothes shop, an invention Peter still struggled with. He didn't mind the second glances his habit brought and appreciated the simplicity it offered each day:

'What shall I wear today, Peter?'

'I shall wear what I wore yesterday.'

'Is it fashionable?'

'It covers my nakedness.'

*

He was currently on his knees, not in prayer but cleaning the carpet with dust pan and brush. One day, he would buy a vacuum cleaner but for now his mind was elsewhere. What would the Detective Inspector ask? Would he be treated as a suspect? What did he know that was important? He remembered the look the Bishop gave Jennifer at the end of the meeting and felt deep unease. Would the Detective Inspector wish to know such things or were they best kept to himself? St Augustine called the eye 'the window on the soul' but you could hardly condemn a man for a look, particularly when he was a Bishop.

Abbot Peter would have to be cautious. A man who lives alone can be dangerous when offered brief importance, becoming garrulous, too eager, intoxicated by the attention. And there would be a battle for authority, there always was. He would bestow it upon the Inspector as soon as he arrived, this was his way, bestow authority on the other from the off and then take it back slowly but steadily as time went by. In his arrogance, Abbot Peter worked for no one and bowed only to the exceptional.

And perhaps on reflection, as Peter rose from the floor with a well-filled dustpan, the Bishop and Jennifer deserved each other. Both displayed more weaponry than grace. Jennifer was the VWCW –Very Wonderful Church Warden. Head of the local primary school, she still found time to be Church Warden at St Michael's. People said of her, 'I don't know how she does it!' She'd been particularly wonderful during the *interregnum*. It literally means 'between reigns' and describes the time in a church's life between one vicar leaving and another arriving. In most businesses, leaders are quickly exchanged, with new feet promptly placed under the desk. Not so in the Church of England. The interregnum at St Michael's lasted almost a year during which time legal responsibility for the church fell on the shoulders of the church wardens. And the church wardens were the wonderful Jennifer and the vague Roger Stills, presently on pilgrimage in the Holy Land's West Bank; and if his approach to St Michael's was anything to go by, probably much exercised there by issues of health and safety.

Anton Fontaine had been the only applicant for the post; the only priest to respond to the advertisement in the *Church Times*. He had also been Jennifer's appointment. The Bishop was known to have had reservations as did some members of the parish, if Edwina Pipe was to be believed.

'The fact is,' said Mrs Pipe as she removed the altar frontal and lowered her voice, 'not everyone in Stormhaven wanted a black priest. It wasn't racial or anything.'

'Well, it was racial,' corrected Abbot Peter.

'It was racial, yes,' agreed Mrs Pipe. 'But fair's fair, you had to ask the question: what could a black priest from London, who did dancing and the like, know about an English seaside town?'

'What do you need to know?' Peter had asked, wondering if Mrs Pipe placed him in the same category. After all, what does an Abbot from the desert know about an English seaside town? But she'd ignored him and carried on: 'It was Jennifer who thought him the right appointment and though the Bishop could have overruled, he chose not to. It was almost like she had something on him!'

'Perhaps the Bishop didn't wish to appear racially prejudiced,' said Abbot Peter. 'It's a pie easily thrown and one hard to clear up.'

Mrs Pipe attacked a stain with terrible force.

'Though in my experience,' added the Abbot, 'a decision without some prejudice or other is a rare thing indeed.'

'But then of course Sally arrived,' said Mrs Pipe, letting the stain be. 'So all unease was forgotten.'

'She was wonderful – and reassuringly white?'

'It's Sally who runs the parish.'

Sally was the curate at Michael's. She'd come to the parish after four years as a social worker. An excellent curate who everyone hoped would one day make someone an excellent ... wife. People still thought like that in some seaside towns and, despite coming from Marlborough in land-locked Wiltshire, so did Sally, in a way. It was not public knowledge, but she was not unacquainted with dating sites.

'Just testing the water!' she'd say. 'Nothing serious or anything! It's just a laugh.'

Her most practical gift was remembering everyone's name. She remembered adults' names, children's names, even the names of goldfish and distant relatives in photos on the mantelpiece. 'And how's Gerald getting along,' she would ask Betty, having seen a photo of her great-nephew six months ago on his farm in the Australian outback. No one had asked about Gerald before; no one had even noticed the picture. Betty decided then and there that she would leave everything to Sally.

The children of Stormhaven also loved Sally. She visited their school and made dull lessons fun. One child spoke for many in a 'Parish questionnaire' when she said: 'Sally makes me feel really special.'

Some wished she was their mother. Sally would say: 'You have a very good mother of your own!' even though she didn't believe it.

Less public was the fact that Anton and Sally had shared a brief liaison. How do you describe these things? Mrs Pipe knew because she'd seen them in the vestry when they thought themselves alone. And so Abbot Peter knew because Mrs Pipe had to tell someone and this strange man in a habit was quietly reassuring and the most absorbent of listeners.

'Locked away together in all that close confiding,' said Mrs Pipe. 'I mean, what else can you expect? It must happen all the time. They were certainly close when I saw them! You couldn't fit a song sheet between them let alone a hymn book.'

Some said it was the reason the Bishop opposed the appointment of Anton. They claimed he feared Anton could not be trusted with his young protégé. Sally would go far. But he didn't want her going too far with the Reverend Fontaine and thereby messing things up for her-self. The Bishop had a paternal eye out for Sally.

And Mrs Pipe was right. The relationship between the two had emerged in the steady practice of professional contact. What exactly it became was not clear. Playful flirting? Excited friendship? Spilling desire? Whatever the answer, the relationship turned out to mean more to curate than vicar. Anton pulled back leaving Sally distraught, and subsequent hours on her knees availed little. And the pain overwhelmed her at the most awkward of times. She'd recently walked out of a wedding she was conducting. Sensing the approach of tears, she claimed her contact lenses were playing up and made for the vestry. She returned a few minutes later, red-eyed but in control.

Sally was aware of her error but then she'd had to know. Her mistake had occurred after Evening Prayer. She'd shared a kiss or two with Anton in the vestry. Sally had then pulled away and asked the question:

'We need to know where we're going with this, Anton. Are you thinking of marriage?'

'You are joking!' he'd said.

*

It takes a murder to make you realise how much you know, thought Abbot Peter as he laid out the shortbread on a plate bought in the charity shop. He could read the paper; the boy had just dropped it on his door step. But with the Detective Inspector due any moment, it made sense to reflect further on last night's meeting. Other people and incidents now came to mind.

Take Malcolm Flight, for instance, the Treasurer who seemed to treasure very little. He worked in the supermarket by day and spent the rest of his life painting in the church. Mrs Pipe called him 'The Ghost'.

'I call him "The Ghost",' she said. 'There I was, sitting in the church all on my ownsome, when suddenly from behind the pillar, this figure appears! Well – I fair jumped out of my seat in terror! That's why I call him "The Ghost". You never know where he is. And you never hear him, he just appears.'

Malcolm had fallen out with Anton when the vicar removed his triptych from the church. Malcolm felt this three-window portrayal of the crucifixion of Christ to be his best work. Anton said it was gloomy and depressing and put it in storage: 'People do not come to church to hear depressing tales,' he told Malcolm. 'They've got enough of those at home! We all know you like the dark places, Malcolm, but in that, as in most things, you're a freak! No offence.'

Anton would not have noticed Malcolm's rage and it was unlikely Malcolm noticed it either, not being someone who knew how he felt. He did occasionally explode like a latter-day Vesuvius, when the hot lava inside him forced its way to the surface and then everyone ducked. The last occurrence had been in the supermarket when a colleague had taken his freezer gloves for the second time that day.

'You'll give them back to me!' screamed Malcolm, when they met in the meat aisle, bringing the calm retail operation to a dramatic standstill for a moment.

'It's OK, mate,' said the glove thief, shocked by the force of reaction. 'Here they are, all right, I won't take them again.'

'I've never seen him like it,' he later told Eva on the tills. 'Like a flaming volcano!'

But while that was nine months ago, with a verbal warning from the manager attached, Malcolm's feelings for Clare were more present. Clare Magnussen ran a van rental business and sometimes played the keyboard in church. (The old organ had been broken a while and no one was working too hard to repair it.) In business, Clare was hard, efficient and cool. In church, she was reliable and distant, restricting herself to particular company.

'He's so low-life,' she sometimes said, explaining her dislike of someone. There were a large number of 'untouchables' as far as Clare, who operated her own unofficial 'caste' system, was concerned.

She was rumoured to be worth over a million pounds, not common in Stormhaven. But she spoke little of her money. She had money, it was hers, she'd worked for it and frankly, it was no one else's business. Anton, however, had imagined it his and jokily suggested she give more of it to the church.

'Your vans are loaded and so are you!' he'd said. 'So why don't you make a large delivery here, you old miser! We need the cash!'

He'd also suggested a cosy trip to the cinema, just before the evening meeting, which Peter had overheard.

'I'm not just a vicar,' he'd said. 'And you're not just a very successful business lady. Does the ice queen ever thaw a little?'

Clare had been shocked. It was her shoulder Sally had cried on in the face of Anton's rejection. Now the busy vicar was moving in so quickly on her, Clare was disgusted – if a little flattered.

But you couldn't treat people like that. He would have to learn.

Thirteen

❂

The first step is the hardest, for the first step is the choice, and all else, mere continuation. The decision is taken, the tone set and the feet follow. Certainly Gurdjieff hoped they would, as he allowed his weight and balance to leave the rock edge. Between him and the beckoning void below was nothing more than an untested old rope bridge.

Was this the only way to the Sarmoun Community? He'd no idea and the only one who did was now gone. He did not waste time in reflection, however; circumstances had their own logic. If the Sarmoun Community wished to stay hidden, they would hardly build wide highways to their door. Make truth difficult. No, impossible!

The other reality to consider as he stepped into the void was his solitude. Soloviev had also left him, unconvinced of the continuing wisdom of their journey.

'Are we not brothers in the love of truth?' Gurdjieff had asked on hearing Sol's doubts.

'There are limits to my love of truth, George Ivanovitch,' said Sol. 'I do not want to die seeking it.'

'You die by not seeking it. Is it a half-life you wish for?'

'I'll do my best. I'll make my way, do normal things like marry, have children and perhaps discover more in my waking than you will from the grave.'

'Without truth, there is no waking,' replied Gurdijieff . 'You know these things. That is why you came here.'

'And the Sarmouni will tell us all, I suppose? Everything there is to know – it is written somewhere? A stranger comes to their door, is taken inside and told all things? I don't think so, George Ivanovitch.'

'Once you believed in such knowledge, Sol. Once you believed in the existence of the secret symbol.'

'The journey here,' said Sol, 'it's given me time to think; there is little else to do on the back of an ass. And my question is this: what can any symbol reveal which you and I do not already know? I am thinking that perhaps I am the ass.'

They had both looked at the rope bridge, stretched across the darkness.

'So it's not fear that has brought this change of mind, Sol? Not the deep chasm which makes you a sudden convert to sleep?'

Gurdjieff knew it was finished. They'd had many adventures together; he'd led and Sol followed. But now his companion was keen to be gone, the friendship spent. They'd watched the skyline dim as their old guide disappeared into the distance. Soon it would be nightfall in the mountains.

'I understand, my friend. You must be on your way,' said Gurdjieff.

'I must be on my way, yes.'

'Then you live well and I will die well!'

They clasped each other firmly as they had done many times before. They both then turned, one toward the Silk Road and Bokhara and the other towards the chasm and the mystery beyond.

Neither looked back and George Ivanovitch Gurdjieff now crossed the bridge alone.

Fourteen

The night of the murder,
Tuesday, 16 December

The Bishop had opened the Extraordinary Parish Meeting. A large Episcopal cross dangled in dark wood over his purple shirt. As he always explained, it was from Africa, carved for him by some saint in poverty.

'It's his authenticity card,' Anton would say. 'Mention Africa and suddenly you're compassionate, real, uber-spiritual.'

The Bishop's black shoes were shiny and his briefcase to match. He was an organised fellow and eager to proceed with the business in hand.

'In the name of the Father, the Son and the Holy Spirit, Amen.' From his manner, he could have been ordering paper for the photocopier.

'Amen,' came the mumbled reply.

There was awkwardness in the air for any number of reasons but the email hadn't helped. Bishop Stephen blamed the missing church warden, Roger Stills, who wisely left the country shortly afterwards on pilgrimage. The Bishop had sent Roger the agenda for the meeting, to be circulated to all members of the PCC. Unfortunately Roger also circulated the Bishop's covering letter, in which he'd outlined in some detail Anton's personal and professional deficiencies as well as Jennifer's misguided and damaging role in his appointment. Once it was public, there was much dismay. The Bishop wouldn't apologise, saying only that it was a private email, not intended for public view; Anton laughed it off as he always did, Jennifer was furious and Roger left for the relative peace of the West Bank.

'Well, thank you for coming, my brothers and sisters in Christ!' said Bishop Stephen, in true episcopal style. 'We have a difficult evening ahead of us but we grow in faith not by walking round the nettles but by grasping them! Jesus always grasped nettles!'

The Bishop was in young middle age and ripe for advancement. With his gaunt features and greased back hair, Edwina Pipe had not taken to him either in appearance or manner. But she for one wasn't going to judge him on the basis of how he looked.

'After all,' she said, 'it's not his fault he looks a Nazi war criminal.'

Despite attempts at bonhomie, which could be overwhelming, there was a purifying edge to Bishop Stephen. He spoke much and often about the need for reform. Nothing in the world was as it should be and however much he fingered his African cross and spoke of the dear Kenyan woman who gave it to him, people felt accused and attacked in his presence. And he was on the attack tonight.

'It is good that your vicar, Anton, is with us,' he continued, nodding slightly in his direction, without catching his eye. 'As you know from the agenda, it's his ministry at St Michael's that we are gathered to discuss. I think we all acknowledge that it has been a difficult couple of years for St Michael's.'

'You mean a difficult couple of years for you,' thought Jennifer.

'And we meet here tonight,' he continued, 'to consider how things might be taken forward.'

'In other words, how you might sack me?' said Anton in a flippant manner. 'You've been aching to get rid of me since my first day here. And now Roger has kindly circulated your covering email, I think we can all see why.'

'You should remain calm, Anton, just as everyone else should remain – .'

But the Bishop didn't finish his sentence. Jennifer intervened.

'I've asked Abbot Peter to chair the meeting tonight,' said Jennifer. 'We thought he had the necessary qualifications. He is someone who both loves us and yet stands apart from us. He seemed ideal.'

'Well, that's wonderful,' said the Bishop, his knuckles squeezed a creamy white. 'I'm sure Abbot Peter will do a very good job in his own inimitable way. And who knows: perhaps we'll discover why he still calls himself an Abbot when he's six thousand miles from his monastery and in retirement!'

There was some uncomfortable shifting in seats.

'I joke, of course,' added the Bishop. 'A naughty jester am I!'

'I think we should move on, Bishop,' said Jennifer. 'Abbot Peter?'

*

Everyone later remembered his opening line. Indeed, it became something of a catchphrase in the parish, when something significant happened.

'It's all about the chemistry!' they'd say, for that is how the Abbot had begun on that memorable night.

'It's all about the chemistry,' he said. 'We are a room of such dear people but the chemistry is uncomfortable. Ingredients react against each other, ingredients react with each other and it's a dangerous mix. This is what I see.'

'I see only a problem to be solved,' said the Bishop, in a throwaway manner, 'but don't let me interrupt your desert meanderings!'

'Managers see only performance, Bishop; love feels the energies beneath. And it's those energies we need be aware of. A community has a choice. If it's brave, it becomes a magic potion and rather wonderful. If it's not brave, it becomes – well, it becomes a sea of poison. We must hope we are brave. I think we shall be; I think tonight we shall be heroes.'

But the heroes struggled that night. Of the nine gathered, three would soon die. The six left alive remembered only an evening they would rather forget. Despite the Abbot's best efforts, the meeting started with an explosion and then fizzled towards an unconvincing end. It didn't help that Anton effectively accused Ginger of being a paedophile.

'Twice Mr Hucknell has complained about Ginger giving his son Tommy what is euphemistically called "refuge".'

'You know nothing!' bawled Ginger, rising from his chair.

Abbot Peter met him on his way to Anton and guided him back to his seat.

'We can't be too careful in these matters,' said Jennifer coolly. 'This is a legitimate concern, Ginger. You may have been here a long time but no one is above investigation.'

'Including you!' hissed Ginger.

'And what do you mean by that?'

But Ginger just stared.

'We'll try and keep listening to one another,' said Abbot Peter. 'And questions tend to be more helpful than accusations.'

There was a pause as people put their accusations away; or simply re-framed them. Sally Appleby twisted the knife gently with the observation that perhaps too many changes had taken place too fast under Anton's leadership, leaving people somewhat breathless: 'I know from what folk have said to me confidentially, that they have found it all a bit bewildering.'

Malcolm Flight agreed. He strongly felt that there should be more discussion before things were done, particularly with regard to paintings. He did, however, think the parish finances were in better order now. Clare Magnussen concurred, but said that as a general principle, people should not be pressured to give more money.

'People give in many ways; the church should not obsess about money. I really think this. It does no favours to anyone to try and make them feel guilty!'

Anton said this was all very well and that he was sorry if Clare felt guilty but if there was no money, there was no church. Clare said that she didn't feel guilty, that she was merely saying, at which point Jennifer intervened and talked generally about the need for good communication in any organisation. Ginger was more direct, saying that Anton did not understand the needs of the young people and that he should involve himself more. Anton said that he had suggested closer involvement but that Ginger had always blocked it:

'You like to rule your own kingdom, Ginger. Foreign potentates are not welcome!'

Ginger said that simply wasn't so with the venom of one who knew it simply was. He knew also that Anton had just crossed the line.

Betty remarked that work with children was very important and that there seemed to be more cleaning materials now, which was good but that she didn't always know what was happening in the church what with all the changes, which made cleaning difficult sometimes – and were there any tables left at the forthcoming Christmas Fayre because a friend of hers, whose husband had died, had a lot of junk to get rid of?

'And perhaps we have too,' said the Bishop.

As the meeting regressed, Abbot Peter thought briefly of his father. He always thought of him when he encountered the number nine, though this evening was not the time to explain why. And when he thought of his father, it was not of the weak man with his rule-bound wife who'd adopted him as a baby. His true father had been both bully and adventurer, who discovered a great secret in Afghanistan, became a spiritual teacher and fathered various children with his disciples. 'The guru never sleeps alone,' as they say. Young Peter was one of those who were given away. He was found another home which had never quite been one.

He'd first encountered his biological father at the age of 22 and met him only twice thereafter, shortly before he died in Paris. They'd met in New York, drunk ouzo together and talked. His father was there organizing groups, giving seminars, looking for publishers and being rude to people, which was one way to attract the wealthy to your cause. Peter had felt fascination rather than warmth towards this man, who treated him more as pupil than son. He found in him a mix of the fanciful and profound. He lied a great deal but lied with insight, which gave it a certain truth. Peter particularly remembered one remark his father had made:

'Be outwardly courteous to all without distinction. But inwardly, stay free! Never put too much trust in anything.'

His father had never been courteous but he had stayed free.

But it was the 'miracle of nine' that evening that particularly brought his father to mind. For tonight, Peter was aware of a remarkable occurrence in the parish room of St Michael's. The law of averages demanded that occasionally it was so yet he could not remember experiencing it before. This was remarkable! But whom could he tell? No one here would understand the nature of this miracle. Suddenly he wished to speak again with his father, he would understand.

It was, after all, his father who had taught him the strange and remarkable wisdom of the Enneagram and its nine pointed symbol.

Fifteen

○

The strongest safe is resistant to extreme violence; yet can be opened by a child with the key.

And so it was with the Sarmoun Community. They said nothing, wrote nothing, gave no address, invited no attention and placed dark chasms between themselves and the world. For hundreds of years they had gathered quietly in upper rooms and deep retreat, a brotherhood protecting the nine-pointed secret. Yet if a stranger, against all human odds, turned up at their gate then they were as welcome as the Messiah himself.

George Ivanovitch Gurdjieff arrived barely conscious on the back of a carpet seller's cart. He'd been found wandering on the slopes, nineteen days after leaving Bokhara. Gurdjieff had lied to the carpet seller, an instinctive skill, claiming he was a member of the Brotherhood who had been attacked. He asked to be returned there for medical attention and the carpet seller believed him.

The rope bridge had proved surprisingly secure. Like a dead snake, it was more fearsome in appearance than reality. Gurdjieff had even paused midway, to contemplate the darkness beneath him. He'd smiled at its terror, in open taunt, daring it to take him now. He took on death as he took on people.

'Hell's mouth had no teeth,' he later said. 'It was not my time. It was not my time to join the skulls.'

But delight turned to frustration when no path appeared. After two days of wandering, all hope had ebbed, like the tide of the Black Sea where he played as a boy. He'd got water from a passing shepherd but no sense. The herdsman had known nothing of the Sarmouni and what use is the water of the ignorant? It saves the body, but kills the soul. Had Death merely bided his time? He cursed the shepherd but drank his water.

He even wondered if he should have listened to Soloviev, not something he had ever wondered before. His friend was safe in

Bokhara, while he was dying like a fool beneath the frowning crags of the Hindu Kush. Was this madness or sanity, wisdom or nonsense? By the time the carpet seller found him, he was hallucinating a city of huge wealth where women were attending to his needs with extravagant care and precision. This was very good, this was better. Perhaps this was heaven, as the sun beat down?

He was brought back to earth lying on a merchant's cart, cushioned by fine fabric destined for Samarkand. But he himself was destined for the Sarmouni.

Sixteen

Tuesday, 16 December

The weather that night had matched the meeting's mood, stormy and hell-bent, 'a right bag of spanners' as Edwina Pipe would say. The furies had been building as Abbot Peter had approached the church, the water tossed and surly. One day the sea would overwhelm the steeped shingle and assault the land beyond. One day Stormhaven would experience the watery terror, this everyone knew. A fractured deck chair had flown across his path, a thing possessed, and the parish meeting was likewise. What hope for the landscape of the soul amid the surge of such turbulence?

'I suggest we pause for tonight,' said Peter. With ammunition exhausted and all spite spent, things had come to a natural end and no meeting should go much over the hour. 'Perhaps enough has been said for now. It's hard to be truthful, but we've done our best. Beyond the first truth, however, is the second truth. And to reach the second truth can take time.'

The Abbot had spoken of the first and second truth before but it was a new idea for the Bishop.

'The Abbot will no doubt tell us what on earth he means!' he said. 'We should perhaps leave the riddles to Jesus.'

'The first truth is the obvious pain,' said Abbot Peter gently. 'This has been spoken clearly enough. The second truth is pain's flowering, the emerging resolution and this we have yet to reach. So if it's acceptable with the Bishop, I suggest we go away and consider our part in this fracturing parish landscape. Perhaps we could then meet a week from now and consider how we might become a landscape reborn. I think our seaside town deserves it.'

'A nice thought indeed, Abbot, but I'm afraid we are rather beyond such vagaries,' said the Bishop.

'Bishop –' said Jennifer but her intervention was waved aside.

'I've heard and seen enough,' he continued. 'It's time we came to a decision. It is now well known – due to the publication of my private thoughts – that Anton was not my choice but Jennifer was persuasive and so he came. We have lived with that choice for two years now. But is it your wish that he remains? That is the question and it's simple enough: stay or go? We will vote by hand raised, for as children of the light, we have nothing to hide.'

And so it was the brutal vote took place, each avoiding the glance of the other.

'If you would like Anton to stay, please raise your hand.'

Eyes remained fixed on the floor as consequences were weighed.

'Well?' said the Bishop, tapping his prayer book with impatience.

Jennifer raised her hand and then, with a smile, Anton raised his as well.

'I do have a vote, I trust?'

'Thank you,' said the Bishop, ignoring him entirely. 'And now raise your hand if you would like the vicar to leave.'

Ginger's hand was the first to be raised, followed by Clare's and Malcolm's. Sally was the next to raise hers with an apologetic glance towards Anton. Betty looked straight ahead as she raised hers.

'Abstentions – or "Don't knows" as they should be called?'

Abbot Peter raised his hand.

'I thank you for your time, ladies and gentlemen, and I'm glad that we've been able to reach such a clear decision. My maths says that when five plays against one – the vicar cannot vote – five takes the day.'

'With one abstention, Bishop,' said Peter.

'Don't knows don't change the world, Abbot. But thankfully others have had the courage to do that for you. I'll be speaking with all those involved to effect a speedy end to this unfortunate affair. I declare the meeting concluded. Shall we close with the grace?'

Together they spoke the familiar words: 'The grace of our Lord Jesus Christ and the love of God and the fellowship of the Holy Spirit be with us all, evermore, Amen.'

'Safe travel home,' said the Bishop.

'A journey denied the second truth,' said the Abbot in the Bishop's ear. 'This is sad.'

'It's life,' said the Bishop as he returned his papers to his briefcase.

'It's your life,' replied the Abbot.

'I sometimes wonder if you really belong here, Peter?' said the Bishop, placing an episcopal hand on his shoulder. 'Have you ever thought of going somewhere you matter? Think about it.'

People gathered their things and prepared to leave. Peter noticed Jennifer's look towards the Bishop, one of horror and incomprehension and then a brief exchange:

'It was a joint decision to give Anton the job, Bishop. You included.'

'We both know it was your call, Jennifer and it's been a disaster.'

'Anton has not been a disaster.'

'If you think that, then you're a pretty poor judge of disasters.'

And then Anton spoke up.

'And what if I do not wish to leave, Bishop? What if my leaving would raise more questions about you than me, Bishop? Questions about your strange favourites, for instance?'

But the meeting had become a parting and there was no one left to hear. In time, Anton would make his way to the vestry. It would be the last walk of his life.

Seventeen

Wednesday, 17 December

The Detective Inspector would be arriving soon. Abbot Peter glanced down the road for signs of his approach. He looked for a car of quiet distinction, but saw only a lone paraglider, freshly launched from the cliffs, heading out towards the horizon. It was a clear, cold day and good for flying free.

He stepped away from the window and turned up his electric fire. He had a slight chill from events of the previous night. Someone usually gave him a lift after parish meetings, but last night, the practice of decency had died. Everyone had departed with their own thoughts and concerns, leaving the Abbot to walk home through dark rain and furious wind. His drenched habit now hung drying over the bath. It would need a visit to the dry cleaners soon, crusty with the salt. In the meantime, he had his second best habit to wear.

He'd remained in church after the meeting, staying with Anton. God knows, he was hardly a fan of the man but there was a way to proceed. Righteousness cannot advance through unrighteousness.

'What's done is not good, Anton,' he'd said.

'I didn't get your vote, though, did I?'

'The present got my vote. I was voting against the process in which we were trapped. The way we go about things is important.'

'So's my job and to me, slightly more urgent than the process, whatever that is!'

The Abbot paused. 'What will you do now?' he asked.

'What will I do now? I'll go to the vestry and make a CD of festive music for the Christmas Fayre. Life goes on. If I don't get murdered, that is!'

Fear crippled Anton's smile.

'I think that's unlikely,' said the Abbot.

'You didn't see the look, did you? It was like nothing I've ever seen.'

'What look?'

'Look of a maniac.'

'Who?'

At that point Anton's mobile had rung in loud and jangly tones. He got up to answer it.

'Really?' he said, surprised at what he was hearing. 'Well, that's good, very good! I knew it would be all right, just knew it and thank you for your support ... perhaps you should have said that at the meeting! ... and then it wouldn't have ... good idea ... very good idea ... well, I'm alone now if you want to come round to the church.'

Peter heard no more, for Anton had left the room to continue the conversation, walking through the church and into the vestry. It was one of Peter's memories of Anton, always on the move, particularly on the phone. It was as if he had to walk as he spoke. On this occasion, he left Peter without so much as a nod in his direction and they were the last living words he heard Anton speak, for the vicar of St Michael's did not return to the parish room. Perhaps he forgot he was talking with the Abbot. Or perhaps it was a just a long call. Abruptly disowned, Peter sat for a while and listened to the storm, crashing against this battered place of worship, built on the site of a Norman church. He wished to be in his secret place but knew it was impossible now. And then he saw the candle.

The parish room was a modern development within the church and linked to the main church space by a glass door. Through this, Peter saw the candle flickering by the altar, a weak light in the dark. He decided to extinguish it before leaving, aware that Anton could be careless about such things. Peter would put it out and then head home. He pushed open the glass door and entered the church. The place was dark and steeped in the smell of hymn books and flowers. He walked up the centre aisle, red carpet beneath his feet. Erratic gusts slammed against the stained glass where saints walked with haloes through the storms of life. Three steps then took him up to the altar area. He climbed them carefully, licked his fingers, squeezed the burning wick into quiet submission and sensed a presence in the side aisle. He stopped still on the steps, peering into the deep shadows beyond the pillars. His heart beat with unfamiliar fear. And then something dropped on the metal grate; he was sure he heard something drop. Or was it the wind? No, something had dropped, something metallic. He stood motionless, awaiting night vision, seconds passed, a minute maybe two. He looked for movement but there was nothing and it was late. He took himself in hand. He walked down the altar steps and back down the centre aisle. The storm was making a fool of him, denying him peace.

He returned to the parish room for his coat, turned out the light and left the church by the main door, locking it after him. He cursed as he stepped into a large puddle forming around the blocked drain, appropriate baptism for the stormy journey home.

'This didn't happen in the desert.'

He walked down the old high street. It was sad to see so many shops at the lower end now boarded up and vacant. He crossed over the small roundabout and made his way up the Causeway to the sea front. From here, it was five salty minutes until he reached Sandy View. He turned towards the cliffs, lost to sight in the swirling wet. To the left lay the small homes that lined the front. To the right sat the beach huts, proud on the shingle edge. The sea was ponderous and heavy, troubled by the wind and crashing white wash with random force against the pebble coast. How long would these defences hold?

It was then that Abbot Peter saw the dim shape, a hunched figure appearing from behind the beach huts and now coming towards him. It was a familiar walk but what was she doing here, at this time and in this weather?

'Good evening, Betty!'

'Good evening, Abbot.'

And she carried on walking.

Eighteen

○

'I am glad you made it,' said the Sarkar. 'Really most glad.'

'It is good to be here,' replied the young desperado, taking the floor cushion offered.

'I must say, though, we did have our doubts.'

'Doubts? Doubts about what?'

'We began to fear you might not find us, my friend. You quite gave us the slip after the chasm.'

'You knew I was coming?'

'Of course we knew you were coming. We brought you here, didn't we?'

'No. I was brought here by a man called Mussa.'

'Precisely.'

'You mean – Mussa?'

The Sarkar took a sip of water and drew on his cigarette.

'He works for me.'

'Then he is a good actor. I never would have guessed he was on the side of light.'

'Why so?'

'He played the part of a coward, a swindler and a cheat. And played it most convincingly.'

'Not everything in life is an act, my friend. If the Messiah were available for employment, I would employ him. Until then, I employ Mussa.'

Gurdjieff was unnerved by a sense of recognition. He had met this man before.

*

Three days had passed since he'd entered the gates of the Sarmoun Brotherhood. On arrival, he'd been taken to the wash house, invited to strip and then left alone to step naked and joyful into one of the large tubs of piping hot water. Gurdjieff had a passion for the scalding and groaned in delight. Clean and renewed, he found his old clothes taken and replaced by a sheepskin coat, belt and cap, familiar dervish garments. He liked his new clothes. Here was the Black Sea boy at one with the Hindu Kush! All life is precious and every day a prize!

Full of questions and ripe for revelation, he'd been given a tour of the settlement by one of the monks. 'How many live here?' he asked as they walked.

'There is a community of around nine hundred souls.'

'And these round buildings of stone and thatch which we pass: what are they?'

'They are called Oratories and house members of the community. Each, as you see, is surrounded by vines and herb gardens, for which the oratory community is responsible.'

Gurdjieff could see why people came here. It was a good and peaceful place to live, ordered yet free. Here was movement but not wasted movement. This was his first and abiding impression of the Sarmoun community: movement but not wasted movement.

The monk spoke simply and left gaps between observations. Sometimes, he would walk without saying a word, inviting Gurdjieff to see with his own eyes and ask his own questions.

'You are a quiet guide,' said Gurdjieff at one point.

'People must be taught to see for themselves,' said the monk. 'It's not good to have everything pointed out. It makes people lazy and obese with second hand knowledge.'

Gurdjieff was taken aback. This had not been his understanding of teaching. Wasn't the teacher meant to tell everything they knew?

'But when the guide knows more than the guided?' he probed.

'Then the guide must restrain themselves.'

They walked on further in silence until Gurdjieff returned to questioning of a more basic sort.

'How long has this community existed here?' asked George Ivano-vitch.

'Allowing for one break, when Genghis Khan destroyed the nearby city of Balkh, the brotherhood has been in this place since records began.'

'And when did records begin.'

'We don't know – there is no record of that.'

Guide and follower laughed together. It was the guide's only joke and one he clearly treasured.

'And what do you all believe? I have heard different things.'

'We believe many things,' said the guide. 'We contain many approaches to life. But our motto is this: work produces sweet essence. That is the fire around which we gather.'

'What sort of work?'

'Work is spiritual, physical and mental.'

'It's true. Everyone seems to be doing something.'

'Each member is a specialist in some sphere of activity: one might be a gardener, another a mathematician, another skilled in falconry. There are many skills. Here also are those skilled in medicine. We approach now a herbalist, for instance.'

An old man ahead was on his knees, tending a thick-leaved plant, rather ugly and small, with little by way of flower.

'He grows the holy Chungari plant.'

'A holy plant?'

'It is called the herb of enlightenment.'

'It doesn't look much.'

'Neither did the Christ. But a beautiful aroma, I think you will agree.'

As they drew close, it was like sweet honey in the air.

' Literally, Chungari means 'howness' and is consumed by Dervishes at special times.'

'Ah! The fuel of intoxication!'

'It's non-narcotic.'

They drew close to the shrub. Gurdjieff reached out to touch but the monk's hand forbade him.

'You can neither touch nor taste,' he said. 'This is not the time.'

It was to be a familiar and frustrating feature of the Sarmoun Community in these early days. Amid so much explained, so much was not. The visitor here experienced both openness and secrecy. You were made welcome but made also to wait.

'You seem frustrated,' said the guide.

'Everything in this place is hidden!' exclaimed Gurdjieff.

' "Dervish" is Persian for "One who waits at the door". You will not wait for ever.'

*

'After we met in Bokhara, I decided to help you,' said the host and in an instant, Gurdjieff realised with whom he spoke. This was the thin-fingered man he and Sol had met in Bokhara, in the room where they drank lemon. 'Yes, I thought you displayed a grand spirit, determined and desperate. I saw quickly that your friend felt otherwise and I tried to separate you from him. It seems he did that himself later on. But you were different from most who enquire about the community. I felt you might not only want the truth but know also what to do with it.'

'Hardly the impression you gave,' said Gurdjieff, flattered but tetchy. 'We almost gave up after meeting you. Had we not met Mussa we would have left Bokhara the following day. We'd never been so poorly treated as we were there.'

'We do not encourage visitors yet delight to see them!' said the Sarkar with a smile, eyes dancing beneath his cobalt-blue turban. 'We are rather contrary in that way. But as I'm sure you understand, human motives are less than pure and people do not always seek us for the right reason.'

'And what is the right reason?'

'To nurture truth at the expense of self.'

'Who on earth does that?'

'Precisely. Most use truth to beat others and so lose it in themselves. Here, we use truth to die to ourselves and so keep it alive.'

'So what truth can you tell me?'

The Sarkar smiled. Would this be the man? Would this be the man to take the teaching to Europe? There was both genius and tyrant sitting before him.

'I am aware of a symbol,' continued Gurdjieff with impatience. He was tired of all this waiting. 'A nine-pointed symbol. That is why I came. But this is a secretive place.'

'It is an open secret.'

'An open secret closed to me?'

'Open secrets closed only to those who will kill them.'

'And am I such a one? Am I a killer of truth?'

It was time for decision. They had welcomed this young man into the community of the bees. Would they now allow him to taste the honey? Was it time the symbol was explained?

'I think you are a friend of the truth, George Ivanovitch. An awkward friend and rather uncouth, but a friend nonetheless.'

The young man expanded in pride. He would not be pushed away any more. He would take on this ancient and discover the secrets of the Sarmouni.

'So to repeat myself, Sir – what truth can you tell me?' he asked.

'I can tell you everything.'

'Everything?'

'Everything that has significance. If I do not know it, it is not significant.'

'A big claim.'

'A simple truth. Would you prefer I lie in self-effacement and pretend a more stupid self, like a giant in the clothing of dwarves or a lion claiming he is nothing but a fly?'

The enquirer thought of a test. He was always testing, he'd tested people all his life, never trusting.

'So you can tell me if I shall be famous?'

'Intriguing perhaps but not significant.'

'Can you tell me how many stars there are in the sky?'

'Awe inspiring but again, not significant. Numbers do not determine glory.'

'So what is significant?'

'That today might be the last day of your life.'

George Ivanovich laughed mockingly. 'But doesn't everyone know that?! Everyone knows today could be the end of it all!'

The man in the turban paused.

'Everyone knows it, my friend. But not everyone feels it. Everyone knows it as a theory but it's only significant if felt in the marrow of your bones. Do you feel it in yours?'

The man in the turban stroked his beard and looked suddenly frail, his face gaunt with mortality. And then he continued:

'What I offer is a different sort of knowing. I describe what it is to be human, the inner energies that create and destroy. Strangely, these things are not widely known. We know our height and our weight and the size of our shoe, things which dictate nothing in our lives; yet remain ignorant of the inner forces which dictate everything, which daily make us who and what we are.'

'You claim we are puppets in the hands of these forces, our strings pulled unknowingly by their hands?'

'You glimpse the truth. Truly, we do not know what we do and neither do we seem too concerned.'

Gurdjieff was not happy with this answer. For the first time since his arrival, he believed he was wasting his time. 'We do not know what we do,' said the man. Yet he, Gurdjieff, knew exactly what he did. He'd met charlatans before, claiming some special knowledge, some special way to hide their own sick minds which wanted only power. Or money. Indeed, it was a good deal easier to count those who weren't fakes than those who were. A list of the former was a short one. His thoughts, though, were interrupted.

'But in particular, I describe you!' said the Sarker, with sudden delight, his eyes dancing.

'Me? But how can you claim that? You do not know me!'

'On the contrary, I know you better than you know yourself.'

'Then you know my birthday?'

Testing again, seeking truth. He hadn't come all this way for nonsense which appealed for a moment and disappointed for a lifetime.

'I know what gives you birth.'

'And what is that?'

'We will not be personal so early. We'll not grab hastily at the truth plant, for fear of crushing it. Those who are not ready for the truth, they kill it in their rough and stupid handling.'

The enquirer pondered these words in the heat of late afternoon.

'How do you know these things?'

'Let me show you something.'

Between host and visitor was a small table covered by a clean white cloth. The host now pulled the cloth from the table. There before the young man was a strange mosaic in polished wood, a mysterious symbol, a circle whose circumference displayed nine points.

'It looks like the devil's tool,' said the visitor.

'The devil may borrow it but I prefer to think it belongs to God. Indeed, some call it the nine faces of God.'

'And what do you call it?'

The host covered the symbol with the cloth, hiding it once again from public gaze.

'Tradition names it The Enneagram,' he said.

'And you?'

'I follow tradition.'

A white dove landed in the cave's entrance. Peaceful and pure, it paused a while, before flying high into the sky of the Hindu Kush.

Nineteen

The knock on the door found Abbot Peter gargling mouthwash. After twenty five years in the desert, where camel breath was not confined to the camels, dental care and fresh breath had been one of life's late discoveries and eagerly embraced.

He opened the door to a pretty young girl with black hair and olive skin.

'Can I help you?' he asked, at once beguiled and irritated she'd come at a bad time. He might have enjoyed talking with her.

'Is this Sandy View?' she asked.

'It is, my friend, but if you've come for the charity bags, I'm going to need another day. I forgot all about them and I'm now waiting for someone, due any minute. Otherwise I'd ask you in.'

'Then let me confess something too.'

It had been a while since the Abbot heard a confession and this wasn't the time.

'You're very welcome to return –.'

'I'm the one for whom you wait,' said the girl.

An edifice of preconception collapsed within Abbot Peter.

'Oh I see.'

The girl smiled jauntily.

'To assume makes an ass out of you and me,' she said. 'Isn't that what they say?'

'Mainly the smug, in my experience,' replied the Abbot.

The girl's demeanour suggested that she continued to enjoy her victory.

'So you are the Detective Inspector?' he said.

'The clues were there.'

'Not many.'

'But enough perhaps.'

'Circumstantial evidence maybe.'

'That's all you need to build a case.'

'Something you do very well, no doubt.'

'Thank you.'

'No reason on earth why a Detective Inspector should be a man, of course.'

'That's true.'

'Miss Marple was ever-popular in the desert. A sweet old lady but pushy and dangerous. My guess is that you too are pushy and dangerous.'

'Flattery, flattery.'

Peter noted she took this as a compliment.

'The surprise does not stop there, however,' said the girl who was clearly now a woman. 'There's something else to be revealed.'

'Really?' said Abbot Peter.

'Oh yes,' she said, smiling.

Peter paused, allowing their first exchange to pass through him.

'Isn't one burning bush enough?' he said. 'A second might have left Moses confused.'

'Who have you never met?' asked the woman.

'That would be a long list.'

'Other people have met theirs.'

'It's quite early for riddles.'

'They're all around us.'

'Don't tell me you're an angel. I've met angels and they generally bring nothing but trouble.'

'Whether I'm an angel or not, I don't know – but I am your niece.'

Abbot Peter inhaled deeply, strangely moved. He had not met a family member for over thirty years and had only the vaguest picture of his family tree. Indeed, as he'd once told Mrs Pipe when she'd been fishing for information: 'From my present knowledge, Mrs Pipe, it's more of a stick than a tree.'

'My niece?' he finally managed.

'Your niece.'

'I have a niece?'

'And one more thing.'

Abbot Peter could not imagine one more thing. His mind was already a flooded valley of broken fence and wall. He held the door frame to steady himself.

'And what is this one more thing?'

'We'll be working together on this case.'

'The crucified vicar?'

'The same. We'll be working together. You've been granted Special Witness status. For good or ill, we're a team. My name's Tamsin Shah by the way. Now may I come in?'

Twenty

Stormhaven was unusually busy with both gossip and forensics as the facts of the matter emerged. The crucified vicar had been nailed to the cross on the wall of the vestry in St Michael's. Early reports from the pathologist suggested the nails had been hammered home at midnight and that he died around 2.00am. He'd been taped to the cross and drugged with chloroform, prior to nailing. He was reckoned to have died of a heart attack and was known to have a weak heart.

News travelled fast and Malcolm was later to recount a conversation in the supermarket early that morning.

'Crucifixion is just the worst thing ever for a weak heart,' an earnest customer had said to Eva on the till.

'Is that right?'

'Terrible.'

'That's something to avoid then.'

'Where possible.'

And then as Eva passed some mushroom soup across the scanner she reflected further on health issues.

'So it's like butter then.'

'Sorry?'

'Well that's bad for the heart isn't it?'

'It is. But crucifixion's worse.'

Only insiders, however, would have known why the cross was in the vestry. It had formerly stood in the main body of the church, on a stand above the altar. But Anton had found it too depressing for such public display in services.

'The church needs to cheer up!' he'd declared. 'And move on. We are allowed to be happy, you know!'

Someone said an empty cross spoke of Easter, the human body no longer held by death but the vicar hadn't seen that at all.

'We mustn't get sentimental,' he said. 'In the end, like an electric chair or guillotine, a cross is nothing more than an instrument of execution.'

And so it had become once again. His own.

*

Peter had ushered her inside, though whether it was his niece or the Detective Inspector he welcomed, he wasn't sure. She'd refused the shortbread but seemed pleased at the offer of green tea. He'd bought it in error in the supermarket but it was a good mistake, broadening the horizons of his hospitality. He now had a choice of teas.

'Builder's tea or green?' He liked the sound of that. 'So what is a Special Witness?' he asked, once the catering was complete. 'I may not want to be one. As Socrates said, "There's so much I have no need of".'

He suspected he did want to be one. It was a continuing weakness that he was moved when asked to do something, as if some part of him, some unresolved aspect of his abandoned psyche needed this affirmation. And the step from murder fiction to murder for real had its own challenge and allure. He was a hunter, a hunter after truth and as he thought again of the little boy who was Anton Fontaine, he wished to hunt his murderer down.

'It's an idea on trial in the area, to promote a more earthed and insightful investigation,' said Tamsin speaking like the police at a press conference. 'A member of the public who is recognised as a trusted citizen of the affected community can now be brought in to assist the police. They're involved in all aspects of the case, kept fully informed of developments and work closely with the officer leading the enquiry.'

'Which in this case is you?'

'Which in this case is me, yes. Chief Inspector Wonder has always thought I could go far, and when this came up, he couldn't second me to the East Sussex force fast enough. He was a little hesitant about the use of a Special Witness for this one – it's going to be high profile obviously, with a lot of public interest – but I persuaded him.'

Abbot Peter could imagine that, could imagine the persuasion.

'If the scheme goes well, it could mushroom very quickly. We want it to succeed.'

'The South Coast police leading the way?'

'We're always leading the way. The Met gets the press, but the imaginative work is elsewhere.'

'The skill, I suppose, is in choosing the right Special Witness.'

'That is important.'

'A bad one could do serious damage.'

'I'm sure that won't be so with you,' she said.

Abbot Peter smiled the smile of one who knew his own worth. The idea was ridiculous.

'Well, will it?' she asked.

There was both threat and panic in Tamsin's voice. Abbot Peter responded with silence, returning to the solitude of his breathing as Tamsin became restless. It was time for him to take some of the authority back.

'Well?' she asked.

'Well, what?'

'Would you like to be a Special Witness?'

'Why choose me?'

'You were recommended.'

'By whom?'

'I can't divulge that. They thought you'd be perfect for some reason. They said your whole life is an investigation.'

'True in a way.'

'And other soundings seemed positive. There will be certain forms to fill in, confidentiality agreements, that sort of thing. And you'll have to work hard for your money.'

'I'm paid?'

'There is an allowance, yes.'

The Abbot dreamed briefly of a vacuum cleaner.

'Well?'

'Do you always fire so much at people in such a short space of time?'

'We need to move quickly. There's a vicar's body hanging in the vestry and the Chief Inspector is already being harassed by the Bishop.'

'I can sympathise. But why the panic in your voice? Who's harassing you?'

'I harass myself.'

'I understand.'

'So down to work.'

'Maybe. But I'm still thinking about what you said earlier.'

Tamsin's impatience was further inflamed.

'What did I say?'

'You said you were my niece.'

'So?'

'It's hardly a casual opening line.'

'It got me through the door.'

'And that's all it meant?'

'This isn't really the time, Abbot.'

'When is the time to find lost family?'

Tamsin resisted.

'It isn't pertinent to the case in hand,' she said.

'Pertinent? I haven't heard that word for a while.'

'And the case is my job right now.'

Abbot Peter waited as the sea heaved, rose and collapsed on the stones. Things come and go, nothing remains and silence holds all. It was Tamsin who relented.

'I'm the daughter of a half-sister you'll not even know you have. Okay?'

'Tell me her name.'

'Is it important?'

'It might be polite.'

Abbot Peter was considering another possibility. Was this newcomer a burglar or trickster? A fake phone call earlier and a simple visit now, before clearing him out. He had heard of such things. With her pretty face, many would succumb. Perhaps she had a less winning accomplice waiting outside. He hadn't heard her car arrive. Perhaps there was a van parked a little down the road. And then he was wondering if she was the murderer herself, now come for him. Why had he let her in? News of a vicar crucified, followed by the arrival at his door of a pretty young Detective Inspector who claimed also to be his niece? The whole thing was unravelling in his mind and in danger of looking absurd. He would test things; he always tested things.

'Tell me her name,' he said. 'The name of your mother,'

'Do your tree lights not work?' said Tamsin, noticing the quiet Christmas tree in the corner.

'They worked briefly, looked rather fine and then gave up.'

'The tree looks a little sad without them.'

'They'll be back. And the name of your mother?'

It was a battle of wills, as outside, gulls swooped in screeching delight. Inside, it was the focused against the devious.

'My mother's name is Marguerite,' she said.

'Marguerite?'

'Yes.'

Abbot Peter smiled and blessed the time and tide of life. 'Then you must remember me to her,' he said. He was satisfied. He did know of a half-sister called Marguerite, the child of another of his father's devotees. They'd never met but that was no surprise. He'd not seen his mother Yorii since the adoption and had been in the desert much too long to pursue the loose ends of his father's other sexual outgoings. But Marguerite had a daughter and here she was now. A stranger is suddenly a relation and something is changed.

'I will be a Special Witness,' he said. 'And I will be a good one. We have detective blood in us, in a way. Did you know that?'

'I don't really do families. The wording on my Mother's Day card is very carefully chosen.'

'Nothing too congratulatory or grateful? I understand. But did you ever hear about your grandfather?'

'Not much, no. He was reckoned to be rather odd in my home, referred to with sighs and raised eyebrows. I'm not sure he can help us.'

'On the contrary, he can help us a great deal.'

'How?'

'Well, he was so keen to find the truth he went all the way to Afghanistan. And what he found there might prove useful here.'

'Whatever,' said Tamsin managing to sound neither congratulatory nor grateful.

Twenty One

○

'The Enneagram is a model of perpetual motion,' continued the Sarkar. 'More particularly, it is a model of perpetual creation and destruction.'

Gurdjieff sat motionless as he listened. All things were about to be explained. Would this be enlightenment or disappointment?

'I will not tire you with the maths of it now, suffice to say the Enneagram symbol came into its present form only recently – in the fifteenth century.'

'Five hundred years ago is hardly recent.'

'It is in the truth game, my friend. It was then, of course, that Central Asia founded the modern theory of numbers by giving zero a separate symbol.'

'We can study the maths another time, perhaps,' said Gurdjieff. He had not come here for maths. He could count money; that was sufficient learning of numbers. 'It is the human side of the story which interests me; both the creation and destruction, as you say.'

'It is a mystery which I reveal to you, George Ivanovich, and mystery cannot be boxed. Those who box mystery, kill it. Do you understand?'

'I understand.'

'Yet it is also a mystery easily discerned and the veracity of which is readily perceived, even by the dull of mind.'

'An open secret.'

'Indeed, an open secret about you, me and anyone who ever walked the earth.'

'It's universal.'

'And you will not find these things written down in any occult literature. Indeed, so great an importance was assigned to it by the enlightened, that they considered it necessary to keep all knowledge of the work a secret. As you know, we continue that tradition of secrecy here.'

'I am well aware of that.'

He had not forgotten the disdain shown to Soloviev and himself in the market place of Bokara; his hands still bled from gripping the rope over the chasm and both his face and back bore the stain of heatstroke. He had suffered for their secrecy.

'The Enneagram excels most obviously in its understanding of Man,' said the Sarkar.

But suddenly Gurdjieff wished only for an understanding of women and in particular, the pretty girl who had just entered the cave. She approached them both and placed some water on the table. She was thanked by the Sarkar, who appeared a little surprised at her entrance. She glanced at the visitor and found his eyes settled on her. She was neither displeased nor greatly concerned, but having heard of the Russian traveller, she had wished to see for herself. Visitors from the world beyond were not common and the world beyond appealed to her. She wished to be away from the mountains of the Hindu Kush. Her first impression was of a swarthy young man, handsome in his dangerous way. And she knew all about dangerous men.

'This is Yorii,' said the Sarkar. 'She is the daughter of one of our skilled carpenters.'

'I am honoured to meet you, Yorii,' said George Ivanovitch standing up to deliver a low bow.

Yorii nodded in appreciation.

'Are you staying with us long?' she asked.

'I'm unsure,' he said, smiling while looking to the Sarkar for help. 'I am a guest, so it is not for me to say.'

'Gurdjieff speaks well,' said the Sarkar. 'As he says, he is currently unsure and must remain so for a while. Who knows what patience and learning will bring? No life can ever be fenced in by prediction.'

The Sarkar dismissed the girl with a pause and slight movement of the head. The men were to continue alone. She bowed her head and left.

'We were talking about creation and destruction,' said the Sarkar. 'That which brings life and that which destroys it.'

Gurdjieff was listening again. He knew how hard it was to discern between the two.

Twenty Two

Abbot Peter was subdued as Tamsin drove him along the seafront towards the scene of the crime, previously known as St Michael's church. Without a car of his own, he usually enjoyed the luxury of a lift but not on this occasion. There was little pleasure for Peter in what lay ahead.

'And now we must go and meet Anton,' she'd said.

'I already have,' said the Abbot.

'But only when he was alive, so there's much you haven't seen.'

Peter had no desire to see the body but Tamsin said it was necessary to see what was done and how. He'd said he could use his imagination, but she said that police work was not about imagination but facts, the hard facts and, for Peter, they didn't get much harder than gazing on the crucified.

'I do know about crucifixion,' he'd said.

'You know about a crucifixion two thousand years ago, but we're not investigating that one. We're investigating last night's crucifixion of Anton Fontaine and you haven't seen that. I'm not religious myself, but I think we'll find the two bear little relation to one another.'

'There are only so many things you can do with nails and a cross.'

'Where are you on the autism continuum?' she replied, as they drove up the hill towards the church.

*

The church was cordoned off. Formerly a place of worship, it was now mere corridor and passageway for scene of crime officers who cared little for their surroundings. They were here to solve a murder not pray for the world. Abbot Peter walked with Tamsin through the church towards the vestry. Much in demand, she spoke with efficiency to each of the men who waylaid her.

'We're not here to tiptoe around religious sensibilities, Sergeant. We're here to find a murderer.'

'Yes, Ma'am. And the lady who does the flowers?'

'Is not allowed in. End of story.'

'She says the flowers are already bought.'

'Your point being?'

'Just seems a wicked waste.'

Tamsin looked at him with dry incredulity.

'Those were her words, Ma'am. "A wicked waste", she said.'

'Sergeant, at this particular moment, that's you. A wicked waste of my time.'

'Yes, Ma'am.'

'No flower lady. '

'That'll be Edwina Pipe,' said Abbot Peter.

'Then tell the Pipe woman to take them to a hospital or funeral parlour.'

'She won't be thrilled,' added Peter.

'No, but they might be. And isn't that meant to be enough for Christians?'

The Abbot left her to her business and approached the vestry alone. He had no appetite for what lay ahead and stalled. Behind the door hung the crucified body of the man to whom he'd spoken to last night. Peter was one of life's observers, but while he had an endless appetite for psychological darkness, the sight of physical pain held a strange terror. So here he was between a rock and a hard place. Behind him was the harridan Tamsin and before him, the vestry door. Which way to turn? His hand moved towards the handle.

Twenty Three

'The crucified vicar story.'

'What of it?'

'Well, I was just wondering how we were going to work together on this one, Chief Inspector.'

The voice on the phone was smooth and compelling.

'I wasn't aware we were a partnership, Mr Channing.'

'A right relationship between press and police is one of the great social partnerships, Chief Inspector, at the very heart of a healthy democracy!'

Wonder was slightly aggrieved that Martin Channing had managed to get through. He'd clearly charmed the switchboard but that would be the extent of his victory this morning: Channing, as editor of the *Sussex Silt*, was much too dangerous to be allowed near this investigation.

He may have been a newcomer to the south coast, but everyone now knew Channing. He'd just turned fifty when, three years ago, he chose the well-worn path of the rich from London to Brighton. It was the Prince of Wales, later to be King George IV, who'd started this trend in the late eighteenth century and it had never really stopped. London was for work, Brighton was for pleasure but Martin Channing combined the two, bringing his hobby with him. The former editor of a middle-England national – 'chauffeured to Downing Street on a regular basis, those were the days but semi-retirement now, really, it's not a proper job!' – he edited the *Sussex Silt* and was apparently having the time of his life.

And the *Silt*? Everyone bad-mouthed the paper, you had to, it was one of the basic tests of human decency. At dinner parties around Brighton, believing in UFOs was entirely your choice; you could even hold a candle for private health care, the amendment of the human rights act and council-assisted places in private schools for the children of white witches. But whatever cause you espoused, you had to hate the *Sussex Silt* or face the disapproval of the politically righteous.

'If the devil came back as a newspaper, he'd come back as the *Silt*!'

'And so say all of us!'

The only footnote to all this decency and correctness and right thinking was that everyone read it. No one admitted to reading it, no one wanted to read it but everyone did read it. 'My mother insists I get it for her. Really! But what can you do? And I did flick through a few pages when I visited last Saturday – appalling, of course!'

For a paper no one read, sales were huge which thrilled the advertisers and made it a publication with no little power. The genius of Channing was to bring to its pages just the right balance of moral outrage and despicable sleaze. The paper printed the darkest stories whilst at the same time complaining that decent people should not have to read such things. Readers could at once feel titillated and self-righteous. What more could anyone want?

'As you know, Chief Inspector, we do like to get to the bottom of things at the *Silt*.'

'Yes, rock bottom on occasion.'

'The truth is rarely pleasant.'

'And the truth is rarely in your paper.'

'Well, we all work under pressure, Chief Inspector, police and press alike, so let's make a pact.'

'A pact?'

'I won't mention the numerous miscarriages of justice perpetrated by the police if you'll look past the occasional error made by the *Silt*.'

'You make this sound like a negotiation, Mr Channing.'

'All life is a negotiation, Richard!'

Richard? There it was again. He's Richard when someone wants something. With his mother, it was only Richard if he was being told off.

But Channing wasn't finished: 'And if we can help the police along the way, then clearly it's a win/win situation for us both.'

'The case is under investigation and there'll be a press conference when we have something to say.'

'But who's interested in the manicured revelations of a press conference, Chief Inspector? When with inside information, we could get the public to do your work for you.'

'And how does that work exactly?'

'I mean, how was it done, for instance? Put some meat on the bone for me. Is it true the vicar was naked? I'm hearing he may have been naked. Appalling if it's true, not what anyone wants to read about – a naked vicar involved in some sex game presumably? We do not want our readers having to dwell on those images.'

'So don't mention the nakedness.'

'We'll have to mention the nakedness, Richard, because facts like these might just jog someone's memory.'

'Only the murderer's I think. Who on reflection is probably one of your keenest readers.'

'That's a bit cruel, Richard! But we're the good guys here and you do know that I'm just a phone call away if there's any way we can help.'

'I'll bear that in mind.'

'Yes do. I sincerely believe, that at its core, the press, like the police, is a public service.'

'Quite.'

'Our motto is the truth; our practice is the fearless advocacy of the truth!'

The Chief Inspector, a history buff, recognised the quotation.

'Isn't that from the first edition of the *News of the World*, when it was founded in1843?'

'It was a fine vision.'

'It was, yes,' said the Chief Inspector, with enough emphasis on the 'was' to make his point. Channing took the hit but sought the rainbow in the rain.

'I'm denigrated by many, and perhaps deservedly so – God knows, I'm no saint, would never pretend to be – but I hope you at least see a little more of me, Chief Inspector, see beyond the cartoon figure to someone who really wants to make a difference here on the south coast. I suspect you do.'

'I think we understand each other,' acknowledged Wonder, liking the role he'd just been given.

'You're too clever, Richard, you can see through the flannel! Here I am, as one naked before you!'

'So you won't stir things, Martin?'

Martin? Now he was doing it.

'You have my word, Richard.'

Twenty Four

Abbot Peter knew about crucifixion, at least as a religious professional. The crucifixion of Christ was the famous example of this
barbaric form of execution but the Romans crucified people in their
thousands, leaving their rotting corpses up for as long as they would
hang. It was an inefficient form of execution but then that was part of
its appeal. Death could take hours or days, depending on the
strength and will of the victim. But bodies hanging in such pain and
humiliation were reckoned a good deterrent to lawbreakers. No one
much wanted to join them there.

It was Jesus, though, who made the cross famous; he alone who
ensured that necks across the world would be decorated with cruci-
fixes, silver and gold. How a fashion accessory could emerge from
such an event remained a mystery to Peter for it was blood and
agony from beginning to end. Prior to execution, Jesus' back would
have been scourged, using the 'flagrum' – a whip of leather strands
with small pieces of bone and metal attached. Such was the damage
done to the spine by this device that unconsciousness and sometimes death occurred through loss of blood.

If the victim survived, they then carried the cross bar to the site of
execution, where seven inch nails were driven through the wrists.
They would hit the median nerve, sending pain up through the arms,
shoulders and neck. The body was then turned slightly, to allow the
feet to be nailed to the pole. The cross was then swung up into the air,
at which point the body strain was such that dislocation of both
shoulder and elbow joints was inevitable. With only shallow breathing possible, loss of blood and lack of oxygen could then cause
severe cramps and unconsciousness.

Remarkably, medical opinion still debates what ultimately causes
death for the crucified. Archaeological evidence is rare, for the
simple reason that crucified bodies were never buried; and the one
that was, unhelpfully claimed resurrection. But the death of the

crucified was not a complete mystery. Although the fatal blow for one victim might not be that of another, amid loss of blood, collapsed lungs, multiple dislocations, cardiac rupture and unrelenting agony, perhaps heart failure, hypovolemic shock, exhaustion or asphyxia were the most common ends.

But now Abbot Peter must look on the crucified himself and a sense of shame passed through him. He'd always spoken mockingly of Jesus' weak followers who had made themselves scarce after his arrest. Only four brave souls had the guts to stand by the cross in solidarity with Jesus, three of them women and one of those his mother. 'Fair weather friends' Peter called the others in his sermons – 'friends who disappeared when the Roman heat was on.' And now he understood why. Who'd want to witness that? They'd been terrified and so was he. Behind the vestry door was the crucified vicar with whom he'd spent many hours. And he too wanted only to run away.

God help you when your dream comes true, thought Abbot Peter. He had so wanted to meet a Detective Inspector. And right now, as he pushed open the vestry door, he was rather wishing he hadn't.

Twenty Five

The killer took the notebook from the shelf again. It had found a role in life at last. It was now the murder diary. Or the diary of a murderer, was that better? Book titles were so hard. This probably wasn't the intended use when the notebook was wrapped in festive paper and left below the Christmas tree in church. But we cannot legislate what others will do with our kindness and nor should we try. The murderer started to write:

The church is a beehive of activity. Strange how quickly everything is changed. Busy bees in their investigation clothes investigating. Though to me it feels more like a game of snakes and ladders. What a nasty game, I could never play that. But hopefully they will encounter more snakes than ladders.

I saw that pushy woman detective with Abbot Peter traipsing behind. It's like watching the Queen and Prince Philip. I hate pushy women, really hate them. It's good to use the word "hate". That feels good and I think I can use it now I've killed. Before you kill someone you imagine yourself too nice to hate. But after killing someone, you're free of all that self-deception, all that nonsense. Everyone hates; but some of us are honest enough to acknowledge it and blessed are the honest.

My fans may want me as the sole murderer but it takes two to tango. Murder requires teamwork. If you can call it that.'

Twenty Six

Peter gazed on the naked figure of Anton, taped and nailed, head hanging, the shock on his face, blood dry around the wrists, feet taped but not nailed. No nails in the feet. Strange. Had the murderer experienced a failure of nerve? Been disturbed? Or simply lost interest?

Scene of crime tape denied Peter the closeness he desired. Before entering, he had wanted only distance but now longed only to be close. He longed to touch Anton, bless the cold body, kiss it even, but was under strict instructions. And so he stood and gazed at a measured distance like a visitor in an art gallery. It was the saddest of pictures, a black Christ – no Messiah certainly, but still a keeper of the divine spark, and now savagely pierced.

'I'm sorry they were not better days, Anton,' he said, looking into the surprised and open eyes.

He wished to speak to him, give body to his thoughts. It's what talk therapy does, it puts inner things out there, gives them air and visible shape. Abbot Peter needed this now. 'I'm sorry for the fears you had to run from, my friend, and the abandonment at the end. You were worth more than your last night on earth. You laughed it off, you always laughed it off; you laughed it off and moved on because to feel it would have killed you. But now something else – or rather someone else – has done that. Who was it, my friend? Who killed you, Anton? Do you have anything to say?'

Peter paused, waiting for the dead to speak. Perhaps the body would rip its arm from the wood and write the murderer's name on the wall.

'Did you see them, Anton, you must have seen them ... you knew they were coming, you spoke to them on the phone ... and how was it done and why? ... and don't worry, I won't judge ... how could I ever judge?'

Just then, the door opened and a scene of crime officer popped his head round. If surprised at finding a figure in a monk's habit talking with a dead man, he didn't show it.

'If I could be left alone for a moment,' said Peter.

'Of course,' he said and the door closed again.

Peter looked again on the figure but knew Anton had gone, Anton the person, Anton's spirit, these things had gone, no longer having need of this carcass. Peter's time was done, there were more voices outside. This wasn't an art gallery or even now a church; this was a murder scene, a brutalised space and still an open wound.

'Goodbye, my friend. And whether you will care, I don't know – but I will find the one who did this.'

Act Two

'The Enneagram describes nine different journeys of the human psyche. It describes the journey away from our true selves when young and the return journey that becomes possible in adult life.'

Act Two

Twenty Seven

The Reverend Sally Appleby, the curate at St Michael's, had done a good job making things ready for Tamsin and Abbot Peter. They were to use her office for the day's interviews.

'I hope you'll be comfortable here,' she said. 'Not as clean as it should be! But you've rather caught me out.'

Her spotless office would be a pleasant setting. It was up the small metal staircase and next to the Gallery which looked down onto the Church. The gallery itself was not much used. The church hardly needed an overflow and so this was a place for gathering dust and forgotten church artefacts. Sally's room, on the other hand, was a light space and on a clear day, you could just glimpse the sea over the rooftops. Her distinctive perfume hung in the air while fresh images of Christ and the saints looked down from the walls. Sally was a suspect of course, how could she not be, but on that Wednesday morning, eight days before Christmas, it seemed an unlikely home for a murderer.

'I've spoken to everyone,' she said. 'They're all in a complete state of shock, of course.'

'I quite understand,' said Abbot Peter.

Strange to say, but Sally and Peter had passed like ships in the night over the eighteen months of their acquaintance. Something inside her drew back from him and he'd allowed the distance to remain. They met as polite colleagues in shared professional endeavour but nothing more.

'I've tried to reassure everyone,' she said to the Abbot. 'I've told them that I'm here for them; that they must call me night or day, if needs be.'

Peter noted Sally hard at work establishing her pastoral superiority. The message was clear: Sally was caring for everyone; and any who wanted care would certainly choose her over him.

'Let me introduce myself, Sally,' said Tamsin, stepping forward to clarify roles. 'I'm Detective Inspector Tamsin Shah and I will be leading this investigation.'

'Very pleased to meet you,' said Sally, 'Another woman in a man's world!'

'I've never seen it like that myself,' said Tamsin. 'We all make our own way, I think.'

'Oh, definitely,' said Sally, changing gear. 'I've always very much believed that … very much so.'

'And Abbot Peter is to assist me as Special Witness.'

'Really?' said Sally, taken aback. 'And what does that entail exactly? Being a Special Witness?' She seemed a little flustered.

'Not my idea, I hasten to add,' said Abbot Peter with a smile.

'It simply means that Abbot Peter is part of the investigation team,' said Tamsin. 'And as such, privy to all material uncovered.'

'I see.'

'Abbot Peter has become a detective, you might say.'

'I'm sure everyone will be reassured by that,' said Sally. 'Well, most of us, anyway!'

Abbot Peter could imagine the Bishop being less than pleased and Sally as well, it seemed. There was a slight pause as both Tamsin and Peter waited for Sally to leave. But she didn't.

Sally said: 'We must hope that Abbot Peter isn't the murderer then!'

'Clearly everyone is a suspect at the start of the investigation,' said Tamsin.

'Everyone except for Abbots?' asked Sally.

'Abbots quite as much as anyone else, perhaps even more so,' said Tamsin. 'The church has a poor record when it comes to massacre. But on this occasion, we were quickly able to eliminate Abbot Peter from our enquiries. Free of suspicion, he then became a strong candidate for the post of Special Witness and came with a warm recommendation.'

Tamsin smiled at Peter, who was quietly wondering how he'd been eliminated from the enquiry quite so fast. As the last known figure to have seen Anton alive, he had expected hard questions. Perhaps later, he would ask why they never came.

'Who?' asked Sally.

'Sorry?'

'Who recommended him?'

'Operational information, I'm afraid, but getting down to business, you found the body, didn't you, Sally? You were the first one on the scene.'

'I was, yes.'

'Perhaps you could tell us about your discovery,' said Tamsin.

The detective had decided to kick on. She had thought of holding Sally over until later, but why wait? She had no wish to waste time and the sooner the curate was removed from her bubble of special status the better. She could play the wonderful priest in her own time; for now, she was just witness and suspect.

'You were in the church very early weren't you?'

Sally sat down on the spare chair.

'I was in at 6.00 a.m.'

'OK. Was that normal?'

'I sometimes come to church for my private prayers in the morning.'

'Do they not work at home?'

'I find the atmosphere of a place of worship helps; knowing that other people have prayed here for years.'

'It didn't help the vicar.'

'No. Well, bad things can happen in holy places too.'

'Archbishop Oscar Romero was shot dead in a hospital chapel in San Salvador while celebrating Mass,' said Peter.

Sally nodded. 'Great man,' she said.

'He was killed by a government assassin. The day before his assassination, he'd called on the country's soldiers to stop supporting the government's abuse of human rights.'

There was a pause which threatened to become a minute's silence for the murdered of San Salvador but for Tamsin's sharp interjection.

'Meanwhile, back in Stormhaven,' she said with deliberation, 'this morning you just happened to come in early, Sally?'

'As I've said.'

'Indeed. And so how exactly did you make the discovery?'

And now Sally blushed.

'I came in through the side door of the vestry as normal. It wasn't locked which was unusual. But I went in, and – well, there he was.'

'What did you see?'

'I saw Anton hanging there, nailed to the Good Friday cross.'

'And why was the cross there? I'm not an expert but it seems unusual in a vestry.'

'It is unusual, rather stupid if you ask me. It was Anton's idea. He didn't want it going back into the church. He didn't like pain or reminders of pain.'

'And how did Anton look when you saw him?'

'It was awful. His face was shocked. And he looked cold.'

'What else did you see?'

Sally allowed her eyes to drop to the ground, in a rather coy manner. For a moment, she looked like Princess Diana.

'I want you to tell me everything you saw,' said Tamsin. 'You're the one who found him.'

Sally was struggling to speak her lines.

'His wrists had big nails through them,' she said. 'But he was also held by a large amount of sticky tape round his arms. It seemed -. '

' – it seemed what?'

'Well, my first thought was that he'd been taped to the cross first – then nailed. That was just my thought.'

'Anything else strike you?'

'His feet were taped as well but not nailed.'

'OK. Anything else?'

'There was a lot of blood. I've seen some pretty bleak scenes as a social worker, but nothing to compare with this.'

'What else can you tell us about the body?'

Sally again looked at her feet.

'He was naked,' she said.

'Completely naked?'

'Except for the dog collar. A dog collar had been placed around his neck.'

'What can you tell us about that?'

'It was his dog collar. Well, it was like it at least. They're just pieces of white plastic, after all. Some priests cut up washing-up liquid bottles when they lose them. They're just as good.'

Tamsin was not interested in the varied roles of old washing-up liquid bottles.

'Do you have any more to say about the dog collar?'

'You mean the writing?'

'You tell me.'

'It was Ginger who saw it first.'

'Ah yes, Ginger was with you?'

'He wasn't with me, that's a misconception.'

'Whose misconception?'

'I'm just saying it isn't how it appears.'

'How does it appear?'

'Well, that we were together … when we weren't.'

'You were together in church but not together?'

'I think I can see what Sally's saying,' said Peter.

'So you weren't kissing or anything?'

'No!'

Sally blushed again, a deeper red now.

'It's important we know,' said Tamsin.

'He came in through the other door,' said Sally.

'The door from the church?'

'That's right. He was there on business of his own.'

'What sort of business?'

'You'd have to ask him that.'

'We will obviously but I just wondered if you knew?'

'Well I don't.'

'Carry on.'

'I screamed and he heard me and came immediately to see what was wrong. I had no idea he was there but was very glad he was.'

'I'm sure you were.'

'I was in a state, I don't mind admitting. He was a complete angel.'

'Was it normal for him to be in the church at six in the morning?'

'I don't know what's normal for him. You'll have to speak with him about that.'

'Well, again, Sally, we will but I just wondered if you had an opinion on the matter.'

'I don't have an opinion, no.'

'Surprisingly opinion-free when it comes to Ginger.'

Sally sat quietly.

'And what happened then?'

'Ginger checked for breathing. It was then that he saw the writing on the dog collar.'

'And what did it say?'

'It said: "Should have done better".'

'That's all?'

'That's all.'

'And did you have any reason to kill him, Sally?'

'Me? Well, no, of course not!'

'No cause for anger? No reason for resentment about the way you'd been treated, either personally or professionally?'

'No. He was just my vicar. What can I say?'

'And what about Ginger?'

'Ginger is a kind man who wouldn't hurt anyone.'

'That's not everyone's view.'

'Then they don't know him.'

Tamsin paused.

'From what I understand, you both had a sack full of grievances against Anton Fontaine.'

'That's a sack I'm not aware of,' said Sally, with controlled rage.

'And we still have the unexplained early morning gathering. Quite by chance, you are both in the church at 6.00 a.m. the morning after the murder.'

'If you really think I was Anton's murderer then you are very stupid,' said Sally.

'Not wise words, Sally,' said Tamsin. 'I will find out what you two were doing here.'

There was a knock on the door. PC Neville poked his head round.

'Just to say there's no sign of her, Ma'am. We can't find her anywhere.'

'Who's that?' asked Sally. 'Is there someone missing?'

'Thank you for your help, Sally,' said Tamsin, getting up quickly. 'You may go now.'

The unspoken hostility remained as Sally was asked to leave her office. But Tamsin wasn't quite done: 'I'd add only that we must be careful that pastoral concern, or indeed any feelings of a more personal nature, do not in any way become respite or protection for the guilty. Do you understand me?'

'I believe so,' said Sally.

'We're dealing with a dangerous individual here, who operates quite beyond any normal moral compass.'

'Rather like you then,' thought Sally.

'We mustn't mistake collusion with compassion,' said Tamsin.

It was a cold farewell.

Sally said: 'Of course,' after which she collected her bag and left.

When she was gone, Tamsin turned to Neville, as young and fresh-faced a copper as was either legal or decent.

'In future, Constable, when you have operational information to disclose, you wait until the room is free of suspects. Do you understand?'

'Yes, Ma'am. I'm sorry.'

'She could be the murderer.'

'I'm sorry, Ma'am.'

'Too late for sorry, Constable.'

'Never too late for sorry,' smiled Abbot Peter.

'Maybe in your world, Abbot, but not in mine.'

'So who's missing?' asked Peter.

'Clare Magnussen.' And then turning to the Constable, 'You've tried her work and home?'

'Nothing, Ma'am. And it's out of character apparently. She's never been absent from work without warning. The Bishop says he gave her a lift home and since then, no sign of her. And we don't think she slept in her bed last night.'

'Why not?'

'Yesterday's post was uncollected by the door. It looks like she came to last night's meeting straight from work and never made it home.'

'And the house searches? Have they delivered anything?'

'No, Ma'am. We're doing our best to get round. But with two of the team off sick and Mick on compassionate leave –. '

'Compassionate leave? Whatever happened to coping?'

She looked round in derisive dismay.

'Just keep the fit busy, the unfit on our radar and let me know as soon you know anything. That will all be for now.'

'Yes, Ma'am.'

The policeman left, closing the door carefully behind him. Tamsin and the Abbot were alone in Sally's office.

'Well?' asked Tamsin.

'You're not strong on manners,' said Peter.

'Neither was the murderer.'

Twenty Eight

And now Clare was remembering … allowing herself to remember.

It hadn't seemed worth it in the past, despite Jonathan the nice psychotherapist. And he was nice, a decent sort. But now she was allowing the memories of her mother who had hit her from when she was very young. Why? Why does someone do that? Who knows? But for some reason this mother, the mother given to Clare, the carer given to Clare, didn't care at all … in fact she seemed to hate her youngest daughter. And every time, when the hitting was over, she'd always say the same thing: 'Don't bother telling anyone, Clare – they'll never believe you'… .

And she never did tell anyone. She never told anyone of the years of random violence from her mother, violence ignored by her father who was usually out, but not always, sometimes he just played the saxophone … that's how you knew if he was in; you'd hear the saxophone playing … and then one day, in her early twenties, she did tell someone. She'd told a psychologist at a dinner party and he just confirmed her mother's prediction. She had begun to tell her story over the dessert. After a while, he said:

'It simply can't have been as you say, Clare. People like you are in special units or drugged up with medication. They're not doing the sort of job you're doing.'

So her mum had been proved right. No one would believe her though it had been as she said, worse in fact because she'd told the psychologist only a little of what went on.

And she had survived … she'd begun to regain control in her early teens when on one occasion her arm went up to stop her mother's strike. It just happened … after that, her mother never tried it again, just emotional punishment from then on, but always losing power. And then with Clare as an adult, the years of denial, the shroud of evasion, the final refuge of scoundrel parents …

Some called Clare tough as old boots, some simply called her cold, but she'd survived and regained control until now ... she was drifting in and out of consciousness, disappearing then returning with such clarity of thought, trapped, losing strength, no voice to call out, held down, pressed hard, held in, darkness, heartache, familiar smells, stone floor and remembering, distant things, distant things never touched for the sadness they bled, the overwhelming sadness, the overwhelming bleeding, the abandonment ...

Stretching out now, Clare was stretching out, reaching out for someone, the sound of a car, voices, they could be voices, is there anyone there ...?

Twenty Nine

Tamsin and Abbot Peter sat on a bench with their sandwich lunch, looking out on the cold green sea. Peter broke the silence.

'I don't want you to take this amiss, Tamsin.'

'Ominous. My defences are suddenly raised.'

'Because I know you're the detective here.'

'Good. But what exactly are you preparing the ground for?'

'And you're a hunter, of course, dangerous and sharp-toothed.'

'Thank you.'

'I certainly wouldn't want you on my case!'

'You'd be too easy.'

'Ah, cocky as well!'

'No one in the south of England got higher marks than me in my Inspector's exams.'

'Then I am in awe of you.'

Peter paused, allowing time for the applause to be heard. He started on his tuna sandwich, reassuringly moist and filled to the edges, just as a sandwich should be.

'But tell me,' he said, 'Do you know what every good interrogator knows?'

'Of course. Don't give them an inch.'

'Almost the opposite in fact.'

'Not in my manual.'

Peter took another bite from his sandwich and chewed slowly.

Tamsin spoke first: 'Well get it out then! You're like a storm waiting to break.'

'It's nothing really.'

'But it's a nothing that's starting to get on my nerves.'

'It's just that the good interrogator knows you don't get anywhere with the suspect until you break down the barrier between their world and yours.'

Tamsin thought for a moment. 'Exactly! That's why I pressure them.'

'Well, that's one way but only one way and rarely the best.'

'Always the best. It's why governments continue to use torture.'

'And why secret services around the world are told so many lies. Victims will say anything to make the pain stop.'

'That's the point.'

'But "anything" may not be the truth, Tamsin. The reign of Henry VIII was the story of endless people confessing "the truth" – a long list of things they hadn't done just so they could get off the rack. They knew they'd be executed soon after but at least it wasn't the rack.'

'Is there a point to this dull history lesson?'

'It's horses for courses, Tamsin, and sometimes a soft word or a joke is the better way to join the two worlds together. Humans are liars, I grant you, we can't help ourselves – but strangely, we're more likely to be disarmed by kindness than terror. And once disarmed, once the barrier between the two worlds is broken, then the real talk begins. And the hope is that it's truthful talk.'

'Shall we get back to work now?'

'We are at work.'

'Not in my book.'

'We're working on how we might access the truth. And by the way, who recommended me?'

'I can't tell you. Operational information. If you knew, you might go easy on them, seduced by their flattery.'

'Good point.' He ate a little more of his sandwich before adding: 'But the only good one you've made in the last five minutes. We must understand the psychology of the killer.'

'I don't want to rain on your mental parade,' said Tamsin, wiping some crumbs from her lap and sighing a little.

'I sense damp in the air.'

'But in my experience – my professional police experience – psychological profiling is as often wrong as right.'

'Well, I can't answer for your brief professional experience, Tamsin, and I grant you that some of the sickest people on the planet are psychiatrists. But the right person with the right psychological tools is a dangerous enemy.'

'And you're that person?'

'I don't know if I'm that person, time will tell. But I certainly have the right tool: the most profound analysis of human motive ever discovered.'

'And that is?'

'The Enneagram.'

'The *what*?'
'We'll talk this evening.'

Thirty

○

The Sarkar poured himself some water and sipped sparingly. The man in the cobalt blue turban did not rush things and Gurdjieff was struggling to concentrate. He fidgeted a little, looked into the distance, then over-compensated, staring too hard into the eyes of the speaker. The mysterious Yorii was out of sight but not completely out of mind.

'You must strive for attention,' the Sarkar said, 'and all will be well.'

'I understand, Sir. I want to learn.'

'Then you will learn! You will learn of the nine soul structures of humankind.'

'This is the teaching of the Enneagram?'

He had decided that questions were the best path to staying alert.

'The Enneagram describes nine different journeys of the human psyche. It describes the journey away from our true selves when young and it describes the return journey that becomes possible in adult life.'

'The journey away from our true selves and then the journey home?'

'That's right, the destruction and recreation of each soul. And at its heart is this claim: each of us has chosen one of those nine ways, one of those nine paths, as our model.'

'You mean one of the paths is our path in particular?'

'Indeed. We may relate to several, to all in some way or other. But one path above all others controls our particular selves. Some people call the path away from true selves our 'compulsion'.'

'So our compulsive behaviour is behaviour which takes us away from our true selves; in other words, that which destroys us?'

'Correct. These compulsions are the basic construct of our personality and significantly define our life. After all, we create around us what we are within.'

'A frightening thought.'

'In one way, but also rather hopeful. We only have to notice the compulsion to find the world a far more wonderful place.'

'That makes sense. So, let me understand – the Enneagram describes nine ways of being? First a journey away from truth, dominated by our personality and then a journey home to our true selves which we left behind.'

'You are a good student.'

'And each individual has chosen one such way?'

'In a manner, though there was little conscious choice, for the path was set in the early years of life, when we had feelings but no words to describe them. But you are broadly right. There are nine spaces on the symbol, numbered from one to nine each describing a different path. And everyone dwells in one of those spaces; everyone has chosen one of those paths.'

'Do you know which path I have chosen?'

'I could hazard a guess.'

'And will you tell me?'

'No.'

'Why not?'

'The journey to the shrine is the shrine itself.'

'How do you mean?'

'It is for you to find your space.'

'Why so?'

'The Enneagram is concerned, above all, with your intentions. It is not what you do that matters, but why you do it – this is the key. And that particular investigation is best carried out by you.'

'That is a subtle and uncomfortable investigation.'

'The investigation of motive? Indeed. We have here in our hands a sharp knife, which cuts to the marrow of our existence. We must handle this knife carefully.'

George Ivanovitch was less concerned with careful handling than with finding out more. He wanted to hear each space described but first had a more general question. 'And tell me – is there anyone beyond the Enneagram's reach? Is this a time-bound understanding or perhaps just for the people of Asia or the Americas or the North Pole?'

'No' said the Sarkar. 'It's both a timeless and universal symbol. All are within its reach. Every human who has ever lived, in whatever part of the world, they each walked one of these paths, each lived a specific number from one to nine.'

Gurdjieff was relieved. Anything less than a timeless and universal understanding would have meant prompt and disappointed departure. He had come here for deep truth, truth which would not fade with time or travel.

'So is the Enneagram a religion, a new way to follow?'

'Not at all. It is insight not religion. It can be used by those with faith and those with none. It asks only accurate reflection on our self.'

'Not a popular pastime.'

'But fruitful for those who attempt it.'

The desire in Gurdjieff almost stained the air in its urgency. They had talked round the subject enough. He wished to hear the nine states described.

'So now you will reveal the nine different spaces, the nine different paths?'

'In a while,' said the Sarkar, *'and not here.'*

'Not here? Then where?'

'We must walk to the Seeing Stone.'

Thirty One

But Tamsin couldn't wait until evening to hear about the Enneagram. What was gained from waiting? How did the saying go? 'Patience is a virtue, catch it if you can, found seldom in a woman and never in a man.' Rubbish. Tamsin was with the men on this one; waiting was for losers. And so that afternoon, as they sat in Stormhaven police station, awaiting further news from the pathologist – 'don't expect someone quirky or amusing like in the TV programmes' she'd warned Peter – she also demanded that he get this Enneagram nonsense out of his system so they could get on with the case.

Peter said: 'We haven't got time now.'

'We've got plenty of time,' she said, 'at least five minutes, maybe ten. That's long enough to assess the evidence. I don't want your life story – just the bare bones of the theory, taught you by your father?'

'That's right.'

'Fine. But I hope when I tell you the whole thing's nonsense – not to pre-judge at all – you won't get all precious about it as though it's some irreplaceable family heirloom. Fathers are wrong sometimes – wildly.'

'His English was poor, I grant you. My father, your grandfather, was an Armenian Russian and speaking with him was a little like speaking with a child; but a child with disturbing insight.'

'How was it disturbing?'

The Abbot prepared for Tamsin to be offended.

'He said everyone was asleep to their true selves.'

'I see.'

'He said that each person was an idiot, sleepwalking through life.'

'Not a teaching designed to win friends.'

'No, but he did win devotees.'

'Most nutcases do.'

'Those prepared to face their own idiocy. And this is where the Enneagram symbol became important.'

'This child's drawing here?'

Tamsin looked at the roughly-drawn circle drawn on the back of the envelope, with nine marks equally spread round the circumference and each with a number by it.

'That's right. Forgive the graphics but this symbol describes nine ways people forget who they are; nine different ways to lose your true self and become unhappy – and rather dangerous in the world.'

'And you say everyone has chosen one of these ways?'

'Very good, I'm impressed.'

'So every human has a number, from one to nine?'

'I'm beginning to think this was part of the Inspector's course.'

'Or is it just that I learn quickly?'

'And this number affects who they are and how they behave.'

'So how do people discover their space?'

'To find it, you have to discover what sort of idiot you are; or to put it in a more acceptable manner, you need to discern your central compulsion around which your phoney personality grew.'

'And what if I don't believe my personality is phoney?'

'Then you are most deeply asleep.'

Tamsin went quiet, a resistant silence the Abbot was familiar with. 'And you believe that all this can help find murderers?' she asked.

'I do.'

'Because you know people's numbers?'

'It's a gift I have, unfortunately.'

'You know their number even if they don't know it themselves?'

'Very often, yes. And this is what made the final parish meeting before the murder so interesting. I suddenly realised that the nine of us gathered in that room represented the entire Enneagram symbol. There was one of each number present, from one to nine.'

'Like an Enneagram training course!'

'If you like, yes, though I've always tried to avoid those.'

'And what are the chances of this miracle?'

'Very slim and I probably would have forgotten all about it. Yet once events unfolded, I began to reflect on the nine types of idiot in the room that night.'

'Including yourself, of course.'

'Believe me, I know my idiot well, even if on this occasion he wasn't a killer. But I did ponder which idiot was, which particular idiot had cracked in these circumstances and why. Which compulsion in that circle was so inflamed and painful that murder became the only way? Find the fault line and we find the murderer.'

'So what number am I?'

Thirty Two

'Is this allowed?' asks Betty.

'I think we're all consenting adults,' says Ginger.

'I just want to make sure everyone's all right,' says Sally.

It was her idea that all those who attended the fateful meeting the night before should gather at 6.00 p.m. in the parish room, the only church space presently available to them.

It was the first time they'd been together since the meeting, though there were one or two absentees. Anton was dead, Clare and the Bishop were missing and Abbot Peter investigating.

'Strange to think that the five of us were all sitting here last night,' says Malcolm.

'Seems like a world away,' says Jennifer.

Ginger then speaks: 'I note no one is sitting in Anton's seat.'

They all look at the empty chair where the vicar had sat to hear the evidence against him and ultimately, to receive his cruel marching orders: death by raised hands.

'And no Clare?' asks Jennifer.

'The police are still looking for her,' confirms Sally. 'I haven't heard anything more from them.'

The implication being that as soon as they knew anything, she'd be the first to know.

'But should we be talking at all?' asks Betty, concerned about the rights and wrongs of them gathering in this manner. 'After all, we're the suspects. It's obvious they think one of us did it.'

'I think you're in the clear, Betty!' says Sally.

'What about the Bishop?' asks Ginger.

The Bishop was not with them either. Sally had decided against inviting him.

'It could have been the Bishop,' says Ginger. 'We all know what he thought of Anton.'

'Which makes him an unlikely murderer, too obvious,' says Malcolm knowingly. 'You have to find the hidden relationship.'

Ginger says: 'Sometimes murder is obvious, Malcolm. Sometimes there's nothing complicated about it at all. Trust me.'

'I really don't think it's him,' says Malcolm, who'd never spoken to Ginger before, as far as he could remember. Sometimes violence separates; sometimes it brings together and on this occasion, it was the latter. The fact that these five people now sat in the same room talking, revealed how unspoken cliques are smashed by circumstance. Here was a new community, suspicious, frightened, shocked, needing to talk and each quietly wondering if they were sitting next to a sadistic killer.

'It's never the Bishop,' says Jennifer glibly, like some tired hack-writer at a script meeting.

'Why's that?'

'Because Bishops are too concerned with their careers! A murder can seriously damage a CV – though not as much as being gay, of course.'

After a day at school playing the wonderful head, Jennifer had a lot of sarcasm to get out of her system.

Sally adds: 'I didn't ask the Bishop because I thought he'd be too busy.'

'And probably he'd try and take over,' says Ginger.

'Not that Bishop Stephen doesn't have his fair share of secrets,' contributes Jennifer. 'And murder investigations tend to flush out plenty of those. I hope we're all ready for that? All ready for our secrets to be laid bare?'

There is an uneasy pause.

Sally says: 'I don't think we should sit here accusing people.'

'So why are we here?' asks Betty, who has now started knitting.

'Well, to look out for each other. I'm still your curate and these are difficult times.'

'But you might also be our murderer,' says Malcolm with a smile.

Sally blushes and looks irritated.

'And how likely is that, Malcolm?' asks Ginger.

'Isn't it always the one who finds the body?'

'You're talking nonsense, so mind your mouth.'

'Children, children!' says Jennifer.

Ginger's anger is almost a physical presence.

Jennifer says: 'I have to say, Ginger, that if you'd been sent to my office by a teacher, I'd tell you to go back to the playground and find a role other than that of Sally's minder. It's not helping you or her.'

'I'm not Sally's minder. She doesn't need a minder.'

Jennifer's raised eyebrows and knowing smile undermine Ginger's words.

Betty says: 'I think it's very sad about Clare.'

'We must just hope and pray,' says Sally, glad the subject has changed.

'But does that actually mean anything?' asks Malcolm.

'Does what mean anything?'

'I mean, it's what we always say, 'we must hope and pray,' it's the standard line, but how's it going to help? How's hoping and praying going to help Clare now?'

His voice began to crumble.

'She could be anywhere,' says Sally. 'She's an independent woman.'

'No,' says Malcolm. 'She's dead.'

'Well how could you possibly know that?'

'I just do.'

Not long after that, Betty decided she was going home, unsure the police would be in favour of this unofficial meeting, particularly after Sally confirmed they knew nothing about it.

'You didn't ask them?' says Jennifer with astonished amusement. 'What are you like, Sally!'

Others followed Betty soon afterwards, leaving the curate alone to lock up. She'd liked to have gone into the main body of the church but that area remained off-limits and seemed a step too far.

It hadn't been quite the support group she'd anticipated.

Thirty Three

'Stormhaven is a place of rest and quiet for both resident and visitor alike. A place to change down a gear or two, take a break.'

Peter was reading from a brochure as they sat together in Sandy View at the end of the first day to review the case. Tamsin had asked for a brief background to Stormhaven, never having set foot in the place before this morning.

'You mean it's boring?'

'Not at all, no. People transpose their inner boredom onto places, quite unfairly of course. Stormhaven is merely unpretentious.'

'Code for "no decent shops".'

'The shops struggle, I agree, but the gulls swoop and scream and the elderly park along the seafront, looking out on the waves from the warmth of their cars.'

'Don't go into advertising.'

'It has the air not of a town past its best but of one that perhaps never quite reached it. Stormhaven tried to be noisy and fun but failed.'

'It could almost be you, Uncle.'

'But of course things have not always been thus.'

'Don't tell me. The town once housed the court of King Arthur.'

'No, Stormhaven is one of the few places not to make that claim. But Alfred the Great's palace was found at nearby West Dean which he used as a defence against the Vikings. And during the thirteenth century, this was a major port in the south of England, exporting wool, importing wine and it was very wealthy.'

'Sounds like a Waitrose sort of place.'

'Pretty upmarket, yes. But then the fourteenth century was less kind. Raided constantly by the French, the place was sunk commercially with the arrival of the Black Death. By the middle of the century, the town was largely burned down and residents were both few and depressed.'

'So no change there then.'

'They'd lost their harbour to Newhaven, a few miles down the coast – they still hate the people of Newhaven – and were so poor they couldn't afford to send a representative to parliament.'

'Waitrose closes and a Morrisons opens?'

'For the residents of Stormhaven, the humiliation was complete and the humiliated are not pleasant people to know.'

'Why do you say that?'

'It's just an observation.'

'No one likes being humiliated.'

'No, and the humiliated fight back. Believe me, there have been dark episodes in the history of the town; things about which no one is proud.'

'Spoken of in hushed whispers?'

'Indeed. But with the coming of the railway in 1864, everyone expected change. Here was a new chapter in their civic history and high hopes abounded. There were plans for a magnificent pier, five seaside gardens and bold Victorian buildings along the front. They would transform this backwater into a proper seaside town, with all the fun of the fair and arcades for public amusement.'

'I'm sensing a "but" in the air.'

'A large one. The money ran out long before any pier was built or visitors came. Instead, they all went to Brighton with its gay royal air, easy access to London and famous Pavilion.'

'You can't blame them. It beats a blanket and thermos on the Stormhaven stones.'

This had never occurred to Abbot Peter but made sense of his love for the place.

'Perhaps that's why I'm so happy here,' he said. 'I've always been attracted to failure; so much more interesting than success.'

'That's what all failures say. That's why they're failures.'

*

They'd conducted preliminary interviews with all six suspects; the seventh, Clare, was still missing. Peter was enjoying the history but Tamsin wanted to get on.

'I'll tell you the dark past of Stormhaven one day,' he said. 'Show you how desperate people behave.'

'I think we've just seen how desperate people behave. I mean, how many crucifixions does it take to make you notice the present? Or do you only experience life that's over 500 years old?'

'I am seduced by history, but thankfully you've shaken me from my slumbers.'

'And by the way, I trust you won't bring your lust for failure into the investigation. Once it's all over, worship at its shrine by all means, but until then – .'

'Failure is at the heart of every murder, Tamsin.'

Peter was suddenly struck by a truth but one too elusive to be grasped and held.

'What?'

'Failure is at the heart of every murder.'

'You've said that.'

'Only the failing kill, an interesting thought. Only those scalded in their search for the sacred and now running from their pain kill people.'

Tamsin sipped her wine while glancing through her notes.

'Cod psychology is only distantly related to police work, Uncle.'

Abbot Peter smiled, and, sensing her discomfort, focused on the day.

'When I reflect back on the interviews,' he said, 'I think mainly of the large number of lies.'

'Sorry?'

Tamsin lifted her eyes from her notes.

'During the interviews, a lot of untruth was being peddled out. I'm used to misinformation as a priest and counsellor but I didn't realise the police got quite so much of the dark stuff as well.'

'All the time. So I'm glad your lie detector's working.'

'Oh, discerning evasion is easy. It's the truth that struggles to emerge.'

'So which particular porkies jumped out at you today?'

'Five spring obviously to mind.'

Tamsin was surprised by his precision.

'There's nothing so satisfying as a list. So let's hear it, Uncle.'

'Sally said she had no reason to be angry with Anton. Malcolm Flight said he left the church after the meeting. The Bishop said he drove Clare home. Betty says that the reason for her late night walk was to get some air and Ginger said that he was catching up on some paperwork in church this morning. All lies.'

Peter had Tamsin's attention.

'The counsel for the defence might ask for evidence,' she said.

'I know from both Mrs Pipe and Clare how badly Sally took her rejection by Anton.'

'They told you that?'

'They did, yes.'

'Why?'

'It's what people do, they tell me things. They won't tell a soul, but they will tell an Abbot.'

'Malcolm Flight? An honourable man in my book. Dull obviously and a bit of a freak, as Anton said, but honourable.'

'Maybe he is, maybe he isn't. But he was in the church late.'

'How do you know?'

'I'm pretty sure I heard him. He dropped his keys, you see, or at least I think he did. More particularly, the oil is still wet from his painting and he was in the shop all day yesterday. He must have worked on it after the meeting.'

'Not bad. But the Bishop lying about taking Clare home? Why on earth would a Bishop do that?'

'I don't know why. Perhaps he has a messy life too? For the moment I'm merely saying it isn't true.'

'How do you know?'

'Jennifer saw him driving alone in his car.'

'Perhaps he'd already dropped her off.'

'He was still two miles short of her home. And it was raining.'

'Perhaps the wonderful Jennifer is telling a lie. She seems to be the only one who hasn't told one yet.'

'She could be. She lies as well as the next person, probably better. All we can say is she hasn't been caught out yet.'

'And Betty?'

'I met her on the seafront when I was walking home much later. She appeared from behind the beach huts and was a picture of fury. Whatever it was that took her out last night it wasn't the desire for a little air. You had to have good reason to be out in that storm.'

'Which just leaves Ginger's early morning attendance at church. Don't tell me: you were out for a run at half past five and you met him carrying a hammer and a bag of nails.'

'More flies are caught with honey than vinegar.'

'I beg your pardon?'

'Are you merciless with everyone?'

'Mercy is not one of my weaknesses.'

'It could, as I say, distance you from truth.'

'It could also help me nail the murderer.'

'And how appropriate that will be: the crucifier nailed. A toast to justice.'

'To justice.'

They clinked glasses of red wine.

'So why do you think Ginger was lying?'

'No evidence as such. He simply doesn't do paperwork. It would be like me taking parenting classes. And of course he never rises before ten o'clock. No youth worker gets up before ten o'clock, he told me so himself; until today, when the vicar happens to be murdered. And Sally happens to be doing a morning shift as well.'

Tamsin seemed invigorated by these dark observations.

'It's always good to get the initial lies out into the open. It feels like we're lifting the stone a little, peering underneath and witnessing a mass panic of the creepy-crawlies. But it does at least seem certain that he died of a heart attack between midnight and 2.00 a.m. this morning.'

Tamsin took a further sip of wine, and then added: 'Though more pressing than Anton's time of death is the question of when rigor mortis set in with Bernard Silsbury.'

'Who's he?' asked Peter.

'Our pathologist.'

'Ah. Proving a little slow, is he?'

'Slow? How will anyone know when he dies?'

Peter looked out to sea. 'He'll know a peace he doesn't know now. People like you wind him up.'

'You mean people like me who are trying to solve a murder?'

'From our brief acquaintance, he's a master in the passive-aggressive arts. And in his fight with you, time of death is his greatest weapon. He knows you want it and knows it is he who must deliver it. Most humans are unworthy of power.'

'Well, his power is limited in this instance. I don't think his final report will hold any surprises for us. Rigor mortis sets in around three hours after death.'

'Starting with the eyelids, I believe?'

'How do you know that?'

'One of my monks at St James was a former pathologist in Milton Keynes.'

'Moving on ...'

'Clive was his name,' continued Peter. 'Nice man. He decided to start his life again, and with his savings, opened a shoe shop in Cyprus.'

'As you do.'

'But he soon realised that he knew nothing about shoes, and cared even less, after which he made the short move across the water to Egypt and became Brother Clive.'

'So it wasn't a general calling to shoes but a particular calling to sandals.'

The Abbot smiled.

'He never lost his fascination with rigor mortis, though, often describing how it worked its way down through the body.'

'That must have made for some fun nights at the monastery.'

'And of course complete after twelve hours, as I remember, by which time it's reached the lower extremities, going into reverse after about thirty-six hours.'

'And Anton's was nowhere near complete at 9.00 a.m. this morning. It had reached down to his torso but no further, so around 2.00 a.m. sounds right.'

'Clive always said that time of death was one of the most crucial parts of the pathologist's work but also one of the most difficult to get right, with so many variables in the equation. "There's a thin line between science and mystery", he'd say.'

'I don't need the mystic Clive to tell me that no pathologist can give a definitive time of death after a quick look at the body.'

'Yet that's exactly what you asked for today.'

'Well, you always try, don't you?'

'*You* do.'

'I just wish Bernard could at least give the impression that he wants the case solved, that we're on the same side, that in fact I'm the good guy here, not the murderer, and that giving me this information won't help me cover my tracks and escape to the Costa del Crime shortly after.'

'So are you one of the good guys, Tamsin?'

Thirty Four

And now Clare was remembering her uncle. He'd sometimes come to stay in the summer and take her to church on Sundays. Most of Clare's friends hated being taken to church – 'It's so boring!' – but Clare? She loved it. It was safe, no one hit her there and it was quite the highlight of her week.

And once, after her uncle had left for another year, she decided to go to church by herself. So aged ten, she escaped the house on Sunday morning and took herself to morning worship. She managed it for a couple of weeks before her father found out. After that, he locked her in her bedroom on Sundays. He wasn't having a daughter of his growing up with any of that nonsense in her head. And then he went back to his saxophone.

Since those days, church had always been an act of rebellion for Clare, a cry of independence from those so careless of her childhood. And perhaps there was a god, she'd sometimes sensed that, particularly at midnight mass on Christmas Eve with the candles burning, the choir singing and expectation in the air. But for the abandoned girl, god or no god, the place of safety was enough, the feelings of relief still running through her adult bones, free of the horror that was her home.

She'd never quite got free, though. Do you ever get free? She'd never – and this saddened her – quite discovered the intimacy destroyed by her mother. She would have liked a relationship, someone to love, someone to love her but she seemed to frighten people away, the invisible wall around her; and those she didn't frighten, she'd push away herself, repulse, kill them with cold in case they came close.

No one close, never again, no one to be given that power over her, that crucifying power, and through it all she'd done well, she'd come far, she should be proud; not on medication, not in care, she'd done well, so well, still reaching out, there was such glory in her, she sensed that glory now, such beautiful colours in her, such eternal origins, way before her mother, way before her father, such a coming home and had she ever been so happy? Reaching out, her hand free now, happy, free air ....

Thirty Five

Abbot Peter poured her a little more wine. Tamsin allowed herself just half a glass, aware of her drive home.

'I may have to stay the night,' she said.

'Well, that's possible,' replied Peter with all the enthusiasm his reluctance could muster.

'It's all been very sudden, you see. Last week I was living in Arundel.'

'Very posh. '

'And now suddenly I'm here in less than congenial police digs while things are sorted.'

'I do have a spare bed,' he said.

'Good.'

'The room's not in mint condition but offers partial sea views and is a convenient eight minute walk from the station.'

'Of course the murderer may not have been there at 2.00 a.m.,' said Tamsin, ignoring the estate agent's pitch. 'In fact my strong guess is that they weren't. No one hangs around the scene of the crime longer than is necessary.'

'A bit careless, in a way then.'

'Why so?'

'As we know, crucifixion doesn't kill by itself. Not in the short term, at least. Those who were crucified with Jesus had their legs broken to hasten their end. It meant they were no longer able to lift themselves to breathe and died of asphyxiation. Without the legs being broken, they'd have to die of other causes and that often took time.'

'I missed the lecture on crucifixion at training college. You'll have to explain.'

Peter gave Tamsin a brief lesson in Roman execution.

'One thing is for sure,' he concluded. 'You don't die in three hours on the cross, unless unusual circumstances intervene. It does make you wonder what we are looking at here.'

'Perhaps the murderer or murderers didn't want him to die,' she said. 'Perhaps they just wanted to teach Anton a lesson. Perhaps they are as surprised as we are to wake up this morning and discover he's actually dead. What they wanted was not death but the drawn-out pain, the lonely hours and the eventual humiliation of discovery. The vicar crucified and naked for all the world to see, with his epitaph scribbled on the dog collar: 'Should have done better.'

'Possible. If that was the case, his assailant could not let themselves be recognised.'

'There was a lot of blood. They would have needed protective clothing which could double as a disguise.'

Abbot Peter pondered.

'Any news of the house searches?'

'They've produced nothing.'

Tamsin said this as though someone had failed; as though anyone half-competent would have found something.

'Somewhere nearby,' she said slowly, 'there's protective gear covered in blood, a decent hammer, some big nails, roles of tape, gloves, a knife and a good supply of chloroform.'

'But we haven't found them yet.'

'No, and until we do, we have problems. I think I'll stay, if that's okay. This is very strong wine.'

'Sorry?'

'I think I'll take you up on your offer and stay.'

'Ah, right,' he said.

Had it been an offer? For Peter, it had been more of a polite remark. Nothing was more precious to him than his solitude and Tamsin, like the Norman Conquest, was a serious invasion. Hospitality for the Abbot was making people feel at home when he wished they were.

'I don't have any spare sheets, I'm afraid, so you must have mine,' he said, slowly opening the doors of his heart. 'They've only been on a week.'

'I don't want your sheets.'

'I don't mind.'

'No, but I do. It wouldn't be hygienic. Do you have a sleeping bag?'

'I'm not sure. I have a spare toothbrush, hardly used. But something tells me you won't want that either.'

*

It was an odd 'Good night'.

Ever-resourceful, Tamsin had turned a spare tablecloth into a sheet, double folded the single blanket and placed on that a back cover from a chair in the front room. From the same chair came a

116

cushion, now a working pillow. It was a sort of warmth, as she lay listening to the cold sea falling on the shore, advancing to the high point. She had at least shared the Abbot's toothpaste, putting some on her finger, rubbing her teeth and swilling round. Tomorrow she would return to her police digs and bring some sheets of her own. Or perhaps she'd buy them if Stormhaven rose to a department store, which, on reflection, seemed optimistic. But really there was little point in a spare bed without sheets, unless her uncle wished it permanently spare. Perhaps he did? Most of his possessions seemed to have been gathered from the shore line and it would be some time before one of his beachcomber friends found clean bed linen snagged on one of the groynes.

And the house rules which her uncle had laid down? She could live with those.

'I just ask two things,' he'd said as she'd busied herself with the practicalities of her stay.

'House rules?'

'Sounds rather grand, but if you like, yes. Good fences make good neighbours and all that.'

'Agreed. So what are they?'

'We take our shoes off at the front door.'

'Slippers or socks from thereon in?'

'Yes, please.'

'Fair enough. And the other rule?'

'My study remains out of bounds.'

'Why, what goes on in there?'

'I do.'

She'd found this rule slightly offensive but was coming to terms with it slowly. Peter had offered no further explanation, which established it as something non-negotiable and somehow outside the remit of any subsequent discussion.

As for St Michael's, tomorrow she'd have to decide whether the planned Christmas Fayre could go ahead at the weekend. It was only two days away and much preparation had gone into it. Sally was in favour of it proceeding and really, there were no policing reasons why it couldn't. Perhaps there were pastoral reasons but pastoral reasons were not her concern. There was a murderer listening to these same waves tonight. That was her concern. And out there somewhere was Clare. Could she too hear the waves? Hopefully.

Tamsin was sound asleep by the time the brick crashed through the window about half a mile away. It was the front window of Jennifer Gold's house, head of the local primary school and church warden of St Michael's Church where the vicar had recently been crucified. The brick had a message attached and the message was this:

'We know it was you.'

Thirty Six

○

'Is there far to go?' asked Gurdjieff, feeling both the heat and the climb.

'And you young and fit!' replied the Sarkar, striding ahead up the steep path. 'Perhaps you're just young!'

'It's good for a man to know where he's going!' Gurdjieff called out, sulkily.

'We never know where we are going!' replied the man ahead, turning for a moment. 'We just imagine we do.'

Though the path was unforgiving, it was not merely the physical demands that caused Gurdjieff pain. The discomfort lay also in being led by another, when he was the one who led. It was he, George Ivanovich, who had always been the one at the front, demanding trust from others. Roles were now reversed, however. Here was a man demanding that he follow and follow blind, which did not improve his mood.

They walked a further hour in separate state. Gurdjieff was thinking of Yorii. Since their encounter in the cave, they'd twice met on the compound. Gurdjieff had been given gardening duties and these took him all over the settlement. The first encounter took place when he saw her talking with a friend. Yorii introduced him to her companion as 'the Russian with the mad eyes.' In response, he'd said it was better to be mad when the sane were so clueless. This seemed to go down well, making them giggle and raise their eyebrows.

Their second meeting involved no laughter. It took place a few days later, when Gurdjieff, on entering one of the Oratories, was struck in the face by a large beam of wood, carelessly carried. If he expected sympathy, however, he was to be disappointed. It was the carrier who turned on Gurdjieff in fury, saying he should look where he was going. Gurdjieff, still sore, needed no invitation to return the angry words. The carrier became increasingly foul-mouthed and threatening, his breath betraying intoxication. Yorii then appeared and tried to intervene. The carrier knocked her savagely to the ground and lurched hurriedly on his way.

'I'll get him,' said Gurdjieff. 'Do you know him?'
'He's my father,' said Yorii.

*

Up ahead, the Sarkar came to a halt and beckoned George Ivanovich forward. Emerging from shadowy wood into bright open space, Gurdjieff felt his spirits lift. Standing on the heights, the valley sprawled silently and splendidly before them. Away to the right was the community they had left that morning, snug and separate on the mountain side. They had walked a distance, most of it uphill and Gurdjieff dripped with sweat.

The Sarkar sat on a rock in a state of calm. 'Work makes for sweet essence,' he said.

'Not if you're a foul-mouthed carpenter,' thought Gurdjieff, as he took from his back-bag a bottle of water and drank keenly.

'And the trusted must himself learn trust,' added the Sarkar. 'You find trust hard?'

'Perhaps.'

The men took in the view. It was a magnificent and detailed panorama.

'I like to come here,' said the Sarkar. 'It's a place of such clear vistas. Come and sit on this stone!'

He indicated that Gurdjieff must now take his place on the rock. The Sarkar climbed down and the young adventurer climbed up. Once there, he was inwardly consumed by a sense of honour:

'That the Sarkar should give me this stone throne, so smooth and holding!'

He looked out across the valley, king of all he surveyed.

The Sarkar said: 'The place where you now sit, I call it "The Seeing Stone". You step out of a dark wood and suddenly you see everything! The Enneagram has a similar effect. It too is a clear revelation.'

'I had heard rumour of darker things.'

'Darker things?'

'Some fear it.'

'If a fear of the sea denied you the pleasure of swimming, you would not be considered wise. It is the same with the Enneagram. Do not allow the fear to deny you delight.'

'Are people right to fear it?'

'In a manner. Certainly the Enneagram enters the forbidden places of the human soul. But it does so only to heal. It visits the darkness only to make light of it. It is good to make light of life, do you not agree?'

'It sounds well enough.'

'The Enneagram, like the Seeing Stone, is concerned with seeing and light. In particular, it's concerned with the nine types of humankind.'

'You said that some called it the "Nine Faces of God".'

'So they do. The world is unity but there are nine different facets of this unity.'

'And one of these facets belongs to me?'

'The Enneagram excludes no one. You shall find yourself there as sure as day follows night.'

'So describe these nine dispositions.'

'You press me like an Egyptian jewellery seller.'

'You make me impatient!'

'No, I reveal your impatience. It is not the same.'

Gurdjieff shrugged in frustration.

'But you will tell me?'

'That is why we have come to this place,' said the Sarkar.

Thirty Seven

Whatever Tamsin's doubts, St Michael's Christmas Fayre was going to be the best ever! This is what Sally said and others agreed. They were going to rally round and make it so. There had been one or two against the idea at the committee meeting, feeling a Fayre to be inappropriate, 'what with the tragedy'. They suggested something in the New Year, when things 'were more normal'. For most, however, life went on and death disturbed little.

Some people said, 'If I know Anton, it's what he would have wanted,' and this was hard to oppose. The first party to transfer their desires onto the deceased usually win the argument.

Others added that 'It would be a victory for the murderer, if the Fayre is stopped.'

Well, no one wanted another victory for the murderer.

And Stormhaven had its history to consider: 'St Michael's Fayre has taken place for over 800 years! We will not allow the murderer to break the chain of history!'

The unspoken challenge was that they would not allow the police to break it either.

Some were also aware that it would be an administrative nightmare to postpone things, and expensive. We must not speak of expense at such times but it was a factor. The publicity was printed, the flowers bought, the cakes baked, the stall tables delivered and the income allocated. They were going to make it a Christmas Fayre to remember.

And so the cogs of parish life turned. Fliers were placed in newsagents' windows, delivered by Betty; stall holders were contacted by Sally; entries for the children's painting competition were collected from the school by Ginger; Jennifer reminded the children in assembly – the last one of term – and the Mayor was reassured that, apart from the vicar being fatally nailed to a cross, all was wonderfully well.

If she was honest, the mayor had been hesitant at first, unsure about the best move in these unusual circumstances. Where in the mayor's 'Advice for Office' manual – so helpful on issues like expenses and the proper titles of local dignitaries – was the chapter on 'Attending parish fayres when the vicar has recently been crucified'? She had no desire to step into a public relations disaster and you never knew which way the local press would jump, particularly the *Sussex Silt*.

'Mayor set to dishonour dead priest' had been the headline half way down page five yesterday, but the story itself was less aggressive than the headline, merely explaining the dilemma which she faced. Someone had said it would dishonour Anton. But there's always someone to say anything and plenty of more positive views were printed as well; and so having taken local soundings, she decided to accept the invitation. She was later to declare how stirred she was 'by the wartime spirit shown by the parish' – even though, as a pacifist, she added, she didn't approve of war. Just the spirit.

Any lingering concerns the Mayor might have had were finally put aside when Sally spoke to her on the phone: 'We really need a figure of unity at this time,' Sally said. 'A leader around whom we can gather in these dark hours.'

'I understand,' said the Mayor, who liked this idea. She longed to be more than just another Councillor with a toilet chain round her neck.

The Bishop had also liked the idea when Sally pressed him to attend: 'Bishop, we really need a figure of unity at this time,' she'd said. 'A leader around whom we can gather in these dark hours.'

Bishop Stephen agreed to be that man. He had been due to visit a pig farm near Heathfield as part of the 'Christ and the countryside' initiative. He could picture it now, wading around knee deep in pig dung with a big grin on his face for the cameras. 'Always smile at the pigs,' said his press officer from the safe distance of his computer terminal. 'Otherwise they'll have you in a caption competition.'

'They'll have me in a caption competition whatever I do,' he'd said. 'A pig and a bishop? It's just too easy.'

But now he had an escape. Christ and the countryside could wait; he'd go to the Christmas Fayre at St Michael's.

Of course, Sally knew the truth. She knew that she was the figure of unity in the situation rather than the mayor or the bishop. How easily people were flattered into actions that suited her. She'd done it all her life. Behind the leadership of others, she would lead and be needed and be loved.

Thirty Eight

Once again the notebook came down from the shelf, as the murderer took seriously their duty of record. The diary of a murderer or the murder diary; they were still deciding. They would like to talk with someone about their role in the story, their lead role. That would be better. But in the absence of such space, some amused jottings at the absurd nature of it all:

'I know how people see me, but people only see others in one way, through a very narrow eye glass. So people see me but they don't see me. They all make their assumptions and their assumptions are wrong.

I've done them a favour in a way, that's my understanding. A big favour. I watch them walking around going 'tut, tut, isn't that terrible' and feeling very self-righteousness and full of their own moral rectitude. And it's all because of me! Can't they see that? When you can call someone else terrible you feel so much better about yourself. God knows why. You're just as terrible yourself if you could see it.

The world needs murderers. We are the downtrodden saints. Holmes needed Moriarty – they don't write crime stories like those anymore – and Jesus needed Judas. We don't hear sermons on that, but I've always thought it. Jesus needed Judas. I hope they appreciate what I've done for them and their sad little lives.

We could call it the Judas Appreciation Society.

Thirty Nine

Thursday, 18 December

'I'm beginning to wonder about the good people of Stormhaven,' said Tamsin as she sat with Abbot Peter on a bench in the High Street.

They were enjoying the public privacy of a busy place, and with a clear winter sun in the sky, reflected on the morning's events.

'Firstly, they can't forget their vicar quick enough. There was no chance of the Christmas Fayre being postponed!'

'It is a popular event.'

'And secondly, they throw brick messages through people's windows at three in the morning.'

'Desperate times.'

'And Jennifer of all people! Head of the local school and church warden! Hardly the prime suspect.'

'Snob.'

'It's a fact. Study your criminology.'

'*We know it was you.* Those were the words on the brick?'

'Yes.'

'The question is, who is the 'we' and what is the 'it'?'

'Well, the 'it' is pretty obvious. It has to be the murder.'

'Other things do happen in Stormhaven.'

'I must have missed them. And remember, police are not huge fans of coincidence.'

'It's a surprisingly random universe.'

'It may be but within the random, crime remains a little pocket of predictability. Once the facts of the matter are out, things quickly become certain. And in this case, it appears someone is certain even now.'

Abbot Peter made a face. He did not worship at the shrine of anyone else's certainty. Certainty had the worst of historical track records.

'Perhaps Anton will come back and tell us. I have this strange feeling we haven't heard the last from him.'

'Do you suggest we visit a medium?'

'No. In my experience, the dead come and find us if they need to.'

'A ghost is not admissible evidence.' said Tamsin.

'Then more fool us. Still, we work with what is. The charge on the dog collar was that he was a failure as a vicar. How do you think he would have pleaded?'

'How am I supposed to know? No one admits to failing at work. They rationalise it. It's someone else's fault. They were unlucky. It was just the wrong time. It's a terrible thing to be told you're a failure.'

'Have you ever been so called?'

'Me?'

'Yes, you.'

'No! And I don't plan to be.'

'Yet we all are.'

'We're all what?'

'Failures.'

'Speak for yourself.'

'Oh I do but not just myself. Strands of success are rather isolated phenomena in the textures of our lives.'

'I don't see that at all.'

'And neither, I think, could Anton. Personal failure would not have been something he could consider. He sits through a meeting in which his boss, staff and most of the congregation disown him. It's a sort of crucifixion in itself. But he doesn't care!'

'Well perhaps he should have cared!' said Tamsin, with some feeling. 'Perhaps that's why someone had to crucify him! Because he was so lousy at his job!'

'It wasn't you, was it?'

Tamsin got up and started walking towards the church. Peter watched her go.

'Well, are you coming?' she asked, turning around. 'We need to speak with Jennifer.'

Abbot Peter did follow, but slowly. Something significant had entered his mind but again, like a mouse across the kitchen floor, too quick to be caught. It had disappeared down through the hole in the sub-conscious, leaving no trace but the droppings of frustration.

Forty

The glaziers were mending the window as they spoke. SOCO had been and gone, removing the brick and message for testing, though no one expected much. It would be surprising if a gloved hand had not thrown the brick and the message was *Rockwell Extra Bold*, a standard computer font. It seemed likely a man was responsible or at least a strong arm. It had arrived through the window with some force.

Yet inside, the house was now calm; a yellow space of minimalism and tranquillity. Mrs Pipe had once said Jennifer rushed through life like a 'thrown stone', strangely prescient in the circumstances, but she returned at the end of the day to a peaceful setting. It was efficient, simple and expensively natural. She had been cleaning up when they arrived, using white vinegar.

'I use it for all surfaces,' said Jennifer when the Abbot remarked on the surprising absence of chips. 'There's really no need to use any man-made cleaning products. No need at all.'

Peter could imagine a school assembly on the subject. Jennifer did good school assemblies, everyone was gripped. But who'd tell the children that their head teacher was a murderer? Those would not be easy words to choose and Abbot Peter hoped no one would have to.

'I was absolutely terrified,' said Jennifer, as she recalled the night before. 'I was awake, thinking about school things when I heard the smash.'

'And you knew instantly it was your home under attack?'

'I did.'

'And what did you do?'

'Well, I lay there for a moment, scared rigid. I was trying to think of a possible weapon to use. And then I remembered an old piece of piping left by the plumber in the airing cupboard.'

'Which you found?'

'Yes, I put on my dressing gown, grabbed the piping and then walked slowly down the stairs. I don't know what I must have looked like, copper pipe in hand!'

'And in a way, it's of no great consequence,' said the Abbot who had never understood people worrying about what they must have looked like.

'And then I was wondering about the Nativity rehearsal,' continued Jennifer. 'If I got attacked, who would handle it? I've been the one overseeing the nativity this year and I do want it to go well. The kids deserve it.'

'I'm sure it will,' said Peter. 'I'm looking forward to it. You can't put a price on a good nativity.'

'Well, you say that, but a school in Brighton is charging £4 a head for theirs this year.'

'Did you hear anything else?' asked Tamsin, moving swiftly on from the marketization of the birth of Christ. 'After the breaking glass, I mean?'

'Nothing. I stood and listened for a while and heard nothing. By the time I found the brick on the floor, I was pretty sure I was alone.'

'And how did you feel?' asked Abbot Peter.

'How did I feel? How would anyone feel in those circumstances?' Jennifer was slightly exasperated.

'We don't know and can't ask because anyone doesn't exist,' said Abbot Peter calmly. 'That's why I was asking you.'

'You must have experienced something similar, Abbot.'

'Me? Not really. My desert monastery was built to withstand attack from all sides, a regular old fortress! No stones through windows there.'

'Why would a monastery be a fortress?' asked Jennifer, suddenly intrigued.

Tamsin gave Peter a look of warning which, if he saw, he chose to ignore.

'In the early days, around the seventh century, the Bedouin were less than pleased with its presence. We imagine everyone wants a nice monastery in their back garden but it simply isn't so. Things came to a head in the fourteenth century, obviously, when they ransacked the place, burned the library and killed most of the monks. Those were unpleasant days.'

'But seven centuries ago,' said Tamsin.

'Yes, things come and go, though, don't they? The Bedouin are a great deal more accepting now, more focused on their own survival in these changing times.'

'You must come and do an assembly on it,' said Jennifer. 'The kids would love it.'

127

'That would be a great honour, but in the meantime, we return to my question.'

'Which question was that?'

'I was wondering what you felt.'

Suddenly the focus was back on Jennifer, who might have imagined her attempts at distraction had worked.

'Well, you feel invaded. That's how you feel.'

Abbot Peter nodded while noting her inability to personalise her feelings.

'I can understand that.'

'And the note?' asked Tamsin, still irritated by the desert diversion. 'What did the note mean?'

'I have absolutely no idea.'

'I suppose it means someone thinks you're guilty.'

Jennifer looked out the window for inspiration.

'I wondered about it being an old pupil, stirring things up,' she said. 'Or a parent. Perhaps that's more likely. Children tend to forget, but parents, never! When you see your child as an extension of yourself, you take any criticism of your offspring personally.'

'Are there any current difficulties in the school which might have led to bad feeling?'

'There are always difficulties in a school. Growing up is difficult. Life is difficult. I face angry parents every day, all claiming injustice, incompetence or both. But nothing has occurred to make me expect this.'

'So an old school vendetta is possible,' said Tamsin. 'A murder in town gives someone the chance to get their own back on the Head, after a perceived slight in the past.'

'It was the only thing I could come up with.'

'Unless someone genuinely thinks you're guilty,' said Tamsin. 'Is there any reason why someone might feel that?'

'It's ridiculous. As Abbot Peter knows, I was the only one who voted for Anton at the meeting. He was my protégé. Anton is the last person I'd want to hurt.'

'So who's the first person you'd want hurt?' asked Tamsin.

'It's a manner of speech.'

'But my question still stands.'

'Don't we all want to hurt someone?'

'Someone in the parish even?'

Jennifer calmed herself and placed her hands on her lap. She was suddenly a Head, reporting back candidly to the governors.

'I believe some people in the parish – and some beyond – have treated him appallingly, yes.'

'And you think one of them to be the murderer?'

'Oh, I know so. Some people just have to win.'

'Who?'

'I have more than enough on my plate without doing your job.'

'But you have your suspicions.'

'Everyone has their suspicions.'

'And someone's suspicious of you.'

'True. Or perhaps someone's just angry with me. There's a difference. I tell the children that resentment is anger kept artificially warm. That's how I try and explain the brick. It's important psychologically to explain these things. Otherwise, it's hard to proceed.'

'And Clare? Do you have any idea where Clare might be?'

'I have no idea at all. Who knows? It's not like her to disappear, but in the end, she's an independent woman. She could be anywhere. Perhaps she's gone on holiday; she likes her holidays.'

'Do you like her?'

'I admire her. She's done very well.'

'But you don't like her.'

'She reminds me of the royal family.'

'Why so?' asked Tamsin.

'She perceives herself as rather special. She wants you there in appreciation, but not too close. No one got too close to Clare.'

'Got?'

'I mean gets. I'm sorry, but it's suddenly like she's dead. What other explanation is there?'

Forty One

'You're rather in my face,' said Tamsin.

'And you're rather in my office,' replied Ginger, towering over her.

'Do you always work with no light?'

'Do you always push open doors without knocking?'

'The murderer didn't knock and until they're found, neither shall I.'

'I was just going, anyway.'

'Which explains the light being out?'

They stood face to face in a dark room, only partially lit by the wall window out onto the Church hallway.

'I'm a great one for the environment, Detective Inspector and I hate all unnecessary pollution.'

He looked at her as he spoke and for a moment, Tamsin felt like one of the pollutants he abhorred.

'Shall we go?' said Ginger.

It wasn't an enquiry.

But Tamsin didn't go. Instead, she turned on the light and saw a clean and ordered room. There was a small picture of Martin Luther King addressing a rally and a poster of a South American Bishop, with the words: 'Murdered for love'.

'I don't think that's a wise way to behave,' said Ginger.

'Not wise? Why wouldn't it be wise to turn on the light? Let there be light, surely?'

'You shouldn't do those things. You don't have the right. It's my room and my light.'

'Do you pay the bills?' asked Tamsin, taking a seat. Ginger did not respond. 'No? So who does pay the bills?'

Again he did not respond.

'So the church pays the bills. Sounds like this room is church property to me, then,' she continued. 'Do go if you must. I'm happy to stay and amuse myself.'

There was a knock on the door. Ginger looked quickly to Tamsin and then moved to answer it.

'You said the lights would be out,' said an irritated Betty before anyone could say anything.

Forty Two

Not far away, Abbot Peter knelt in the side chapel of St Michael's. He'd left Tamsin and her enquiries to seek retreat from the changes and chances of this fleeting world. Here was seclusion, entered through a curtain, like the holy of holies in ancient times. He had taken off his shoes, lit a candle and placed himself at the railing, which surrounded the altar. The altar was bare but for the figure on the cross. Peter contemplated him with fresh eyes. Head bowed, the Christ figure seemed resigned to the nails; sad not struggling. It was as if he had known things would come to this, almost '*c'est la vie*'; whereas Anton had looked surprised and the surprise had stayed with Peter.

He'd come to the side chapel because if something is worth doing, it's also worth not doing.

'We do things better if sometimes we don't do them,' he'd say. ' "Teach us to care and not to care", as T. S. Eliot instructed.'

People were work for the Abbot, always had been, and rest only really came in solitude. He could cope with people as long as he knew when they'd be gone. To this extent, the ordered hours of the monastery had suited him. The prayer bell may have rung at 4.00 a.m. But he would be carried by liturgy and routine through the day and he was always alone in his cell by 9.30 p.m.

Those were different times, however, and ordered hours were now disordered. They'd been disordered by a foolish 'yes'. He had been flattered into acceptance of the Special Witness post. He'd submitted to the request of a pretty lady; to the manipulative asking of a niece. She was undoubtedly a clever girl, but pushy. And now it seemed she was to spend another night at Sandy View. She'd made the announcement on the way back from Jennifer's, saying it made operational sense.

'Operational sense?' Truly, this was a new language for Abbot Peter.

A police car would bring her things over, including sheets and some fresh fruit. Peter was unsure how he felt. The offer of a bed the previous night had been a generous whim, not a declaration of permanent intent. It would be nice to see her, of course; they had much to catch up on. But did he want her staying? People were work and sometimes relations were the hardest work of all.

Amid such contemplation, he saw the hand reaching out from behind the altar, a desperate stretching hand.

Christ was not the only dead body in the side chapel.

Act Three

He got up to open the window. The cold air rushed in as white breakers hit the shore. Tonight, they were waters of judgement. He knew what must be done.

Forty Three

○

George Ivanovitch sat on the Seeing Stone. The air was still, the valley silent.

'You are to imagine a room in which nine people are gathered,' said the Sarkar.

'I understand,' said his pupil.

'At first sight, they may appear the same. Perhaps they are all of one colour or share a craft, family or creed. But in this room of nine people, whatever their outward links, they are inwardly different. And though they appear similar and perhaps do similar things, they will do them for very different reasons. The Enneagram looks at the root of action not the action itself.'

Gurdjieff listened. From the moment he'd found the manuscript in the underground vault, he had waited for this moment.

'So let us move around this group of nine souls and describe each personality, using a number to describe each.'

'I'm ready.'

'So we start with Point One. The One is industrious for good as they perceive it. When unhealthy, of course, they are self-righteous, resentful, moralistic, myopic, blaming, rigid, dogmatic and with a rather fixed view of the world.'

'I see why people fear this knowledge. It is less than polite.'

The Sarkar was unswayed.

'Ones seek the correct way, the right way and believe the right way is their way. Perhaps they procrastinate sometimes for fear of making a mistake. Feeling the blame when young, they do not wish to be wrong again. They possess inside them a judge, an inner critic who declares them always guilty. So to escape and deflect, they in turn declare others guilty. They tell people what they should do and ought to do. They are angry people – angry that they and the world are not good – but avert their gaze from this trait believing that good boys and girls should not be angry. Left unacknowledged, their rage becomes resentment. Never put

the blame on a One, my friend. They will come for you. But like every number, they are both nightmare and glory, and in health, when living from the mercy pool where self-hate dies, they are clear thinkers and visionaries for good in a world they no longer judge but perceive as quite perfect now. Here is their true majestic self – serene, shining, noble, laughing, ordering, applauding and quite happy to admit mistake. Wonderful. Shall I move on?'

'Tell me all nine. I listen well.'

'So be it. Point Two. Can you see them?'

'I see them.'

Gurdjieff was enjoying this game.

'The Two has a great outward energy but for what? Some call them 'The Cat', flattering endlessly to get what they want and what they want is for others to need them. They need to be needed. When unhealthy, of course, they are out of touch with their needs, fixated with relationship, resentful if neglected, superior, smothering, patronising and rather self-important saints. They ask always the question, 'How are others disposed towards me?' Their inner desire is to be indispensable; to be needed by everyone they know. They are content not to lead; happy instead to be indispensable to a leader. If their care for others is not appreciated, however, their pride is hurt and resentment runs deep. Pride is the stone they trip on daily, pride dressed as caring: 'It is others who need help not I!' This is how they think. But pride merely covers their lack of inner substance. Once they see this, however, once they discover and touch their true inner will, they move from nightmare to glory. Exchanging pride for humility they live a most creative role in the world. Discerning their own needs they are free now to care without caring – nurturing, compassionate, connecting, perceptive, intimate and responsive, their true majestic self awakes! Wonderful.'

Gurdjieff remembered being seduced by a woman such as this. She had never forgiven him when he walked away and now he saw why.

The Sarkar continued: 'The Three is different again.'

'They are all different!'

'Indeed. And the Three will be known for inspiring confidence in those around, though perhaps a little more than is merited. When unhealthy, of course, they can be cold, calculating, secretive, self-promoting, corner-cutting, prestige-seeking and quite numb to their emotions, well-defended from how they feel. They are activists, confident in their moves, needing action to drown frightening introspection. So they drive things forward, desiring success and victory over others. Threes are the golden people in a way, efficient and attractive, people whom others would like to be like. They are also the most deceitful, hiding their motives even from themselves. They crave success because their self-image is defined by it. They crave activity because they fear *the exposure of their inner life to the light. They simply dare not fail and will do all things necessary to ensure they do not. Success is their only identity, until one day, they come home to a kind universe in which they need not defeat or outperform everyone. From nightmare to glory! They learn loyalty, a bigger cause than themselves and now shine a rather brighter light. They are hopeful, truthful, humorous, loyal, self-aware, engaging, authentic and with boundless energy, true rather than phoney gold. Their majestic self awakes! Wonderful.'*

'I've met them,' said Gurdjieff, 'but perhaps not understood them.'

'Then let us continue and I now describe the Four, a rather special number.'

'Special?'

'That is how they imagine themselves, perhaps. They consider themselves special in some way, attracted by the authentic and tragic. Birth, intensity, abandonment and death – this is their territory! When unhealthy, of course, they are controlling, self-pitying, demanding, alienated, blaming, elitist and coloured by despair. They are the white dove cooing, melancholic, moody and in love with sweet sadness. They keep their distance from those present and obtainable, desiring instead the unavailable, the impossible and the absent, the fantasy. Even as they pull people towards them, they push them away. They are the abandoned ones, creating beauty out of pain and darkness from their envy. At their tragic heart is the worthlessness of the abandoned, a sense that their origins are fatally flawed. Hence the pursuit of the special and a fantasy sense of worth. Their genius emerges as they bring their profound awareness to the reality and joy of this present moment, this practical now, where all is quite well. Here they become luminous, personal, content, authentic, intuitive and relating. From nightmare to glory, they discover their infinitely valuable and original selves. Wonderful.'

Gurdjieff recognised one such as this immediately, though whether it was good news, he could not say. His heart beat faster.

'Next!'

Forty Four

Peter sensed a man behind him as he knelt in the side chapel; one who had arrived unseen. Malcolm Flight was probably six foot tall but carried himself as a smaller man; as one not important in the world. With a straggly beard of brown ginger and sandals even in the rain, he was a stranger on the earth, like his hero Van Gogh.

The Abbot remembered last year's Maundy Night vigil. It had been an especially cold event, with the church heating broken. Everyone huddled together in the parish room for the night, drinking tea and improvising blankets. Except Malcolm. He knelt alone on the stone floor of the church. At 5.00 a.m. he got up to make some coffee. He found almost everyone asleep, but was soon back in the cold church with his drink, kneeling again on the stone, where the Good Friday cross was laid out on the floor, the cross which had recently found further use.

'I'm glad she's found at last,' he said.

'Who?' asked Peter.

'Clare.'

Abbot Peter looked towards the hand stretching out from the side of the altar.

'I can't believe the police didn't find her,' said Malcolm.

'They haven't been looking for her.'

'Then perhaps they should have been looking.'

'Clare was not a missing person. She was an independent woman with means and free to go wherever she wished.'

'I told them she might be here.'

'Where?'

'In the church.'

'Why did you think that?'

Malcolm Flight stood in silence.

'That's how everyone describes her,' he said with bitterness, ' "an independent woman" – but what's that supposed to mean?'

There was hostility in his voice.

'At the very least, it means she was free to go wherever she wished.'

'She's not free now,' he said. 'But then, which of us is?'

The Abbot stayed on his knees at the altar rail.

'So what is your part in all this, Malcolm?' he asked. 'Is there anything you wish to tell me?'

Malcolm rolled a cigarette and lit it.

'Not here, Malcolm.'

Malcolm looked at Peter and then put it out on the back of the box.

'You didn't go home after the meeting, did you?' he continued. 'You were here in the church.'

'I would be careful what you say.'

'Why should I be careful?'

'Stupid words, they cause trouble.'

'Which of my words are stupid?'

'Stupid words are like escaped ferrets. They rip at the poor rabbit's throat.'

Peter was taken aback. 'That's a violent image,' he said.

Malcolm breathed in deeply.

'Do you perhaps have a particular rabbit in mind?' asked Peter. 'Perhaps you had a pet rabbit?'

Malcolm paused. He was known for his slow release of information and a life of deep secrets.

'I don't keep pets.'

'You have other interests?'

Was Peter now being too pushy? Press too hard and Malcolm would close like a clam.

'My occupations are shelf filler and painter. My vocation is contemplation.'

'A fine vocation,' said the Abbot appreciatively. 'Though not necessarily a lucrative one.'

Silence.

'Did you need Clare?'

Malcolm brought his hands together in tense union. Each squashed the blood from the other in restless struggle. And for the first time, Abbot Peter noticed how strong they were and how ready for work.

'It doesn't matter if it was a violent image, Abbot. The only interesting question is this: was it a true image?'

True image? Or, as the Latin had it, *vera icon*: the cloth of legend used by St Veronica to wipe the brow of Christ on his way to crucifixion, left stained with the outline of his face. It was a holy relic in the Vatican to this day.

141

'Beware the true image which plays false, Abbot. That is what I say to you.'

'You're saying there is one here who is not what they appear?'

'I do the accounts, remember.'

Peter had entered this sanctuary in search of peace. But with a corpse before him and disturbance behind, he now felt only dissonance. The protruding hand of Clare was pale and lifeless, the forefinger pointing in death to something beyond. But to what? If you traced the eye line, it took you straight to the vestry door. Yet likely as not, this was random directing. Unless Peter was mistaken, here was a body dumped, dragged perhaps, wedged in and left. Perhaps an act in haste?

'What have the accounts got to do with it?' asked Abbot Peter.

There was no answer but rain against the glass. Malcolm Flight, 'the ghost', had left as silently as he'd arrived. Peter turned to the altar once again. The Christ now looked directly at the body that lay sprawled beneath him.

So what, or who, had brought Clare to this holy place? It was time for this sanctuary of grace to be invaded by the law.

Forty Five

○

The Sarkar was gazing across the valley with a smile.

'I'm ready,' said Gurdjieff, still king on his stone throne and eager for more.

'The Five is sometimes likened to the fox, they wish to see but not to be seen. Detachment is both their glory and their grave. They see things deeply but not always truly, blinded by the emotional isolation they believe will save them. When unhealthy, of course, they hoard unshared things, become separate people, withdrawing, secretive, uninvolved, compartmentalizing life. They are restrained with time given to others. Distant and thinking, they withdraw themselves from people, feelings and possessions. They regard all people as a threat to their survival. Fives are content with little material wealth but how they fear inner emptiness. They hoard knowledge, of whatever sort, like a squirrel hoards nuts. Strangers in the world, knowledge gives them power and the foolish Five imagines it will save them. Healing for Fives comes when they leave their self-denying isolation, engage with their long-lost feelings and take their place in the world. From nightmare to glory! Here they reveal deep knowing, spontaneity, vulnerability, transparency, a great sense of investigation; and here they become a window on the universe. Now they see like owls but act like lions, embodied wisdom as their true majestic self. Wonderful.

''You describe yourself!' said Gurdjieff.

'Look to your own heart.'

'But it is you.'

'I describe the Five,' said the Sarkar, smiling.

'And the Six?'

Gurdjieff was enjoying this. It made so much sense of other readings he'd undertaken and observations he'd made. Much was still a mystery but he was excited by the truths he was hearing.

'The Six seeks security but where will they find it?' said the Sarkar.

'That is their life quest. Untrusting of themselves, they seek another to

trust or a cause to believe in. When unhealthy, of course, they are cowardly, insecure, indecisive, paranoid, argumentative, accusatory, doubting little bigots. They are fearful people, scanning the surroundings for possible attack; wishing always to know where they stand. They think much but they don't think well; they think a hundred possible outcomes, imagine problems long before they happen and most never do. They can be rule-bound, wary of breaking laws for fear of stepping out of line. And we note their ambivalence towards authority figures, sometimes reacting with craven submission, another time, with angry opposition. Greatness for the Six arrives when they learn to trust their substantial selves, discover their own true selves to be the authority they've been seeking. From nightmare to glory! From here on, they instruct the world not in fear but in courage. They are serene, strong, hospitable, protecting, questioning, loyal, bright, trustworthy, clear in their perceiving, their majestic self revealed. Wonderful'

'Soloviev!'

'My answer to you is as before. We must first know ourselves before pronouncing on others.'

'I like Sixes,' said Gurdjieff. 'But fear makes them stupid. Soloviev should have come with me here.'

'Fear overcame loyalty and he had no inner strength to hold onto. It must have been a terrible struggle inside.' Gurdjieff thought back to their last moments by the chasm but quickly put away such thoughts.

'We have three more numbers, Sir, and after Six comes Seven.'

'The Seven may charm you, win you over.'

'Really?'

'Sevens are sometimes called butterflies, bright but always moving, never staying, restless, colourful and dancing away from pain. So we might call them The Butterfly, though some prefer The Monkey because of their monkey minds. When unhealthy, they are eager for distraction, shallow, insensitive, rationalising, attention-seeking, fearful, angered by restraint, shame-avoiding, emotionally cold and quite unable to take responsibility for their actions. They touch lightly on life, picking what suits, like a thief at a banquet. They avoid sadness, and worship at the shrine of their mistaken imagining. They are those on the run from the moment, from the now, the great idealists, imagining better and best round the corner. They are future people because they cannot trust this present moment, cannot trust life's beautiful unfolding.'

'They sound like frightened people.'

'Of course. Fear fuels their flight from present to future, fear and shame of their abandoned and unacceptable selves. You look shaken, my friend.'

'No. Why should I be shaken?'

'But of course in their substantial selves, their home selves, they are the true contemplatives. From nightmare to glory! They leave their planning and their frightened future behind and allow the delightful unfolding of the present where they are truly acceptable to themselves. Having passed through the garden of sadness, they are spontaneous, calm, content, playful, testing, positive, connecting, creating, encouraging, cool decision-makers, reflective joy-bringers. Here is true contemplation and their true self. Wonderful.'

Gurdjieff breathed deeply.

'Contemplatives?'

'Indeed.'

'Who would have guessed? Eights?'

The Sarkar drank some water from his bottle and rubbed his eyes. The sun was high in the sky of the Hindu Kush. He got up from the rock where he sat and walked a little, stretching arms and legs. He climbed up now onto a higher rock, which looked down on the Seeing Stone where Gurdjieff remained.

'The Eight is one who likes to confront,' he continued. 'To confront is what they do, how they work. They wish to boss, lusty for power and all else besides. When unhealthy, of course, they are over-bearing, impulsive, insensitive, brooding, raging, stubborn and running from self-blame. The Eight is a leader, openly displaying force and at home with anger. They have been compared to the African rhinoceros and their life to a Spanish bullfight, always wanting blood. They seek power for themselves but dress it up as justice. They are people who are against others, who like to oppose, people who must carve out their own kingdom or die in the attempt.'

'Why so?'

'They have never been allowed to be weak so they fear weakness in themselves; and fearing it in themselves, they batter and bruise it in others. But beyond this diminished creation, born of shame and fear of weakness, is their substantial self, strong not for their own gain but for the weak and needy. From nightmare to glory! Here they are vibrant, direct, truthful and unifying. The world is no longer a battleground but a unity. They reveal innocence of intention and become great challengers of deceit. They will be like a strong tree in whose branches many can rest and find protection. Their true majestic self! Wonderful. '

'And so to our final number?'

'And our final number is the Nine, there at the top of the circle, the number which holds all others in a manner. Indeed, sometimes the Nine is more aware of other's needs than their own.

'So how will I recognize them?'

'They will avoid conflict; this is one feature of their lives.'

'They're hardly alone in that.'

'It is particularly so with them and there are reasons. They do not like the rage they have buried so deep and conflict stirs this. So the Nine is the mediator, one who seeks peace and harmony around them. When unhealthy, of course, they become neglectful, complacent, lost in others' needs, slothful, stubborn, comfort-seeking and dwellers in the land of false peace. Sometimes the Nine is called The Sloth or The Elephant. They can appear peaceful and self-deprecating souls but are stubborn, set within and move for no one. As I say, anger is their buried feeling, one not allowed when young, erupting only occasionally in a flood of hot lava. They give themselves little worth and therefore the world little worth; a deep river of cynicism flows through them. Unresolved anger leaves them at the doorway of despair and depressive states; and their insecure self can be spiteful. But when secure, when they wake the self they put to sleep and connect with action over avoidance, these people can hold and love the world like no others, great and magnanimous leaders! Here they are outward-facing, generous, unifying, reassuring, patient, guileless, receptive, mediating, strong bringers of harmony. From nightmare to glory, the majestic self awakes! Wonderful.'

'And that is the human race?'

'We have barely started, you understand.'

'Of course. But that is the human race?'

'Scarcely ruffled the hair of this creature we call the Enneagram'

'Quite so.'

'Certainly my brief descriptions are entirely inadequate.'

'I understand, but –.'

'I have lived with it for forty years and still regard myself as a novice, a beginner in so many ways. You have known it for five minutes, so stay humble, stay cautious, stay open, stay listening and uncertain. Uncertainty is fertile.'

'And I've noted that. But still, with all those hesitations, conditions and provisos, the nine states you have just described, that is the human race?'

'That is the human race.'

'Will you teach me more?'

'Oh yes. There is much still to learn.'

'It seems to me you have described nine types of idiot,' said Gurdjieff with a smile. 'We must each discover our own brand of idiocy.'

'An original thought. I have never heard it put that way, but yes, true. Nine brands of idiocy! You will learn more in community, of course.'

'And then?'

'Have you ever thought of going to Europe?'

Forty Six

Council worker Christopher Thornton was unhappy with himself and couldn't sleep. What he had done, it really wasn't right and his guilt, not up for discussion. But then what had he ever done which had been right? And when had guilt not been his companion? He'd done things which had the appearance of virtue but, in truth, were just convenient for him. He'd taken the easy path, the line of least resistance. This was how it felt as he fingered himself in bed. He liked to finger himself but tonight found neither pleasure nor response.

In some ways, it was stupid to allow such thoughts. All he had done was add a name to a list, for God's sake! He wasn't Stalin. He wasn't Pol Pot. And the client – well, the queue jumper – was a deserving cause, no question about that. And they always said the money was not a bribe but a gift, just a way of saying thank you for their efficiency and kindness. But you can't make a winner without making a loser and the loser was out there now, hurt. Well, of course they were hurt and they were hurt because of him.

And today they'd rung him up. He thought the matter finished with, weeks had passed without a sound. But now they'd stirred the pot all over again. They'd rung him up and made their case, pleaded desperately, heart-rendingly in a way. But Christopher didn't care and had simply zoned out and lied to be rid of them. Least line of resistance; the fact was, the usurper was more pressing and he didn't want a battle. He'd played the concerned and caring listener and claimed forces beyond his control to be responsible. Yes, of course he knew how important it was and yes, he would do all he could to rectify the matter.

He wouldn't of course. That was just another lie in a long list of lies – his life seemed one extended game of 'Let's pretend' – and this wasn't why he'd joined the council. And he hadn't joined the council to take bribes.

He got up to open the window. The cold air rushed in as white breakers hit the shore. Tonight, they were waters of judgement. Council worker Christopher Thornton knew what must be done.

*

And not far away, in the stillness of the night, a further entry was made in the murder diary. They weren't lonely. How could they be lonely? But this notebook was certainly a friend, a trusted keeper of secrets. No, not secrets – that implied some sort of shame and how could there be shame? Such were the murderer's thoughts as they wrote in their careful, almost childish, hand.

'I am glad they've discovered Clare's body. Apparently I left a hand hanging out in the prayer chapel, though I don't believe I did. Did I leave her alive? Did she struggle for a while, try to get out from behind the altar? I don't think I would have wished that on her; I'm not completely heartless.

In fact I'm not heartless at all. I just have a different heart.

I was surprised they didn't find her earlier, of course. I wanted to get her away from there but how could I? The place crawling with police yet no one found her. Shows how few people pray, I suppose. Everyone loves the idea of a prayer chapel. No one actually uses it … once again I am the truth-teller.

Clare was not in my plan but the great strategists adapt in the field of conflict. The battle plan and the battle are two different things. That's what my father used to say. How am I doing, General?'

Forty Seven

'Chloroform again and then a knife in the stomach,' said Tamsin, as they sat in Peter's front room. 'There was a struggle but the chloroform overpowered her. Clare was unconscious when wounded.'

'When wounded?'

'She didn't die immediately.'

'I see.'

'She may have survived in some state or other for another twenty-four to thirty-six hours.'

'So she may have been alive yesterday?'

'Almost certainly.'

'While the police walked to and fro, she was dying behind the side altar.'

'Yes.'

'We are most blind when we are most busy.'

'So it seems.'

'There she was, trying to get out –.'

'You've made your point!'

Tamsin's rage at the incompetence could be kept in no longer.

'Don't take this personally,' said Peter.

'I'm not,' said Tamsin airily, 'It's other people, not me.'

She put down the pathologist's report sent to abbot@stormhaven.com.

'Your printer takes an age,' she said. 'Ever thought of getting a new one?'

'I'm never in that much of a hurry.'

'And it groans.'

'It's always groaned, from its very first job. It's one of life's groaners. Everything is a problem, but everything usually gets done. It reminds me of my postman in the desert. We were fifty miles of rock and sand from his previous stop and my God, he groaned. But always delivered.'

'She may have been by the main altar when attacked.'

'Oh?'

'We found a prayer candle on the floor there this morning. It seems likely she lit it. At least no one has else said they lit it.'

'And yet that night, I was up by the altar. I went into the church to extinguish the main candle before leaving. There was no prayer candle burning then. '

'Well, there was one there later.'

'So why?'

'Perhaps she'd murdered the vicar and felt a bit bad about it,' said Tamsin.

'Do you light a candle when you feel bad?'

'I don't know, I've never felt bad. Or lit a candle.'

The two sat in silence for a while.

Then Peter said: 'I feel a review is in order. I feel this case within, but the external outlines would be good to hear again, the hard outer casing of events.'

And so with tea and biscuits in hand, Tamsin and Peter, niece and uncle, Detective Inspector and Special Witness, secular and religious, reviewed what they knew on this second day of the investigation:

'The Extraordinary Parish meeting finished at around nine on Tuesday evening. There were nine in attendance. All then left, except for yourself and the vicar.'

'Though we know that someone was in the church,' added Peter.

'So you say. But everyone claims they left. The Bishop gave Clare a lift, and Sally, Betty, Jennifer, Ginger and Malcolm all left independently.'

'Correct.'

'You then talk with Anton. He leaves you to answer a call on his mobile. It lasts for twelve minutes. He goes off into the vestry and does not return. You decide to leave, enter the main church space and blow out the candle. You imagine you hear something.'

'I did hear something.'

'Later that evening, the murderer enters the building. The side door of the vestry was open, so either they came in that way or left that way. Clare is also in the building by this time. We don't know why. The time of her fatal attack is put at around midnight. By midnight, Anton was probably nailed to the cross, still unconscious from the chloroform. Between midnight and 2.00 a.m. he dies from a heart attack.'

'It is finished.'

'Sorry?'

'They were Jesus' last words on the cross.'

'Well they're not ours. We've barely started.'

Tamsin was not impressed by time-wasting.

'At six the following morning, his body is discovered by Sally and Ginger, both on the church premises. Sally found the side door of the vestry open. Ginger had come through the main door.'

'And then the question marks which litter the page.'

'As you say, there are question marks: you think, for instance, that someone remained in the church and you believe that someone was Malcolm. And then according to Jennifer, the Bishop did not give Clare a lift or rather, not as far as her home. There are witnesses that they left together. Jennifer saw him driving alone still some way short of Clare's home.'

'We know quite a lot.'

'Or put another way, we know nothing.'

'And then of course Betty took in the seafront on her way home,' said Peter. 'It was an unusual route given the storm, while Sally denies any relationship with the vicar, and Ginger asks us to believe that he was doing paperwork at six in the morning.'

'Is anyone telling the truth?' asked Tamsin.

'No one tells the truth,' said Abbot Peter with a smile. 'We are most careful editors of our material. The genius is in discerning not whether people are lying but why they are.'

Tamsin moved on. 'And then the following night, a brick is thrown through Jennifer's window, saying, "We know it was you".'

'The most obvious suspect, as you intimated, is Clare.'

'Your reasons?'

'It's straightforward. She crucifies Anton and then kills herself. Here's someone who doesn't mind whether he lives or dies or knows her or not. By the time he's found, she will be dead. Either way, he's punished and she's free from whatever it is which troubles her.'

'Good circumstantially, but the flaws in the theory are about to stack up.'

'True. Who moved her body and why? Who also removed the knife? How did one person alone carry out the crucifixion? And how does the chloroform fit into the story? Why would someone committing suicide use chloroform?'

'It's the death of a theory, I think, unless there were two murderers.'

'Or more?' ventured Peter. '*Murder on the Orient Express* ... the driver took a wrong turning.'

The weak joke indicated an impasse. Their knowledge was growing but not their understanding of it.

Peter said: 'I think I'll take a walk. I need to be alone.'

'So do I,' said Tamsin. 'I'll come with you.'

It was a quiet night by the sea. The dark water was docile as they made their way along the promenade past the Martello Tower built at the time of the Napoleonic Wars. It had remained a squat and spherical coastguard in Stormhaven ever since.

'It houses the dullest museum in England,' said Peter. 'Cookers from the 1940s and kitchen scales from the 1950s, that sort of thing. Quite why, no one knows.'

'Sounds like Sandy View.'

Peter laughed. 'Oh dear. Is it that bad?'

'It's quaint.'

'You should be an estate agent.'

They walked a little further until they reached the beach huts.

'And this is where I met an angry Betty that night,' said Peter.

'Here?'

'Yes, she appeared from behind one of the huts looking furious. They're in great demand, of course. There's a waiting list of ten years.'

'Personally, I wouldn't wait ten minutes for one of these.'

'Who knows what she was doing?'

'Perhaps it was a secret assignation,' said Tamsin.

'It was certainly a wet one. The rain was torrential.'

'True love knows only sunshine.'

'A romantic premise but not a convincing one,' said Peter, who wondered what such sunshine would be like.

Tamsin said: 'The old do have private lives, you know.'

There was a slight pause. Even the gulls seemed subdued.

'So how's your private life?' asked Abbot Peter.

'Same as before.'

'I see.'

They walked on a little.

'I'm not sure I know how it was before?'

'It was private then as well.'

Peter smiled.

'Why do people imagine that close things will be shared in the family?' asked Tamsin.

'Why indeed? As Jesus said, when his mother insisted on seeing him: "Who is my mother?" '

'He said that?'

'Famously.'

'That must have offended everyone wonderfully.'

'He kept his secrets for friends like Mary Magdalene, where I suppose he felt safe. We do reveal things when we feel safe.'

'That could be a very long wait as far as I'm concerned.'

'Of course the murderer will be aching to reveal themselves.'

'You think?'

'Of course. When things weigh on our minds, we need to reveal. The trouble is, there's nowhere very safe for them at present.'

'I hope not.'

Another pause in conversation but no slackening of pace in the chill night air.

'So no young man on the scene.'

'What sort of a question is that?'

'It wasn't a question. There was no question mark at the end of it, more a reflection really. But even if it was a question it's not so very threatening. It's something anyone might ask in the supermarket.'

'That's why I have my food delivered.'

'And there's nothing wrong with a young man in tow.'

'How about a young woman? Is she allowed?

'Oh, I think so. I once knew a camel like that. She became very upset when any male camel came near her.'

'And do you have one?'

'A camel? No, it would look odd in Stormhaven.'

'Like you don't already. You know I mean your private life.'

'Ah.'

'Do you have something or someone, hidden and wonderful? After so long in the desert you must have energy to burn.'

'Oh well, nothing to report on that score, really,' said Peter.

'Nothing? I thought churches were full of illicit assignations.'

'I'm more tempted by illicit solitude.'

'So who was the last woman to give you a present?'

'Er, well, Sally sent me a nice card to thank me for helping out at the Summer Fayre. I don't know if that counts. Oh, and Betty gave me a picture of her father on the beach in a swimming costume, appropriate to the era. He was standing just over there.'

Peter pointed through the darkness to a place on the shingle. 'I've still got that picture. I find old photos strangely haunting.'

'So who was the last woman you fancied?'

'You don't give up, do you?'

'Never.'

This question was less easy to answer. The last woman he'd fancied was Tamsin herself, when she'd stood on his doorstep at their first meeting.

'Well, I've always thought Jennifer was a handsome lady,' he said, and this was true. He did find her attractive, though the word handsome hardly described the nature of his desire. So it was the truth, just not the whole truth. As he said himself, we are editors all.

They walked on in silence back towards Sandy View.

*

Abbot Peter still thought of Clare as he cleaned his teeth that night.

'Tomorrow we must talk again with the Bishop,' said Tamsin.

'He may have been the last person to speak with Clare.'

'No. She'll have spoken with someone else. You don't return to church on a night like that just to light a candle.'

'So who was she meeting?'

'We don't know. Perhaps the Bishop can help us.'

'Best to summon him rather than to be summoned,' said Peter, before swilling his teeth with mouth wash. 'Get him out of his office, away from his palace. Get him down to the rough and tumble of Stormhaven police station. And disrobe him of his purple shirt as he enters.'

'You don't think highly of him?'

'Self-righteousness is a manifestation of self-hate. His ego has merged almost entirely with the need to be right. It makes true conversation with him difficult.'

Peter wondered if he had been a little uncharitable.

'Apart from that, of course, he's a good man doing his best. '

Forty Eight

It had been kind of Sally to come. She'd even brought a lemon and two tins of gin and tonic which they now drank in Jennifer's front room. No one would have known that the previous night a brick had skidded across this clean and comfortable floor in a tinkling of shattered glass. All was now restored but for one small change. Jennifer had opted for reinforced double-glazing this time.

There was respect between the two of them. They had worked closely during the interregnum and unlike some others in the parish, both knew what was required to run an organisation. Sally enjoyed Jennifer's ruthlessness and Jennifer appreciated Sally's competence. Together, they had successfully handled the transition from one vicar to another. Admittedly, they had not seen so much of each other recently. Both had tended to revolve around Anton and each had much on their plate. But they'd twice shared a trip to the theatre in Brighton and had even talked of a holiday flat in Italy together.

'It must have been terrible,' said Sally.

'It was rather bizarre,' said Jennifer. 'Me and my metal piping!'

'And do you know who it was or have any suspicions?'

'I have no idea,' said Jennifer. 'Absolutely no idea. I told the detective that I thought it could be an angry parent. That was before the Abbot went off on one his desert stories. I'm not sure he's cut out to be a sleuth. He does wander sometimes.'

'I know what you mean. I do sometimes wonder a bit when I talk with him! He doesn't react in the normal manner. It's as if my words are falling into some huge abyss of emptiness. But Tamsin seems very, well, competent.'

'Oh yes, you can see why she's made it to where she has. A touch insensitive, of course, which people do not warm to, but there we are.'

Sally nodded with a knowing smile.

'I certainly had to bite my tongue when she interviewed me otherwise heaven knows what I might have said.'

'And how is everyone else?' asked Jennifer. 'I'm afraid I've been a bit remiss in my Church Wardenly duties.'

'Everyone's fine,' said Sally. 'Bearing up pretty well. Hopefully last night's meeting helped.'

Jennifer gave her no reassurance on that score.

'I'm staying in close contact,' said Sally.

'I'm sure you are.'

'Obviously the news about Clare has shaken people.'

'Yes.'

'Though perhaps the unknowing was harder to take than the truth.'

'What weird psychological animals we are!' said Jennifer. 'Our fears are more upsetting than reality.'

'And of course, Clare wasn't the warmest of souls,' said Sally casually. 'People respected her but I'm not sure they ever quite liked her.'

'You mean she was a cold bitch, Sally. I always have to say the nasty things on your behalf.'

Sally looked into her glass and at the fizz around the lemon.

'And life must go on,' she said.

And life did go on, all around them, close and far away, life of all sorts. Outside, a car drove by noisily like a mobile disco; inside, a leaflet dropped through the door, advertising a new Chinese restaurant in the area, offering a 'special deal' for new Stormhaven customers; a mile away, a despairing local council employee opened his window and heard the waves of judgement; and here in the warm, two ambitious women called Sally and Jennifer contemplated the parish affairs of St Michael's with a little gin and tonic. Life goes on until one day it doesn't.

'Betty seems unhappy,' said Sally confidentially.

'Oh really? Why's that?'

'She's reluctant to say.'

'She's not the Betty she was. It's so sad seeing someone in decline. I remember it in my grandmother. I found it very unsettling as a child.'

'I've said I'm there for her, if she wants to talk.'

'Let's hope she does. It would do her good.'

'She says it's no one's business but her own.'

'You've done all you can, Sally.'

'I hope so. I don't like to think of her suffering alone.'

There was a pause in the conversation. Jennifer was pleasant company for Sally. She wasn't as stupid as other people; and her respect meant a lot.

'And how's the big strong Ginger?' asked Jennifer. 'We all want to know.'

'Ginger? Oh well, who knows? Ginger is a mystery!' Sally blushed as she spoke.

'He does seem to like you. His behaviour at the meeting was a bit boorish but it seems two are fast becoming one.'

'*Me and Ginger*? Oh no, no, he's much older than me. You're fishing in the wrong pool there, Jennifer! Definitely fishing in the wrong pool.'

'Yet you were both there in church at six in the morning. And I shouldn't imagine the police believe in coincidences any more than I do.'

Her delivery was as smooth as cream and Sally was a little startled.

'Well, you'll just have to believe in this one, because there's nothing else to say. Absolutely nothing!'

'If you say it, Sally, I believe it. You are a priest after all and if I can't believe you, who can I believe?'

'You can believe me.'

Sally got up and went to the window. Perhaps it was time to leave.

'I have some yoghurt in the fridge,' said Jennifer. 'Or some cheese cake.'

'No, I'm fine, thanks,' said Sally.

'You're not dieting again are you? You should let your body be for a while.'

'No, I've just lost my appetite what with recent events.'

'Liar.'

'I ought to be going anyway.'

'Stay, Sally. Why not? Get drunk! It would be good to see you loosen up a little. I won't tell on you!'

'It's probably not a good time for loosening up. Not at the moment.'

She took her bag from the sofa.

'So tell me – how did Anton look?' asked Jennifer, leaning forward.

'How do you mean?'

'When you found him? How does a crucified vicar look? I mean, I know we're not supposed to ask and all that.'

'Oh, well it was awful, of course.'

'It must have been.'

Sally sat down of the arm of the sofa to reflect.

'I hear he was naked,' said Jennifer.

'Yes, he was. He was – naked.'

Sally's eyes began to water. Jennifer was quickly up, to put her arms around her shoulder.

'It must have been just the worst,' she said.

'It was.'

'And have you talked about it with anyone?'

'The police offered me a counsellor but I said "No".'

'You're too proud.'

'I just don't think it would be helpful.'

'So what do you most remember? You need to tell someone.'

'The shock, I think. Yes, the utter sense of shock in his face.'

They kept a silence.

'He was a good man at heart,' said Jennifer. 'Others may have regretted his appointment but I never did. Well, that's not quite true, he could be grossly insensitive but I think I prefer that to the grossly depressed Reverend Stone. Anton could have done great things here, if he'd been given a chance. He just needed time.'

'But someone disagreed.'

Sally got up to leave and Jennifer didn't stop her.

'Yes, someone did.'

'Goodnight, Jennifer.'

'Goodnight, Sally. And God bless. Look after yourself.'

She walked with Sally to the door and felt numb as it closed.

Forty Nine

'We should hardly be surprised at the latest turn of events, my dear,' said the Bishop, sitting upright in bed.

He'd read his bible verse for the evening but his mind was still in Stormhaven.

'Which events?' asked his wife Margaret, who across the bed was reading a biography of Carl Jung.

He and Margaret did not now touch; or not in any way that could suggest desire. They'd not had sex for two years and not enjoyed it for seven. Something had died since the wedding. Was this a good marriage? Everyone thought so, for Margaret came to all the public events and that was the test surely? And how Bishop Stephen loved to preach on the benefits of such union!

'Those who pray together stay together!' he would say. He liked snappy sayings and the attention they brought.

'Marriage is made in heaven but worked at on earth!' That was another sound bite he favoured.

'That which God has joined together, let no man – or another woman – divide!' Sometimes he used that one as well. He even encouraged the government to support marriage with tax breaks, though his own marriage had less life than a tomb.

'Good night, dear,' said Margaret as she put down her book and turned out her bedside lamp.

'It's no surprise at all to me,' he continued. 'I have always said that the stones of Stormhaven are soaked in blood.'

'It's just a nice seaside town.'

'Hardly.'

'I really don't understand all your dramatics.'

'They're called the Cormorants. The locals, they're called the Cormorants. Do you know why?'

'I'm sure you'll tell me.'

'It's because they're famous for looting ships.'

'Then they must be very good swimmers. At least shops stay still when you smash their windows. I'm going to sleep now.'

'Then I have a bedtime story for you.'

Bishop Stephen could be a story teller, an educator, he had the gift.

'The "Cormorant" name dates back to 1562,' he said as though reading to an interested group of children.

'Is this a long one dear?'

'Not too long, no. But crucial is the fact that Stormhaven was one of the Cinque Ports.'

'Shouldn't "Cinque" rhyme with "sank"? said Margaret sleepily.

'No, no, that's the French pronunciation – the English say "sink" – rather appropriate for Stormhaven!'

Silence.

'Hastings, New Romney, Hythe, Dover and Sandwich were the originals but others were added, including Stormhaven, and the people of these towns had the right to claim goods washed up on the shore from ships lost at sea – a right that was profoundly abused.'

More silence.

'Of course wind-powered navigation around the cliffs was always dangerous in those days, especially in the dark. But the good people of Stormhaven made it a great deal more so by moving the navigation lights. Can you believe it? They moved the navigation lights to fool the passing ships! And – this I find incredible – they even lit fires on the cliffs to guide ships onto the rocks! And when they sank, they robbed the bodies of drowned seamen when they floated to shore. That's the Cormorants for you! Thank God for the good people of Stormhaven!'

He'd made his point and waited for a response. But as he looked towards his wife, there was nothing but sleep's deep breath and the widening chasm between them.

He was glad she hadn't mentioned Clare in some accusatory way.

Sometimes she did, which was ridiculous, and quite unwarranted.

Fifty

Tamsin lay in the spare bed, contemplating the second day of the investigation. She was glad at least to be back in her own sheets, collected from her police digs at the foot of the South Downs on the outskirts of Brighton. The sooner she was out of there the better. Sharing a kitchen and toilets with four spotty constables and a disturbed sergeant was the downside of her transfer to the Lewes area. The sergeant was recently arrived as well. His wife had locked him out of his home after repeated bouts of physical violence. Two suitcases containing his possessions had been delivered to the front lawn via the upstairs window. Now he and his battered suitcases were in the room across the corridor from Tamsin; and he was finding excuses to knock on her door.

'You and me are alike in a way,' he'd said last week, with alcohol on his breath. 'Both starting again. I suppose that's how fate brings people together.'

Not in Tamsin's world. It was time to go flat hunting.

Her uncle had rather sweetly attempted some home decoration. He'd put fresh flowers in her room and one or two dubious shells. She'd had a bedside lamp delivered, something else the Abbot lacked. Indeed, when she considered his home, it looked to have been furnished mainly by Beachcomber Furnishings Ltd, with old netting, a lobster basket, discarded wicker chairs and sea-soaked crates performing various roles.

To this extent, his laptop in the study looked out of place. When asked, he'd said he was writing a book. She hadn't pursued the matter further because it was not relevant to the case. It was good for the elderly to have a hobby but that didn't mean she had to be interested. Sometimes she had the impression he was thinking more about the book than the case; or at least thinking more about something. He'd spoken about the Enneagram in outline to her, but really she had more important things to think about. You had to

161

prioritise and in terms of relevance, some ancient form of typology was right up there with the day's astrological predictions. He hadn't seemed to mind her rebuttal. He said he quite understood and left it at that: 'There's a time and a place for everything, Tamsin and this apparently is neither the time nor place for you.'

She was glad it was the end of the matter.

*

There was a winter moon tonight, shining cold hope through her small window. She heard the late-night voices of two shingle walkers carried on the wind. She'd left the window open to hear the sea but mainly heard the Chief Inspector's final words to her, as she'd set off from HQ on the first morning of the investigation:

'I want the case solved by lunch, Tamsin!'

He was only joking but he never really joked and everyone in the force knew these cases were the easy ones. The crucifixion of a vicar displays madness hard to keep hidden in the routine of community life and in such cases the madman tends quickly to be found.

'It's nick-a-nutter' time,' said one of the sergeants to her. 'Sprechen ze psychiatric?'

But as the second day drew to a close, the psychopath was still appearing sane; there was another body but no sign of Mr or Mrs Mad.

Tamsin went downstairs and made some tea. She drank it with the front door open and the waves crashing. She stepped outside. You could just see the top of St Michael's from here. Everyone out there was lying of course but so what? Each community has its own deceit. What the police needed were some new facts with which to smash the lies and leave the audience gasping. They needed the murder equipment – the knife, the tape, the hammer, the drugs, the clothes. Where were they? If they'd managed to miss a live body in the church, were they now missing something else there? There would have to be another search.

*

In the room across the landing, Abbot Peter drifted into sleep wondering whether the publisher was just being polite. You could never tell with publishers. His words were encouraging but he was probably just being polite. He may not even have read the manuscript and he did keep saying he couldn't promise anything.

'There's a lot of potential here, Peter. Whether it's the right book for our current list, I'm not sure, but this isn't a "no" – or not a definite "no" anyway. It's a "maybe", Peter, so do stay in touch. Cards on the table, I do wonder if the Americans might not be a better market for the Enneagram. The English tend to be less credulous and rather more – how shall we put it – rational about these things. But who knows? It's just a thought. Keep on keeping on!'

For Peter, publishers were like wife-beaters declaring they've changed: you believe them not because they're believable but because you want them to be, the sad triumph of faith over experience. You hope they'll stop hitting you; or you hope they'll publish your book. It was true: the Enneagram wasn't very English, searching out the psyche in such a disturbing way. But neither was it the avoidant psychology of absurd promise so beloved by the American self-help market. And for good or ill, it was quite impossible to turn into a sound bite.

'Give it to me in a sentence,' one publisher had said.

Peter replied: 'If I could give it to you in a sentence, it wouldn't be worth anything.'

Most publishers, like Tamsin, placed it somewhere between astrology and witchcraft and Peter was sympathetic to their cause. It was hard for outsiders to understand until they had stepped inside the circle, until they felt its fire in their belly, at which point they'd scream in delight:

'Someone knows me at last!'

Tamsin had immediately recognised the personal threat it posed and so dealt it a hasty death blow.

'I think that's something to do on your own, Uncle.'

'You make it sound like a dirty habit,' he'd said.

The voices of two laughing beach walkers carried on the wind, excited by a discovery. He wondered what they'd found. He always wondered what others had found but not because he wanted it. He had no need of anything else for life had given him quite enough to love: first the hot desert and now this stormy coast. What more could he ask? You don't have to know what you're looking for to find it. And as sleep approached, he was thinking of the stone. He was thinking of his secret place, for though he lived alone, he would sometimes feel the need to intensify his solitude. At such times, he would make the grassy walk up the white cliffs and at a particular point, learned from a local fisherman, he'd step over the edge, through undergrowth and thistle, where he'd find a small and hidden chalk path – more of a ledge, really – which precariously led to a cave half way up the cliff face. Who else knew of it, he wasn't sure. But there he would sit alone on a large rock and contemplate the big sky, the circling birds and the dangerous sea below. He called it The Seeing Stone after something his father had once said; it was his secret place, where things became clear.

He must go back there soon.

*

And as Abbot Peter drifted off, there was a late night addition to the murder diary. It sat alongside *Strange Case of Dr Jekyll and Mr Hyde* on the book shelf, a fact that interested the killer:

'*I suppose, if caught, I will be called a Jekyll and Hyde figure, a split personality. Such ideas give comfort to people. Blame it all on nasty Mr Hyde. But Robert Louis Stevenson was not saying that. He wasn't saying there was simply a good person and bad person in us all. That would be stupid. He understood there were many different selves, not just two. We use the self who is necessary in any situation, that's my understanding at least. The cleverest know which self to use to achieve their immediate ends. I have an army of selves each obeying my command.*

I seem at present to be a rather good commander.'

Fifty One

Friday, 19 December

It was the morning of the third day of the investigation. Abbot Peter was making toast, Tamsin at the round table in the living room with coffee.

'So the question is: how do you tape someone to a cross without a struggle?' she asked.

'By drugging them first,' said Peter from the kitchen.

'Taping an unconscious body to an upright cross would require great strength.'

'True.'

The only alternative to two murderers and team work, which remained a possibility, was complicity on Anton's part and both knew it was time this option was explored.

'So Anton allows himself to be tied to the cross,' said Peter.

'Perhaps so.'

'It is the large elephant in the room.'

'So let's stop walking round it.'

'The fact is, when a vicar dies in odd circumstances the possibility of a sexual element is never far from the public's mind.'

'And very close to the *Silt*'s.'

'And they're not alone. Sergeant Reiss assumes I'm a paedophile because I'm an Abbot.'

'Has he said?'

'He doesn't need to. I hear people's attitudes more than their words.'

'Let's be honest, Uncle, there are quite a few vicar/sex-shame stories.'

'I agree, though no more than doctor, estate agent or psychologist sex-shame stories. But the vicar ones stick, I grant you. The pervy priest stories are saved by editors for the big-sale Sundays. The English seem particularly to delight in them. What this says about the priesthood – or the role of the priesthood in popular imagination I don't know, but there we are. Sex is the first thought when a vicar dies violently, with burglary trailing some way behind.'

'And when a womaniser like Anton dies in a sex game – let's make that assumption – it's more likely the murderer is a woman.'

'But perhaps not Betty.'

Tamsin got up and went to the front window.

'And then again why not a man?' she said.

'A man?'

'Why not?'

'So we're looking for a woman – or a man. You're not really narrowing it down.'

Tamsin was on a roll: 'We have no evidence that Anton was gay and plenty of evidence to the contrary. Yet for all his flirting he was still single at the age of thirty two.'

'True.'

'So was this perhaps a love that dared not speak its name?'

'I'm not sure love has much to do with it.'

'And now you're sounding pompous.'

'Better by far than vacuous.'

Tamsin's phone rang. The silence as she listened indicated interest. Peter noted that, unusually, she wasn't harassing the speaker, simply receiving their words. He watched her absorption, her compulsive hunger for the kill. Here was a ruthless woman and more often than not, when Peter used that word, it was in a positive sense.

'A note she wrote at the parish meeting has been found in the vestry,' said Tamsin, as she put down the phone.

'A note who wrote?'

'And, get this: her footprints are all over the table that must have been used for the crucifixion.'

'Whose footprints?'

'Betty's.'

'Betty?'

'She's our murderer. She's being taken down to the station now. Give me half an hour with her, people sometimes say more to outsiders, then join us.'

Fifty Two

'Detective Inspector Tamsin Shah with Betty Dodd, interview starting at 2.42 p.m.'

Betty sat opposite Tamsin in a stark room in Stormhaven Police Station that offered only a chipped formica table and two chairs for furniture.

'I've never been inside a police station before,' said Betty, with a mixture of awe and pride.

Tamsin found the child-like quality of this observation unnerving and a rare sense of care arose in her. Perhaps she was also remembering Abbot Peter's words that more flies are caught with honey than vinegar. She'd use whatever it took to catch this fly; she could do honey.

'I hope you've been treated well, Betty.'

'I've been treated very well, thank you.'

'That's good.'

'A very nice young constable brought me here and made me tea.'

'I'm glad. I think constables were made to make us tea.'

'PC Neville was his name.'

'An excellent officer.' She just managed to get that line out.

'And when I asked for some biscuits he went off and found me a box of Jaffa Cakes!'

'I will commend him personally.'

Unlike Sergeant Reiss who would be furious.

'I'll need to be home by four,' said Betty. 'That's when Thomas comes round.'

'Thomas?'

'He's a cat, not my cat, I don't have a cat of my own – I don't like them bringing in the mice. But he likes to come round and I give him something.'

'Well, we'll do our best about getting you home by four.'

'Thank you.'

'And if we have any difficulties then PC Neville will make sure Thomas is greeted with something appropriate. He loves all animals.' This wasn't the sort of recorded interview Tamsin wanted anyone else to hear; she felt like a social worker.

'But before then, Betty, I just wanted to speak with you about the night the vicar was murdered.'

Betty sat in silence.

'And you have chosen not to have a lawyer with you.'

'Why would I want one of those?'

Tamsin could think of several reasons but wasn't going to help out. Honey had its limits.

'Do you have anything you want to say about that night?'

'It was very wet, I remember the rain.'

'Yes, it was very wet; though of course you must like the rain because you went for a long walk in it.'

Betty again remained silent.

'As far as the seafront Abbot Peter told me.'

'Is it true he's your uncle?' asked Betty.

'If we can just stay with the night of the murder for the moment?'

Tamsin gathered herself again, wondering whether to add a little vinegar to the honey currently failing to catch any flies. 'Do you recognise this?'

She pushed a transparent envelope towards Betty containing some paper with writing on it. Betty looked at it without moving.

'Do you recognise that?'

'Yes, it's mine.'

'And what is it exactly?'

'They were the notes I took at the parish meeting. I like writing if I can't knit. I won the writing prize at school for stories. I've read a lot of stories and written a few.'

'They sound very exciting.'

'Oh, they're not exciting. Life isn't exciting. Life is just hard.'

Tamsin said: 'So these are your notes from the meeting on the night that the vicar died.'

Betty nodded.

'For the recording, Betty is nodding her head in agreement. So you lost these notes, Betty?'

'I did, yes.'

'Do you know where we found them?'

'In the parish room?'

'No, in the vestry. Is that a surprise?'

'Does it matter?'

'The following morning this note of yours was found in the vestry where the vicar was killed. Did you go into the vestry after the meeting?'

'No, I went for a walk.'

'That's right, you went for a long walk in the rain.'

'I like walking.'

'You must do but we still have the problem. How did your notes which you took in the parish room arrive on the floor of the vestry when you didn't go there? If you didn't put them there, who did?'

'I don't know. It could have been anyone. Things often get moved in church. It makes people very angry and then they blame me as the cleaner.'

Betty was right; it could have been quite a few people and the note in itself proved nothing. Perhaps Tamsin had hoped she'd break down and confess all; but Betty wasn't breaking down and confessing all so Tamsin decided to play her other ace. If at first you don't succeed ...

'Something else we found in the vestry was your footprints on the table.'

Betty looked straight ahead.

'The table that the murderer used to bang in the nails. Do you know how your footprints might have got there on that table? It's an odd place for footprints.'

Betty was rummaging through her bag. Was she searching for a knife with which to stab her? It did cross Tamsin's mind but instead of a knife, she drew out a handkerchief on which she firmly blew her nose.

'I've never told anyone this,' she said.

'You can trust me,' said Tamsin leaning forward.

'I stand on the table to clean the ceiling.'

'Do you?'

'It's the only way I can reach the cobwebs.'

'They don't give you a ladder?'

'I can't be doing with ladders.'

'No.'

'I prefer the table, feel safer on it but I don't tell anyone in case they make a fuss about health and safety. Roger Stills, the church warden, he's always going on about health and safety.'

'So you stand on the table to clean.'

'Yes.'

'And when did you last stand on it?'

'Tuesday.'

'The day of the murder?'

'Yes, I wanted everything looking ship-shape for the Bishop.'

It was at this point that Abbot Peter entered the room.

'Abbot Peter has just entered the room at 2.55 p.m.'

'Hello, Betty,' he said.

'Hello, Abbot.'

She didn't seem glad to see him and made no attempt to suggest otherwise. The social skills of polite deception had passed her by entirely. Why pretend you were glad to see someone when you weren't?

'Do you have anything else you want to tell us, Betty?' asked Tamsin.

'I don't think so,' she said, getting up. 'I should probably be getting back now.'

The interview was brought to an end and with Tamsin reluctant to move, almost paralysed in her seat, it was the Abbot who walked Betty to the door of the police station. Betty turned down the offer of a lift, opting to walk but not before speaking with Peter about her funeral.

'You will bury me, won't you, Abbot?'

'I'm sorry?'

Peter was caught out by this particular line of enquiry. Such requests usually came with a preamble and context but not today.

'I want you to take my funeral and bury me when I die.'

'Are you thinking of dying, Betty?'

'I'd like you to do it, Abbot.'

'And what if you outlive me by many years which is highly possible?'

'I just want to know that if I die, and I'm not young anymore, you'll take my funeral. My affairs are in order.'

'I'm not thinking about you dying, Betty.'

Betty stood stock still, staring straight at him.

'I'm thinking about you living!' he continued, his words dying in the air. 'But of course, should our lives work out that way, should death greet you before it greets me, then it would be an honour to take your funeral, Betty and to lower you into the ground of glory.'

A quiet smile broke out across Betty's face, like a weak and watery sun.

'And you've chosen burial over cremation?'

'Yes, I don't want the flames, Abbot. I want to rot, slowly rotting is the best way for me.'

And with that she started walking, hands clasped behind her back, strong determined progress, making towards the seafront as Peter returned inside.

He found Tamsin looking blankly at her notes.

'So do we have the killer?' asked Abbot Peter.

'Work in progress,' she said without looking up.

'I'll take that as a "no".'

Fifty Three

'I don't know why Clare got out of the car.'

The Bishop was insistent. Neither was he in the best of moods having been asked to 'cancel whatever you're doing' and summoned to Stormhaven police station with pressing urgency. The Abbot had been right. Bishop Stephen would have been happier in his episcopal study with family photos and a theological bookcase for support. A Bishop in a police station was very much an away match, prompting an unspoken battle of the uniforms. In the corridors and foyer were the blue uniforms against which he deployed his purple shirt and large cross. One purple shirt with cross trumped a hundred blues in his opinion; he was the Holy Father here and far beyond the stupid reach of the Plod Brigade. But what irritated him the most was the discovery that Abbot Peter was part of the interview team.

'So you did drive her home?' said Tamsin.

'I offered her a lift, yes.'

'As was your common practice I believe?'

'I may have been charitable in this manner on other occasions, if that's what you're saying.'

'That is what I'm saying.'

'As though it's wrong to be kind! I thought we were meant to applaud the Good Samaritan?'

'Loud applause,' said Abbot Peter. 'Always.'

'I'm sure Clare appreciated this regular twosome greatly,' said Tamsin.

The Bishop's face reddened a little; this was Peter's perception as Tamsin continued.

'It was Clare, after all, who was always the beneficiary of this charity.'

'She's on my way home!'

'Sort of on your way home. A slight detour necessary.'

'It was nothing.'

171

'And yet you didn't make it to her house on the night of the murder. Why was that?'

There was a pause.

'She wanted to get out,' said the Bishop, quietly.

'I'm sorry?'

'She decided that she wanted to get out.'

'An odd decision on such a stormy night.'

'I thought so myself. I thought, "What's got into you, you poor girl?" '

'And what had got into her?'

'As I say, I have no idea.'

'So how did the conversation go exactly? Become a reporter for a moment. You were driving along in the rain and you were still at least a mile from her home when she said what?'

'Well, she just said she wanted to go back to the church.'

'I see. Any reason given?'

'No, she just said she must go back. Something was obviously on her mind.'

'I'm sure it was. And you offered to drive her there, I presume.'

'Back to church? No, I had to return home; I had other things to attend to. There are many issues which require my attention beyond the affairs of Stormhaven.'

'So you stopped the car and then what?'

'Well, she got out.'

'Did she say goodbye?'

'Oh yes, she said goodbye and thanked me for the lift and then got out. I didn't see her again.'

'Though you rang her on three occasions soon after.'

'I just wanted to make sure she was all right.'

'Do you ring everyone three times after they leave you?'

'It was late, I was concerned.'

'I'm sure you were but about what?'

'About her safety of course! And with good reason as it turned out.'

'Indeed. And you rang her three times because she didn't answer any of your calls, which is odd given your charitable works toward her. I think I'd always the answer the calls of the Good Samaritan.'

'I don't pretend to know the answer to that.'

'I'm certainly struggling.'

'But then, Detective Inspector, sometimes we must live the mystery. I often have to say that to people.'

'And that's all very spiritual,' said Tamsin, 'but in police work, we have to get to the bottom of a mystery rather than "live it" as you say.

And the mystery here is this: why did Clare get out of your car on a filthy night and, without explanation, return to the church?'

*

'A pretty savage performance,' said Abbot Peter after the Bishop had taken his leave. 'Though we must, of course, beware of negative fixations. They aren't always the path to enlightenment.'

'Negative fixations?'

'You become fixated by dislike. You lock onto someone in negative relationship. From there on, everything they do and everything they are, is wrong, despised, judged. They're demonised, they become demons.

'He's a liar.'

'True.'

'And you shouldn't lie if you have a big cross round your neck.'

Fifty Four

Saturday, 20 December

Council worker Christopher Thornton tidied his front room but a note seemed superfluous. Why give meaning to something that had no meaning? A note said his life mattered and his life had never mattered, had only ever been pretence. If he were a stick of Brighton rock, the words down the middle would be 'I'm worth nothing.' It was disturbing but he couldn't remember any particular moment in his life when he could say, 'This is me'. He could only remember saying, 'Well, I got away with that quite well.'

Some unspeakable shame, he felt it there, the sense that if anyone knew him as he was, then they wouldn't like him, would see through the pretence to the emptiness behind. His mother had said how horrid he could be, so he'd sent his shadow out into the world and the shadow had done well until the beach hut incident. It wasn't the worst thing he'd done – well he hadn't done anything really, just another small lie in a very long list. But it was the money that had tipped the scales, the bribe he'd managed to call a thank you. This was the Rubicon he'd crossed and the reason he left home early this Saturday morning and walked the 300 yards to the sea front where he began the climb up the white cliffs.

'Vive le weekend!' said one jolly old lady coming the other way.

'Vive le weekend,' replied Christopher.

Away to his left was the golf course, distant figures with time on their hands or business relations to develop:

'How about we discuss it over a round of golf?'

It was a world Christopher was familiar with but not part of; and this was the final goodbye. His funeral would be an interesting event.

Who from the office would go? And what would they say about him afterwards as they hung around the flowers before leaving. They'd probably discuss the football or house prices. He couldn't imagine them spending very long on him.

The climb was now steeper, Stormhaven below him and the golf course at the end of its reach. Up ahead was a young runner attempting the gradient but travelling so slowly that Christopher's determined walk was in danger of taking him past the lad. And Christopher's walk could be very determined; such physical force within that he'd never really harnessed or directed. If only he'd known who he was. He understood Samuel Becket's lines, words scribbled on a post-it note in his kitchen, 'There were times when I forgot not only who I was, but that I was, forgot to be.'

And now he stood on the soft grass at the top of the cliffs where only the keen walkers came. Beachy Head was the traditional place to leap, two miles further along the coast and generally, Christopher liked tradition, liked the familiar. But he also liked it here and looked around in appreciation of the wind-swept view. The young runner had made it to the top and now turned wearily inland. Surprisingly, he seemed to be going no faster on the flat than he had on the sharp climb. Perhaps he was a one-gear runner, equal in speed whatever the terrain, never fast, never slow but durable and steady, keeping going until the end and, as Christopher had mimicked him in life, so he'd mimic him in death. He'd keep going to the end.

And then he was being greeted by the strange man in a habit. He'd seen him in Stormhaven before, struggling up the High Street or once in the supermarket talking with the till girl. But he'd never spoken himself. You don't, do you? But now the two met at last as the wind quietened, a still morning air in high places and a strangely intimate winter silence.

'Only committed walkers out today!' the strange man in the habit said cheerily.

'That's true,' said Christopher, glad of the human contact. And then a thought occurred to him: 'Do you hear confessions?'

'I'm sorry?'

'Do you hear confessions?'

'I do yes.'

'Good.'

'Though it's a dying trade, not something people practice much now.'

'I suppose not.'

Christopher laughed inwardly at the spiralling and absurd nature of guilt, as new possibilities now became apparent. He could imagine

175

it: 'Father, I confess that I am guilty of allowing my confessions of guilt to become a little sporadic of late.'

But the man in the habit did not seem like a vulture feeding off the self-condemnation of others.

'Yes, they simply "move on",' continued the strange man in a throwaway manner. 'But I sense you can't do that.'

There was a silence between them.

'So what do you want?'

'I just want to say I'm sorry,' said Christopher.

'What are you sorry about?'

'Many things. But I'm mainly sorry about the beach hut.'

'The beach hut? Well, now you've spoken it and I've heard it.'

'Yes.'

'And that's enough.'

'Really?'

'Indeed.'

'That's a weight off my mind.'

There was another silence as a woman with an energetic Dalmatian passed them.

'We all have our reasons,' said Peter.

'But they're not always good reasons.'

'What is it about the beach hut you're sorry for?'

'Just tell Mr Robinson at the council what I've said. He's a good man.'

'And how will I contact Mr Robinson?'

Christopher placed a card in his hands.

'I'm not so bad, am I?' he said.

'You were never bad,' said Abbot Peter. 'Whoever said that you were?'

'My mother, teachers, where to begin?'

'Then they didn't deserve you.'

There was a thought, but perhaps a thought too late.

'I just want you to remember to tell Mr Robinson.'

'I will.'

'Thank you,' he said as he turned and walked on, only doubling back when the strange man in the habit had continued on his journey back down into Stormhaven.

Christopher looked out to sea beneath dark and blustery clouds. He glanced round, once more reaching out for elusive approval in the wind. And then he ran forward until the land ran out beneath his feet and he was falling, as every leaf must.

Fifty Five

The Christmas Fayre was going very well until Anton's unexpected return.

'Where have you been?' asked Tamsin. 'I feared I'd have to go alone.'

They'd been due to meet outside the chip shop at 2.00 p.m. and Peter was five minutes late.

'Yes, I'm sorry but I just had to see Mr Robinson. Very important.'

'And who is the mysterious Mr Robinson?'

'The first time he's been called that, I should think.'

'So?'

'He's a middle-to-large cog in the council's Recreation and Leisure department.'

'Why does that sound so bleak?'

'I don't know. Is it any different from being a middle-to-large cog in the police force?'

'I think it's the Recreation and Leisure thing. Makes it sound like a complete waste of time.'

'There speaks an activist.'

'Or just a person who gets the job done.'

Peter paused. Arguing with self-justifying attitudes led nowhere. 'He doesn't spill charisma, I grant you, but neither does he spill despair. I think he has a job he believes in, which is rather nice.'

'And you think he has something for us?'

It was a leading question, accompanied by hawk-like stare from Tamsin.

'Oh, definitely. He's getting back to me when he knows more. But he knows quite a lot already.'

'And what did you talk about?'

'Beach huts.'

'Beach huts?'

'Yes.'

'Glad to hear you weren't wasting your time.'

The put-down was short and sharp but Abbot Peter could only smile.

Tamsin continued: 'You can now make up for lost time by telling me what on earth you do at church fayres. This is my first.'

'The brief is fairly simple,' said Peter, as they walked together through the wonderful smell of frying fish and chips towards St Michael's. 'You buy one thing you want and two things you don't. You bump into as many people as possible in a cheery fashion. You comment on the good turnout, even if there's only three of you. You have a cup of tea, say something nice about the cakes and take your gracious leave.'

'Sounds more your bag than mine.'

'You'll make it your bag, Tamsin, I know you will. There's room for all sorts at a Fayre and you'll bring your own particular genius. Indeed, I suspect you'll do so well they'll want you back next year.'

'Don't.'

But Peter's prediction proved true. Once there, Tamsin found she could play this game remarkably well, able to charm stall holders quite as well as she crushed junior officers.

'You have some lovely stones and shells here, Betty!' she said, after a brief perusal of Betty's 'Shingle and Shore' table.

The altered circumstances of their present meeting to their last did not appear to strike Betty as odd. Indeed, Betty seemed in particularly high spirits.

'Well, I didn't find them all myself,' she said, 'I did have help but they're all local. Well, nearly all. Would you like to buy one?'

'I'm sure I will.'

'Which one?' asked Betty, staring straight into her eyes.

'It's such a wonderful event,' said Tamsin, not ready to be pinned down. 'Let me first take a look round and then come back and make my choice. I do like the starfish.'

'The starfish isn't from Stormhaven,' said Betty.

'But still beautiful.'

'It's from the Greek island of Kalymnos.'

'Have you been?'

'No. I've been to Watford.'

'Really?'

'I had an uncle there.'

'It's a lovely place.'

'I didn't fancy it much.'

'Oh?'

'I'm happy in Stormhaven.'

'And so say all of us!'

How did Tamsin manage to sound so convincing?

'Or rather I *was* happy in Stormhaven.'

'I'm sorry to hear that. What changed?'

Momentarily, the social and the professional coincided but Betty would not be drawn.

'This is the seventy-fifth Christmas Fayre I've attended,' she said.

'Loyalty. You're an example to us all.'

'Not always. Sometimes I do quite bad things.'

Like standing on the table to clean the ceiling, thought Tamsin.

Tamsin said: 'I simply don't believe you!' as another customer distracted the stall holder and she made her escape.

Meanwhile Abbot Peter was at Jennifer's teddy bear stall.

'It's an annual thing,' she explained, as she continued with the pricing. 'I ask parents to bring to school any teddies currently out of favour at home. I occasionally have an angry child, claiming kidnap and demanding their teddy back. But it always proves popular. Well, a lot of them are good as new. And for those who find children's toys expensive, it can be a bit of a godsend.'

'I'm almost tempted!' said the Abbot, looking at the array of cuddly friends in an uninterested fashion.

'I'm sure we could find a nice one for you, Abbot. A teddy-less Sandy View doesn't bear thinking about!'

'I'm coping somehow,' said Peter.

'If it's a girl, we'd call her Pebbles.'

'And if a boy, Cliff.'

Abbot Peter was looking to move on and eyeing the second-hand bookstall with inappropriate lust when an arm was placed on his shoulder.

'And you must be the Abbot,' said an older woman, appearing at his side.

'Indeed I am. A former Abbot at least.'

'I suppose you never lose the habit!'

It was not the first time he'd heard this quip.

'I was a real Abbot in the desert,' he explained.

'And you're still a real Abbot here, whatever the Bishop thinks,' said Jennifer.

'I hope you haven't been persuaded to buy a teddy?' said the older woman.

'I've resisted the temptation so far, but there's only so much a man can take.'

'Well, don't let her throw sand in your eyes,' said the woman, looking at Jennifer. 'She could sell a donkey to Eskimos.'

'Welcome to my mother!' said Jennifer, before turning to another customer.

'Are you visiting?' asked Peter.

'I live in Lewes, so it's only a fifteen minute drive.'

'You must be very proud of your daughter.'

'She'll do. She was the youngest head in the county when appointed. Though it's strange to see her quite so happy behind a teddy bear stall.'

'They do grow up quickly, I suppose.'

'Oh, it isn't that, Abbot' she said, 'Not that at all, it's quite comical really ...' and she was expanding on the comical when the raffle draw was announced. The Bishop and the mayor duly came forward to do the honours.

'I hope we can trust these suspicious looking characters,' said Sally into the microphone, as they took up their positions either side of her.

Everyone laughed.

'Never trust a Bishop!' said Bishop Stephen, excited by attention.

Everyone laughed again.

The best raffle prize was Clare's offer of one day's van rental, free of charge, on a day of your choice in the coming year. Now that Clare was dead, there was some doubt as to whether the offer still stood, but the parish had decided to go ahead with it anyway. Other top presents included a large bottle of champagne given to Sally by one of her wealthy admirers and a £50 voucher from the local supermarket. After that, the prizes were less thrilling but acceptable. There was shampoo, bubble bath, unwanted dessert bowls and the best of the teddies offered to Jennifer. There was also a can of tinned pears, though no one knew who had given it.

*

The mayor and Bishop formed a surprisingly good double act. The Bishop made jokes about the lavatory chain around her neck and the mayor said she'd use it to flush away his sermons. The mutual hostility brightened everyone's day until finally, even the tin of pears had found a disappointed owner and the Christmas music resumed over the speakers.

It was darkening outside, but bright inside with Christmas sparkle as people moved towards the refreshments and made final decisions about buying. The homemade jam and pickle stall, a surprising new venture by an entrepreneurial teenager had sold out completely, something which could not be said of the bookstall where Malcolm was reducing everything to ten pence. He had no desire to be bagging them up later, to be kept in black plastic bags for next year. He also displayed his triptych, the one removed from the church by Anton and, gratifyingly, he received many favourable comments about it.

'Why is it not in the church?' said Mrs Jones, a regular non-attender, who somehow still imagined a claim over church affairs.

'Anton didn't like it.'

'Well, I don't want to speak ill of the dead –. '

'Don't hold back on my account,' said Malcolm. 'Nothing good can be built on evasion.'

Mrs Jones found this a little shocking.

'Well, anyway, I think it's a marvellous painting. Definitely should be somewhere.'

But despite the praise, Malcolm found himself glancing towards the prayer chapel and thinking of Clare. He would like to have married her, though she was cold like his mother and it wouldn't have worked. Certainly it had not been a good ending between them but then again, what had she been doing in the church at that time?

*

'Good to see Ginger so engaged,' said Jennifer to Sally as they passed briefly by the tea urn.

The church youth worker was holding an informal 'punch the palm' competition.

'He's a natural with young people,' said Sally admiringly.

'But hardly a regular at church events!'

'He comes when he can.'

'It's so sweet to see you on the defensive, Sally, covering his back for him.'

'I'm not on the defensive! And I'm not covering his back.'

Jennifer's surprise was shared by others, for Ginger did not usually attend these things. What he didn't lead, he didn't touch. And anyway, from his perspective, he was paid to be with the kids not the adults. Today, however, he was the life and soul of the party. Big, strong and gregarious, his palm was taking a good battering from eager young boys and one or two feisty girls.

'Hardest punch is the winner.'

'Who's the judge?'

'I am, stupid. After all, it's my palm so I should know who's hit it the hardest! And believe me, the winner so far is a girl.'

A verbal gender war broke out between the under twelves – 'weakling boys, weakling boys!' – as children quickly re-joined the queue for the chance of another punch.

Meanwhile, the Bishop moved among his flock with a cheery smile until becoming becalmed by the books. When the hands of the Bishop and Abbot touched, reaching for the same tome, they had to talk. Peter was aware their last meeting had been in Stormhaven police station.

'I hear your Christmas tree is struggling,' said the Bishop.

'I'm sorry?'

'I'm told the lights on your tree at home are following your lead and abstaining!'

'Oh, they'll be back, Bishop, in their own time. They don't crave the attention that some do.'

There was an awkward pause.

'So how's Jennifer?' said the Bishop.

'Jennifer? Well enough, I think, Stephen. She tried to sell me a teddy but apart from that small moral lapse, behaving impeccably.'

'I met her mother just now.'

'Yes, I saw.'

'Tremendous woman, absolutely tremendous woman.'

'She obviously made a deep impression on you … in the 60 seconds you spoke with each other.'

'So where Jennifer gets that unpleasant streak from, I have no idea.'

'A blueberry muffin, Bishop?' asked Abbot Peter as a tray of the sweet-smelling beauties passed them.

And then shortly afterwards, Anton started talking. The former vicar of St Michael's, recently crucified, was suddenly speaking loud and clear. He'd always fancied himself as a DJ and after a number of seasonal tracks, including 'O Come All ye Faithful' and 'Winter Wonderland ', he was suddenly addressing the Christmas Fayre:

'And that beautiful piece of music was "The Shepherds' Farewell" by Berlioz,' he said. 'A bit slow but what can you do? And before that – my goodness, an intruder in the studio!'

There was background noise of a door opening and someone entering the room.

'Sorry listeners, but the Naked DJ is surprised by a visitor! Didn't expect to see you here quite so soon! I was just making a CD of Christmas music for the Fayre but it's not anything which can't wait obviously. And for those listening, our mystery visitor in the studio is quite lost for words! Well, there's a first time for every –. '

The church sound system went dead, cutting off Anton in full flow. There was stunned silence in the building. Anton had never been short of a word but few had expected him to offer one this afternoon. And no one moved.

It was Abbot Peter who reacted first, knowing what needed to be done. As quickly and calmly as possible, he made his way from the opposite side of the church to the vestry from where the CD was being played.

'Let me through, please,' he said, as he shouldered his way past people still stupid with shock.

'Was that really the vicar?' said someone as he pushed past them.

He was there in around ninety seconds. The vestry door was open, but the room empty, as was the CD tray in the machine. Someone had got there before him and he believed he might know who that someone was. It was a strange certainty and one rejected instantly.

'Certainty blinds more than it reveals,' as he used to say in the desert. 'When you are certain of something you stop looking. And when you stop looking, you die.' So as he stood in the vestry, just seconds away from the murderer's hurried steps, he noted certainty's arrival and then allowed it to leave, just as Tamsin appeared at the door, holding a starfish.

'Gone?'

'CD or murderer?'

'Either.'

'Both.'

'Someone must have seen something.'

'Possibly.'

Peter sat down on the desk while Tamsin checked outside. With no vicar hanging on the cross now, an air of normality had crept back into the room. He noted the service register sitting beside him and the Sunday school rota on the wall. The shocking nailing had occurred on Tuesday, but it was Saturday now, four days later and the tide of time had done its work, the need to continue, the need to hope, the need to carry on, erasing scars, returning scenery to the untouched tranquillity of former times. But Tamsin saw no tranquillity in Peter's eyes.

'Father Anthony,' he said.

'What about him?'

'Strange man.'

'Most of your friends are.'

'No, he's been dead awhile.'

'I refer you to my previous answer.'

'In the fourth century AD, he left his home in Middle Egypt to live as a solitary in the desert for twenty years.'

'Another half-crazed, unwashed religious escapist?'

'Far from it: he entered the desert not to escape the darkness but to face it.'

'How about we stay with Stormhaven? It seems more relevant.'

'Oh, we're very much in Stormhaven. For as Father Anthony said, 'We do not flee from danger, we advance to meet it.'

Fifty Six

The phone was ringing as he walked through the door. Bishop Stephen picked up the phone and discovered Martin Channing on the other end.

'Christmas greetings, Stephen!'

'And greetings to you too, Martin – though technically we're still in the season of Advent. We mustn't get to Christmas before Mary and Joseph!'

'God forbid,' said Martin, who had never made it to Christmas.

The Bishop felt beguiled to hear the charming voice of Martin Channing. What could he want? He was wary, of course. But if Channing wanted to play hard ball, the Bishop knew a thing or two about the journalistic game.

'I'm just back from the Christmas Fayre at St Michael's, as it happens,' he said.

'Where I hear you were a storming success, Bishop.'

'Really?'

"An inspiring man of God among his people in their time of need,' was how one person described it to me.'

'News travels fast!'

'Well, news is my business,' said Martin. 'If I'm not keeping up then we really are in a mess.'

'It was certainly a splendid event, community at its most inspiring, the faithful making the best of difficult times – and certainly a good news story if it's a good news story you want.'

'You know me, Bishop – I'd cross the desert for a good news story.'

'Then perhaps you should cross the desert a little more often! After all, the *Silt* isn't exactly famous for pages devoted to happy outcomes, appearing more interested in – how shall we say? – bottom-of-the-barrel journalism.'

'A little harsh, Bishop.'

'There's more to life than a few celebrities and the latest ghastly crime.'

Martin Channing chuckled.

'You're right of course, Stephen.'

'Really?'

'Painfully so.'

The Bishop could hardly believe his ears as Channing continued:

'And it's a weakness in the *Silt* which I want you to change.'

'Which you want *me* to change? I would have thought that was the editor's job.'

'Good point well made. You hit the nail on the head as ever. I wish some of my journalists had your perspicacity.'

'Well, I like to think I wasn't born yesterday in such matters.'

'Which is exactly why you should be writing a column for the *Silt*.'

'A column in the *Silt?* You mean a regular feature in the paper?'

'That's exactly what I mean. A weekly feature.'

'Weekly?'

'We need the voice of God, Stephen, the voice of hope, a clarion call to our readership in difficult times. I knew it already but your performance today at St Michael's just confirmed it.'

'Well, if you think I can be of help,' said Bishop Stephen humbly. 'I hope I speak the plain and simple truth.'

'And that's exactly what we want. In fact, perhaps that's the name of the column. 'Plain and Simple – Your Bishop speaks in the Soaraway *Silt*.'

'I'd have to be able to speak freely, of course.'

'I wouldn't want it any other way. This is not Martin Channing's column – this is your column.'

The Bishop was warming to the idea.

'Well, there are certainly some issues I believe must be addressed in society.'

'Then here is your forum – though obviously your readers will want you to start with recent events at St Michael's.'

'Really?'

'Oh, I think that would be a marvellous way to introduce yourself to your new congregation, if I may use that term.'

'Is that wise?'

'Is what wise?'

'Me talking about recent events at St Michael's? I mean, I have my opinions of course!'

'Don't worry, we'd want nothing controversial, Bishop.'

'No, that makes sense.'

Bishop Stephen was reassured.

'Nothing of a sensationalist nature.'

'Of course.'

'Every editor knows when respect is due to a situation and indeed to a community. Marvellous people at St Michael's.'

'Quite, quite.'

'No, we just want your thoughts on the rather ineffective investigation so far, some background on the crucified vicar, your feelings about him and his inadequate leadership – in other words, the plain and simple truth. Start as we mean to go on!'

The Bishop could not pretend he wasn't enthralled by this opening. To be given a public platform like this from which to speak of Christ was, well, a godsend surely? The *Sussex Silt* had its detractors, but many read it and they couldn't all be wrong, surely? Here indeed was a new congregation for the Bishop – weekly sales of 150,000 copies, so a readership of perhaps four or five times that number. This was a congregation who needed him. How could he walk away from them?

'And you feel this might be a weekly column?' he asked, like a man seeking confirmation of the full value of a famous painting discovered in his attic.

'I'm certainly thinking along those lines, Bishop, I'd be a fool not to be. We need you out there on a regular basis.'

'I see.'

'But let's get the first column home and hosed and then make plans – exciting plans.'

'OK.'

'No rush of course, but we'd need copy by eleven o'clock this evening. Might there be a window in your diary for that?'

The Bishop thought there might be.

Fifty Seven

'So what brought my Russian grandfather to the West?'

'Train, mainly.'

Tamsin smiled.

'He must have had a reason.'

'My father had his reasons, yes.'

'Oh, so he's your father now!'

'I think he always was. The grandfather bit came later.'

'So tell me about him.'

'Why this sudden interest in your family tree? Things must be bad if you're now trawling the past for an identity.'

Tamsin remained aloof to the mockery.

'He ended up in Paris, didn't he?' she asked.

The truth was, things were bad. Drained by the day's events, Tamsin sat drinking tea beside the fire in the Abbot's front room. No one in the church had seen anything of the murderer. The darkness outside, the Christmas lights inside and the universal sense of shock all proved to be the distraction and cover the killer required to leave the vestry by the outside door and merge quietly again into the stunned crowd inside the church. No one was quite sure who was by them at what particular time after the raffle. There'd been an issue over the whereabouts of Jennifer until she returned from the toilet, at some personal embarrassment. And Ginger came in from having a smoke to find faces turned towards him. He soon turned them away.

'Can a man not have a cigarette?'

So what had they learned this afternoon? Nothing. They were four days into the case and from Tamsin's perspective, as far from home as when they started and neither did tomorrow offer relief. It may be the Sabbath but there'd be no rest for her, with the press conference she could no longer postpone in the morning followed by a meeting with Chief Inspector Wonder, no doubt tapping his fingers on the desk with impatience.

So tonight, the hunter wanted to forget the chase and sit by the fire. She wanted to hear stories from another land, a distant land – things cosy, reassuring and safe. And so her question to the Abbot about her grandfather, not that there appeared anything very safe or cosy about him.

'He spoke privately of being sent to Europe,' said Peter.

'Sent by whom?'

'Well, this is where things get a little hazy. He claims to have been sent by the Sarmoun Brotherhood, a mysterious community somewhere in Afghanistan.'

'Not everyone believes him?'

'He just didn't say very much about it.'

'Perhaps he was sworn to secrecy.'

'Possibly. And sometimes things are simply too sacred to talk about. Something dies in the telling.'

'They call it the sermon.'

'Very amusing,' said Peter with a weary smile. He could do with being alone tonight.

'But whatever impelled him to come he came with a strong sense of calling: "Unless the wisdom of the East and the energy of the West can be harnessed and used harmoniously, the world will be destroyed", he said.'

'Radical words.'

'And all the more so for the fact that such thinking – thinking that took the teaching of the east seriously – though familiar now was unheard of at the beginning of the twentieth century. The west had Freud, what else did it need?'

'Quite a lot.'

'Yes, well, that's another discussion.'

'And so George Ivanovich Gurdjieff left Afghanistan and got on the train to Paris, end of story?'

Peter laughed.

'Why do you laugh?'

'Even when you don't want to hurry, you still want to hurry.'

'I always want to get to the end.'

'Fair enough, but the journey matters as well. You'll have to put up with one or two delays before his arrival in Paris – because my father had to.'

'So what held him up?'

'Well, after some time with the community, he left Afghanistan with my mother Yorii. They soon parted, though. I was the result of a later union between them apparently.'

'We'll not go there.'

'But he was in action straight away. He first taught the Enneagram in Petrograd in 1916. But the Russian Revolution forced him out.'

'They weren't converts?'

'Revolutions place their hope in external reform and pay little heed to the inner workings of the human psyche. They foolishly imagine that if you change the government, you change the people.'

'Not so?'

'Not at all. It's like an alcoholic buying a new set of clothes. Flash new appearance, same old drunk.'

'So your father moved on.'

'Yes, he travelled through Istanbul, Berlin, and Dresden before finally settling in Fontainebleau outside Paris. They nearly settled in Hampstead in London but it didn't work out.'

'So it was in Fontainebleau that he set up that strange school. My mother spoke of it.'

'He founded "The Institute for the Harmonious Development of Man".'

'Interesting name.'

'Especially since nothing he ever did was remotely harmonious.'

There was a companionable silence as the flickering flames crackled in the hearth. Both knew the storm was about to break, that from here on, if the killer was to be found, there must be daring and danger. Abbot Peter put another log on the fire, discarded wood from the boat builders, collected that morning from the beach.

'And so that's my grandfather?'

'An interesting man.'

'There speaks the proud son.'

'Proud? Maybe, I'm not sure. Writer, Russian intelligence officer, entrepreneur, bully, psychologist, choreographer –.'

'Choreographer?'

'Yes, he turned his teachings into dance because mind, body and spirit are one. He was a great spiritual teacher alongside everything else.'

'And it was him who taught you about the Enneagram?'

'He learned it from the Sarmoun Community and held the symbol in very high regard.'

'The odd drawing you showed me?'

'That's right.'

'The circle and the nine points?'

'It may not look much. But he believed that symbol held all the secrets of the universe. He called it "the fundamental hieroglyphic of a universal language". If you understand that symbol, Peter, he said to me, then libraries become useless! Through that symbol, you can read the world.'

Silence descended again.

'And you think that through that symbol you can read the people of Stormhaven?'

'I can read them in a way.'

'Then I'll race you to the murderer.'

'It's not a competition, Tamsin.'

'It's always a competition.'

'But we're a team.'

'No such thing.'

'And members of a team can't compete without risking serious dysfunction. '

'Welcome to the police force. As the saying goes, "Trust a criminal but never a colleague".'

'Well, that's sad.'

'It's life.'

'Not my life.'

'Okay, so we'll pretend it isn't a race; but we'll both know it is one really.'

Peter sighed; and stirred a little.

Fifty Eight

Sunday, 21 December

London had finally decided to come south.

Until this point, the nationals had been relying on stringers from Brighton's *Evening Argus* and the Lewes-based *Sussex Silt* to keep the gossip pot stirred. Martin Channing had earned a pleasurable amount of money writing pot-boiling pieces for former friends in the trade. But in the end, the lure of nakedness, a crucified vicar and some bracing sea air proved too much and London journalists could no longer resist truth's cry for help.

They stayed mainly in Eastbourne or Brighton where expense accounts could be more enjoyably exercised. Stormhaven did have a hotel but it was not one where any Londoner would wish to stay. As an estate agent told Peter when he arrived: 'We don't want to encourage tourists here. Let them ruin Brighton.'

Such an isolationist policy, when brought to Tamsin's attention, was not easily understood. 'The people here have no vision,' she'd said.

'Perhaps it's just a different vision,' Peter replied, feeling one hotel was more than enough.

'But hotels bring income.'

'And they also bring stag weekends with their special brand of late-night hilarity, vandalism and vomit on the pavements. Budapest may be up for that sort of thing but it doesn't mean Stormhaven has to be.'

'The march of progress always has a price.'

'And the other thing about the march of progress is that it doesn't exist.'

But there wasn't much talk this morning. It had been a hasty breakfast at Sandy View with Tamsin gone by 8.30 a.m. to prepare for the press conference.

'Wish me luck,' she'd said, like a daughter going off for an exam.

'Imagine them all with no clothes on and you'll be fine.'

'What?'

'It takes away the fear and the fearless are free.'

Tamsin ignored him, gathered her things, closed the door behind her and set her face to the activity of the day.

As she drove away, Peter stood at the window, watched her go and felt a frisson of pleasure. The house was his again, like reclaimed land and it was time for a coffee alone, the best sort of coffee, with perhaps a slice of toast with butter and marmalade. He'd bought butter after Tamsin winced at the margarine, and thick cut marmalade would top things off nicely, the majesty of bitter chunks of orange. He'd sit in his study, settle into solitude and perhaps work on the jigsaw, so neglected of late. These were the things he was looking forward to when he heard the knock on the door. Had Tamsin forgotten her keys?

'Peter!'

'Hello, Martin.'

'May I come in?'

'Yes of course.'

'I know you get lonely sometimes.'

'Not knowingly.'

Peter ushered Martin Channing into the room.

'It's been too long.'

'You must want something.'

'Yes I want quality.'

'Please sit down.'

'The comfy chair?' queried Martin.

Peter only had one comfy chair.

'Why not? I can always sit on it later. Coffee?'

'That would be very fine.'

Martin contemplated the quiet Christmas tree.

'He looks a rather sad little fellow.'

'I don't think of him as sad.'

'Are the lights not working?'

'They did work briefly.'

'That's a shame. I mean, if an Abbot can't put on a decent Christmas–.'

'They'll be back. So why aren't you at the press conference, Martin? You're an editor, aren't you?'

'I don't attend press conferences.'

Peter went into the kitchen and put the kettle on, reluctantly adding another cup to the one sitting ready. He returned to the front room.

'I would have thought a press conference might be a good place for the press to be, or am I being naïve?'

'The latter.'

Peter returned to the kitchen.

'How do you like your coffee?'

'Not too strong.'

'One spoon?'

'Perfect.'

Some digestives and chocolate bars appeared with the coffee and then Peter settled on the wooden box, which once held herring. It had been a while before the smell finally left the house, like a drawn-out exorcism. But the container had its own charm, gradually succumbing to furniture polish and proved both occasional table and bench depending on need.

'And the press conference is dull because?'

'Because I want the story not the platitudes and you my dear Abbot have the story.'

Peter had once heard Martin Channing referred to as the only reptile on the planet to wear a bow tie. He was charming, camp in a non-sexual way and entirely amoral.

'People still talk of the lovely piece you did for us on the desert, Peter.'

The discreet laying of flattery's trap did not go unnoticed.

'You have a gift, Peter,' he continued.

'You should tell the publishing world.'

'Perhaps I will. It's only a matter of time before you're discovered. And one thing leads to another in my experience.'

'My desert piece in the *Silt* didn't lead to a great deal.'

On his return from Egypt, he'd met Martin Channing at a charity event and the editor had suggested he write about his time in the desert. Peter's title had been: 'Desert Learning.'

The paper's title had been, 'Why 25 years in the desert drove me mad!'

'Slowly, slowly, catchee monkey, as I'm sure Jesus said,' observed Martin, passing on the digestives.

'It was well-edited piece, as I remember,' said Peter.

'I'm glad you like the job we did on it. I took a particular interest in its progress.'

'I think I mean "much edited".'

Martin smiled.

'Well, no offence, but while you're a fine writer of course, Peter, very fine, reminiscent of Balzac in so many ways, you're still learning the journalistic craft.'

'There was hardly a sentence of mine left standing.'

'You musn't take these things personally, Abbot! The desert may make you a saint but it doesn't make you a columnist. So yes, a little surgery was necessary.'

'A heart transplant, as I remember.'

'No, no, no. Minor surgery only! Nip and tuck really. We just shortened the rather long and opaque sentences, freshened up the vocabulary and removed the cloudy bits.'

'The cloudy bits?'

'When a writer doesn't quite know what they want to say, they get cloudy; they imagine that if they go on for long enough it will all eventually become clear.'

'But it doesn't?'

'You can get away with it in books, Peter, but not in newspapers. We can't have a reader drifting for even a moment or putting the paper down. We must be instant, pressing and urgent. You see how insecure we are!'

'So what do you want from me now? You've used the only story I have.'

Martin sipped his coffee and smiled.

'That so isn't true, Peter.' Martin Channing leant forward, as the real reason for his visit became clear. 'Here we are in the midst of an intriguing murder investigation – and believe me, it doesn't get much more intriguing than a naked vicar crucified, unless we could some-how get the royal family into it.'

'There's still time.'

'And in the middle of it all, Peter, as Special Witness I'm told, is your good self! I think you have another story to tell the readers of the *Sussex Silt*.'

Fifty Nine

'We've run out of hymn books,' said Jennifer to Sally, as she put on her robes in the vestry, in preparation for the morning service.

'There are more in the cupboard.'

'For which Roger has the key, which means it's presently somewhere near Lake Galilee.'

'Well, people will just have to share,' said Sally irritably. 'It's not the biggest crisis currently facing mankind.'

'Of course. And I mean, it's a nice problem to have, all these people!'

'I suppose so.'

'You don't sound convinced.'

On a normal Sunday, St Michael's did not run out of hymn books; but today was hardly normal. It was the fourth Sunday in Advent with the lighting of the last advent candle. But more significantly, it was the first Sunday since the murder of their vicar, Reverend Anton Fontaine, and people wanted an update. For once, it was the 'Notices' – generally reckoned one of the duller parts of the service – that were anticipated most keenly.

Sally said: 'Someone told me, they didn't think he'd actually gone away.'

'Roger?'

'Yes.'

'Funny you should say that, because I thought I saw him in Eastbourne on Friday.'

'You never know with Roger. Perhaps he was just too embarrassed about the email incident.'

Jennifer suggested another reason: 'Or perhaps his carelessness was deliberate. He wasn't a fan of Anton and may have been greatly amused to see him humiliated in that way.'

'I can't deny it's possible,' said Sally.

Roger and Jennifer were the two church wardens at St Michael's but there the connection ended. It's in the nature of things that church wardens don't get on with each other and the reason is simple: one is voted for to balance the other. So if one of your church wardens is Jennifer who can organise the world in her sleep, then you choose Roger as her partner, a man who couldn't arrange a boiled egg without help from his landlady.

Roger moved from one vaguely defined relationship to another and in between, returned to a landlady in Eastbourne whom he'd known at school.

'It's all a bit subdued though,' said Jennifer, as she prepared to leave Sally to her final preparations. 'In there, I mean. Not a seat to be had – but definitely subdued.'

Sally managed a sad smile.

Jennifer said: 'I'll leave you to it then. And you'll be fine.'

There was a haunted look to the curate this morning, hardly surprising given recent events. Jennifer gave her a hug.

'No, you'll be better than fine, you'll be great!'

'Perhaps you could join me in prayer, Jennifer?'

'Is the Abbot not in today?'

'He rang to say he's been unavoidably detained.'

'Busy with the murder no doubt.'

'It seems that way.'

'We could do with the Abbot here today, we really could. He's become an important part of the community.'

Sally didn't answer but placing the stole round her neck said: 'Let us pray.'

Jennifer closed her eyes and at the foot of the now empty cross, Sally commended the service and people into God's hands.

'And finally, we pray for the murderer, whoever and wherever they are, for they are not so different from us and we all stand in need of your grace. Amen.'

'Thank you,' said Jennifer. 'That was beautiful … if rather charitable.'

Sixty

The council offices were Sunday quiet this morning. Peter had been surprised when Mr Robinson suggested the venue. A lone girl sat at the desk, texting.

'Is Mr Robinson around?' asked Abbot Peter.

'Mr Robinson's not 'ere at the moment,' she said, fresh from the cockney academy.

'Okay,' said Peter. 'He did say he was in this morning.'

'Well 'e's 'ere but 'e's on the bog.'

'It comes to us all.'

'He won't be long or anyfing.'

'I'm sure he won't and I'm sorry, I didn't catch your name.'

'Sareen.'

'Splendid,' he said. 'Well, Sareen, I'll very happily wait.'

The receptionist paused for a moment and then gave in to curiosity.

'You're not going to, like, arrest Mr Robinson are yer?'

'Why do you say that?'

''E said you was comin' about the police and vat murder in the church place.'

Abbot Peter smiled.

'Mr Robinson is quite innocent and I don't arrest people anyway – I'm a monk.'

Sareen looked shocked.

'Are you really, like, a monk?' she asked.

'Yes.'

'And I was finkin' you was wearin' fancy dress! Vat is so cool!'

'Well, I'm glad I'm cool. It's not something I hear every day.'

'No, it's well cool to be a monk.'

And with that, Sareen returned to her texting.

'I'll be by the fish tank in the corner,' said Peter. 'In my fancy dress.'

Sixty One

The newsagents which served the Brighton area were doing a brisk Sunday trade. Everyone brought their usual paper, their prejudice of choice. But whatever else they purchased, they also chose the special Sunday edition of the *Sussex Silt*, drawn by a front page headline the size of a shop front.

DEAD NAKED VICAR AND SEXY CURATE IN SECRET FLING

It's a tale with more twists and turns than a goblin's corkscrew! But your stone-lifting Silt *can today reveal startling new facts in the story that's gripping the South Coast and beyond.*

The Silt *understands that the crucified vicar of Stormhaven, the Reverend Anton Fontaine, found crucified naked in the vestry on Wednesday, had recently broken off a passionate affair with his attractive young curate Sally Appleby.*

Speaking exclusively with the Silt *for this special Sunday edition, a prominent church insider revealed the two had enjoyed 'a close working relationship'. Pressed further, they said: 'Yes, there was definitely something between them, and Sally was distraught when Anton called it off. I thought it was very poor behaviour on Anton's part, not the example I expected at all. Poor Sally was devastated. And an attractive girl.'*

There's no suggestion the love-sick curate murdered her boss in some sexually degrading act of revenge. So let's put all thoughts of sado-masochistic sex involving consenting clergy in their vestry love-tryst right out of our minds. Many right-thinking Silt *readers will not want to dwell on the image of a young black vicar hanging naked on a cross. And call us old fashioned, but we at the* Silt *agree. We're better than that.*

But as police drag their feet in the case, 'stumbling between incompetence and cluelessness' as our insider put it, the town lives in fear of further atrocities. The question on the good people of Stormhaven's lips today is quite simply this: 'Who'll be crucified next?'

So let's be hearing from you! Have your say in the Silt. *Have you ever had an office romance? Can it ever end well? And what about sex in the sanctuary? Was the relationship between Anton and Sally 'Holy Appropriate' or 'Damned Disgusting'? Go online to register your vote.*

And finally, have you ever thought of murdering your partner and why? Keep the tone light – this is just for fun! – but £50 to the best stories published.'

'Hell's teeth,' said Tamsin as she put the paper down. She was due to meet Chief Inspector Wonder in ten minutes and this wouldn't ease her path. The press conference had gone as well as could be expected. She'd remembered Abbot Peter's dictum about seeing everyone with no clothes on and it had worked; she'd felt no fear and occasionally smiled even. But now this story from the toilet paper that was the *Sussex Silt*! Who spoke to them – or had they just made it up? No, there was too much there that was true; someone had spilled the beans. And Tamsin was much too busy wondering who it was to notice a small piece below on the tragic death of council worker, Christopher Thornton, whose body was found in the water after he fell from the cliffs yesterday morning: 'Police are interested to speak with anyone who knew Mr Thornton.'

Sixty Two

Tamsin entered in silence and Wonder bade her sit with a nod of the head, as he completed some writing. The threatening quiet continued, and Tamsin thought of the Chief Inspector in his underpants to calm her nerves. On reflection, she preferred him with clothes on.

'I've just had that bloody Bishop on the phone again,' he said with some aggression.

'And your point is?'

Go on the attack, Tamsin, always attack.

'He says the church's name is being dragged through the mud, not helped of course by the charming prose in the *Sussex Silt* today.'

'And that's my fault?'

'I'm not saying it's your fault.'

'Did he not notice the fact that the story was based around a "church source"?'

'He's just saying.'

'But what's he just saying, Chief Inspector? From where I'm standing, the church is dragging its own name through the mud without any help from me.'

'There's some truth there.'

'And while we're on the subject of mud, he was apparently throwing plenty of the stuff himself at the parish meeting he presided over the night of the murder. There are a good number of witnesses to that.'

'I'm sure there are.'

'Oh, and he's lying.'

'The Bishop?'

'He's not telling the truth about what happened when he gave Clare a lift home. You do know he rang her three times after she left his car in the pouring rain – and that she answered none of his calls. Remember that if he rings you again, playing the guardian of the truth whilst fiddling with his massive cross.'

Chinless breathed deeply in the face of this venom. He had no desire for a stand-up with Tamsin but he had to watch his back as well. Those with power should stay chums ... networking, that was the word, and the Bishop might be a Mason.

'He simply feels,' said Chief Inspector Wonder, 'that undue attention is being focused on the church community when an outsider could quite as easily have done it.'

'Do I have to repeat myself?'

'I'm aware of your earlier thoughts on the subject.'

'Anton knew the assailant, he was expecting them. Abbot Peter heard him take a call. He said, 'Well, thank you for your support but I wish you'd said that at the meeting. But I'm alone now if you want to come round to the church.'

She looked up with eyebrows which asked: point taken? 'That sounds like a member of the church community to me, Chief Inspector. How does it sound to you?'

Chinless considered the young woman in front of him. Tamsin was not the most creative cop but she was an activist, a ruthless stealer of other people's good ideas, an effective prioritiser, a project leader and lethal in her own defence. Rank counted for little if anyone came for her; whatever the cost, she didn't like losing.

'And who is the killer?' he asked, changing gear.

'We don't know.'

'No.'

He left enough of a pause to punish.

'I never like it when the press say we're dragging our feet,' he continued.

'It's the *Silt*, for God's sake, found under "fiction" in the library. We're not dragging our feet. It's all made-up by that fantasist Martin Channing.'

'It may be made up but that's entirely irrelevant. People like to believe the negative.'

'You've lost me.'

The Chief Inspector paused, dabbing his shiny forehead with a handkerchief.

'Do you have something to say, Sir?' she asked.

'It's not a complicated case, Shah, and given the small number of suspects, you're – well, how can I put this?'

'I don't know Sir. I'm not paid to be your script writer.'

'Taking your time about it? I mean, I'm sure you're doing your best – .'

DI Shah glared at him but he continued.

'This is your first case as a DI.'

'I'm aware of that.'

'Do you need help? A more experienced copper by your side?'

'No.'

'Well, that's OK for the moment. But it's important you make your mark here. You've trodden on enough people on your way up, Tamsin; they'll be only too eager to help you back down again.'

Momentarily, Tamsin contemplated a black hole opening inside her, terrifying and empty, but it was quickly covered.

'I'm also aware of that, Sir. Do you have anything to say that I'm not aware of?'

'You must understand my position.'

'We're very close to our killer.'

'Really?'

'Oh yes.'

'I hope it's not that nice curate.'

Tamsin found this an odd remark.

'Sorry?'

'I hope it's not the curate who turns out to be the psycho.'

'Sally?'

'That's the one.'

'You have a soft spot for her?'

'She christened my grandson, Terry.'

'That's not a major concern at present.'

'But could she have done it?'

'She could have done it. As the *Silt* kindly reported – and I'll kill whoever gave them that story – she did have an affair with Anton and quite apart from that, I hear relationships between vicars and curates are traditionally rather strained affairs.'

'But you don't crucify someone for being a bad boss!'

'Why not?' said Tamsin, in a matter of fact sort of a way. 'That's all a bad boss deserves in my book.'

Chief Inspector Wonder felt waves of inadequacy pass over him. How he'd reached the position he had was one of life's mysteries. In the eyes of many, particularly those passed over for promotion, he'd been fast-tracked through the ranks on the back of an absence of mistakes rather than a bundle of successes; a high flyer for never having flown too low. But most of all, he'd been affable and pliant, features in an officer which makes others feel good about themselves and which can be easily mistaken for competence.

'She's in a picture on my mantelpiece,' he said.

'Who is?'

'Sally.'

'And you don't want a murderer on your mantelpiece?'

'And I mean the other thing is, does it still count?'

'Does what still count?'

'If a christening is conducted by a murderer, does it still count? Is Terry still christened?'

'How exactly does a christening count in the first place?'

'Well, I'm not sure. I wasn't really listening.'

'If it's any consolation, Sir, no one seriously thinks its Sally, though of course it would be hugely amusing if it was.'

'Amusing?'

'But I don't see it, even if we still don't know what the hell she was doing in church at six that morning.'

'And what does Abbot Peter see? Your distinctively dressed Special Witness – what does he see?'

'Not a lot so far. He struggles with hard facts.'

'How do you mean?'

'He's always trying to look beyond them.'

'And what is beyond them?'

'That's just my point. He says I solve cases from the outside but he solves cases from the inside.'

'He was your choice, Tamsin.'

'I know.'

'Where is he by the way?'

'I just spoke with him. He's been with Recreation and Leisure and is now on his way to Lewes for tea.'

'Is he doing his job properly?'

Sixty Three

Abbot Peter enjoyed the short train ride to Lewes. And while he contemplated two recent corpses in Stormhaven, he contemplated many more beneath him now as he approached his destination. Yes, this beautiful old town had its own skeletons in the cupboard – or rather, in the embankment.

It had been during the building of the Brighton to Hastings railway line in 1846 that hundreds of skeletons were discovered in a pit in the lands of the old Cluniac monastery on the edge of town. Why were they there? After some research, the bones were reckoned to be those of royalist soldiers killed in the monastery precincts in 1264 at the savage Battle of Lewes, fought between the armies of Prince Edward and the baronial challenger, Simon de Montfort.

Not all Victorians were sentimentalists, however, and with a railway to be completed, there was no attempt to honour the dead of 500 years before. With no time to waste, the skeletons were thrown onto trucks by the railway contractors and dumped in the rubbish on the nearby marshland. There they came to form the railway embankment which remained today, ensuring that all trains from Lewes to Hastings, Stormhaven, Newhaven, Glynde and Ore travel daily over the compacted remains of the dead soldiers of 1264.

It was not a fact advertised by the rail authorities; some might be upset. But it remained the primary reason Abbot Peter chose train over bus for these excursions. Such communion with the past took him happily back to his days in the desert. Like many monasteries in the rock and sand of Middle Egypt, it had been the practice at St James-the-Less to store the skulls of former residents; and at St James's, not one of the larger foundations, the place of storage had been the outhouse in the gardens beyond the generator. It could on occasion prove a shocking find for visitors who wandered into the half-light of the shed looking for a rake or hoe. There were over 500 skulls piled on top of each other and one resident, suitably aghast, had caused an unusual avalanche in their attempts at escape.

But for Abbot Peter the skulls in the outhouse brought peace and perspective rather than fear. He never left their speechless company without a renewed spring in his step and missed them even now. Travelling to Lewes by train was at least some recompense.

On arrival, he walked up the narrow streets – or twittens, as they were called – that dropped off the high street and then headed down hill to the east of town. He crossed the bridge over the Ouse which had been the escape route for so many of the soldiers running from slaughter in 1264. From there, he continued on past the cafés and antique dealers of Cliffe High Street. He breathed in the familiar yeasty air of the Harvey's brewery and was soon standing at the front door of 18 Thomas Street, the last in a small row of nineteenth-century houses.

Mrs Gold opened the door.

'You promised me a cup of tea at the Christmas Fayre,' said Abbot Peter.

'Not one I'll forget in a hurry,' she said, ushering him into a clinically clean front room.

'It had its own drama, didn't it?' said Peter.

'You can say that again.'

'Shame we couldn't have used it on the advertising: "Vicar will speak from the dead after tombola". It would have improved the turnout, I think.'

Mrs Gold was not prepared for such flippancy in a monk.

'And is the murderer apprehended?' she asked.

Abbot Peter smiled. FA cups are 'held aloft' and murderers are 'apprehended'.

'The murderer is still free, externally, at least.'

'I'm sorry?'

'Well, there's probably not much freedom within them. Those who are inwardly free don't kill.'

There was a slight pause. Mrs Gold thought this was poppycock but then what do you expect from a monk? If the murderer wasn't caught, they were still free in her book.

'Well, do sit down.'

'Thank you. And you have a lovely house.'

'I'm still getting used to it; down-sizing isn't easy. I wouldn't have thought much of this place a few years ago, believe me. But then I didn't know of Gerald's financial difficulties.'

As far as Abbot Peter could remember, Gerald was her deceased husband whose profligate spending only came to light on his death.

'So what was it you wanted to speak about?' she asked, once they were settled with the tea.

'Teddy bears,' said Abbot Peter.

Sixty Four

'That was off the record and you know it!'

The Bishop was incandescent but Martin Channing unruffled. This was hardly the first such conversation he'd had down the years.

'Off the record, on the record? Aren't we suddenly getting rather legalistic, Bishop?'

'You didn't honour your word.'

'Which word was that, Stephen?'

'We were speaking about a column I might write.'

'And which you did write and I'm sure we can use it one day. But let's be honest, because honesty is always best: what you shared with me over the phone was a good deal more truthful and our concern is for the truth, surely? I mean, did we print anything untrue?'

The Bishop felt like a mouse in a trap.

'No.'

'Or anything you didn't say?'

'It's about what's appropriate, about the context.'

'Oh, Stephen, Stephen, I have more respect for our readers than that! I'm a great believer in giving them the truth and allowing them to decide.'

'But you didn't allow anyone to decide anything. You just gave them some Sabbath titillation.'

'Something which the church signally fails to do!'

'I'll be objecting in the strongest possible terms to the owners of the *Sussex Silt*.

'Your prerogative, of course Bishop but you might struggle to get past our sales figures which is the first point on their moral compass.'

'Typical.'

'But I do hope this isn't the end of our relationship.'

'You've got some nerve.'

'Because I can help you.'

'That I doubt very much.'

'I know things that might interest you.'

'Like what?'

Why was he being drawn in?

'I just wondered, for instance, if you knew about an affair Ginger Micklewhite is supposed to have had with a married woman? Interested?'

The Bishop's pause said it all.

'I mean I'm sure you're not at all interested but a reader has contacted us and obviously we're very cautious about what we print. It was in his last post apparently, prior to his arrival at St Michael's. But I did just wonder if it might have a bearing on the death of the vicar? I mean, "everything's material" as the psychologists say.'

The Bishop should have put the phone down long ago. But he was drawn to the negative and tantalised still by the promise of a column. And so he listened and he listened until he could listen no more, until something inside him said 'No!' and he ended the call without a further word.

It was good to be out of the trap. But he was rigid with rage.

Sixty Five

Abbot Peter knew something was wrong.

He returned to Sandy View around 7.00 p.m. and both saw and smelt disturbance. He'd neither left the bottle of whisky out on the table nor emptied it to the extent now apparent. And then he saw the door to his study ajar when he knew he'd left it closed. He paused for a moment, stilling himself and listening. There was no sound but a gull crying and a car turning. He looked again at the study door and then at the whisky. It was not unknown for burglars to draw freely on house hospitality. Or was this perhaps one of Stormhaven's alcoholic wanderers seeking a hostel. Either might resent discovery and Peter steeled himself for confrontation.

He moved quietly towards the study and then a noise from within, an expletive, a woman's voice. He reached the door, peered through the gap and, with surprise, recognised the back of DI Tamsin Shah, also his niece. She was sitting carelessly, clearly the worse for wear, at the small table on which lay Peter's jigsaw of the Colossus of Rhodes, boldly astride the harbour entrance of that ancient city.

'We're not doing very well, are we?' she said, without looking round.

'I did ask you not to use my study, Tamsin. It was one of the house rules.'

'And I asked you to help me with my case.'

'Meaning?'

'So we've both been let down.'

Abbot Peter watched his anger rise and subside.

'You don't have the power to hurt me, Tamsin but you do have the power to hurt yourself.'

'My glass is empty.'

'And what do you want: applause or consolation?'

'You're a lousy detective, believe me!' said Tamsin. 'Really lousy – leave it to the professionals.'

There was such hostility in the remark it took Abbot Peter a few seconds to allow it to pass through.

'Is this your first case as a Detective Inspector?' he asked.

'How do you know?'

'I was talking to one of your colleagues. They said you were very competent, a fast-track promotion girl. But they also said they wouldn't want to be around on the day that you failed at something.'

'I haven't failed.'

'I know, Tamsin, I know. You're doing an excellent job.'

'Who says?'

'I say.'

'Really?'

'I wouldn't want to be a murderer tracked by you.'

'Then tell that to the Chief Inspector! He had the bloody nerve to say I'm taking my time and asked if I wanted some help? Me need help?!'

'The Chief Inspector is just watching his back. It's what those with a little power do.'

Tamsin managed a smile. 'You know the joke doing the rounds at present?'

'Tell me,' said the Abbot gently.

'Why do Chief Inspectors walk into lamp posts?'

'I don't know.'

'They're too busy watching their backs.'

Abbot Peter heard only the frustration.

'It's time for you to rest, Tamsin.'

'I don't want to rest.'

'Rest now and be brilliant tomorrow.'

'Don't patronise me, Abbot! Don't ever patronise me as if I'm a failure! It's you who's the failure! *You!*'

Suddenly she was lunging forward sweeping both jigsaw and glass from the table, sending pieces flying and the glass smashing against the wall. The Colossus of Rhodes, three quarters complete, lay in disorder on the floor amid glinting shards of something other than diamonds. Silence reigned in the study but not peace.

'I'm sorry,' she said.

'It's quite okay.'

Peter was shocked but gathered himself around remembered words.

'We do what we do until we can no longer do it and then the fresh shoots appear. Tonight you rest, tomorrow the fresh shoots.'

The headache was making Tamsin weary.

'And you? What will you do?' she asked.

'I must go to a special place; I've been away from alone for too long.'

'You're alone most of the time!'

'There are degrees of alone and many shades of solitude.'

He helped Tamsin up the stairs to her room. He returned in a while with some hot milk but she was already asleep. He kissed her forehead and quietly closed the door. He went downstairs to his study. Slowly, he returned the jigsaw to the table, piece by piece, a meditation in itself, a return of order in a disordered world. He then made a thermos of sweet coffee and taking his coat from the back of the door, walked out into the winter night, December twenty-first, the shortest day – and the longest night.

And as he began his ascent of the cliffs, he knew the answer lay in the scattered pieces of the jigsaw. There was something about Tamsin and the Colossus of Rhodes which made perfect sense of everything. He had seen the killer.

Act Four

*'I've done a bad thing, Jennifer,'
he said. They were words of effort,
dredged with difficulty from the
harbour slime of his unconscious.*

Sixty Six

On the longest night of the year, the night which turned out to be the last night of the investigation, the six suspects were variously engaged.

Sally was clearing up after the small evening service which took place in the parish room. She left there and walked through the church into the vestry. There she turned out the lights, noticed the answer phone had two messages but decided to leave them. She still hesitated on entering the vestry and held her eyes away from the cross. Could a room of such hatred ever regain its calm? Not for Sally, for whom this would forever be a disturbing place. Closing the door behind her, she returned to the church, still and dark. She was walking down the carpeted aisle towards the main entrance when she sensed a presence in the building. She stopped and looked into the darkness. The noise came from the prayer chapel, nothing more than someone changing position and knocking against something.

Sally paused, her breathing quickened.

'Is anyone there?' she asked.

Silence.

She was not without courage, but remained a practical soul and moved quickly towards the light switches. If she was to face an intruder, let it be in the light. With a flick of the switch, the church was revealed, obscure corners exposed and there in the prayer chapel, the figure of Malcolm Flight, kneeling, swaying backwards and forwards. Sally made her way towards him.

'Are you all right, Malcolm?'

He looked up at her with pleading in his eyes.

'I don't know what to do without Clare.'

Sally considered the words, spoken less than six feet from where her body was found. He was being ridiculous.

'You were never with Clare, Malcolm,' she said.

'How do you mean?'

'You speak as though you were together.'

'We were together in a way.'

'How were you together?'

'She came back for me that night, you know, the night she died.'

Sally's immediate reaction was to judge Malcolm harshly. He knew nothing about the hurt of rejection. Her pain was real; his was all in his head. But she stayed calm with this pitiful man.

'Clare came back for something that night,' she said. 'But was it really you?'

'I had to leave of course because she could be distant, could be cold and that was the worst, the cold and the distance ... not that pain again, not that ... but had I stayed ...'

'We can't live with "if onlys", Malcolm.'

'I could have saved her.'

'Clare made her choices, Malcolm.'

'And what in hell's name do you mean by that?'

What did Sally mean by that? On reflection, the origins were not so hard to discern. Whatever had happened between the Bishop and Clare had not just been the Bishop's doing. Clare was complicit, Sally had seen it. Had the Bishop misread the signs, felt approached and then rejected?

'The trouble is, I only love what I can't have,' she'd once confided to Sally. Sally didn't know what had happened in the car but Clare had made her choices.

'I just meant that she did what she thought best, Malcolm. And you did what you thought best, whatever that was. What more can any of us do?'

And in saying these words, she thought mainly of herself. Soon she would visit the police station.

*

Betty was watching a programme about elephants, and knitting for Romanian orphans. She'd knitted a lot of jumpers on behalf of that country, different colours, though mainly pink or blue and she hadn't lied in the interview, hadn't said anything that was untrue though whether that mattered now, she wasn't sure.

On the telly, the daddy elephant had disappeared, everyone was worried and Betty knew the feeling. She'd spent many years trying to find her father, idolising him, trying to get back to the man. Sixty nine years ago a silly girl in the office had said 'P'raps your dad isn't all you crack him up to be.' Betty had hit the girl hard across the face, a stinging blow, for which she'd been sacked. She hadn't known her father well, he'd died when she was seventeen, disappeared like the

216

daddy elephant. But she had photos and the beach hut would have made things good, made things right after such a long wait. She remembered him by his beach hut, or perhaps the photos remembered, and she remembered the photos. She'd waited for it all these years, waiting until it was hers, only for it to be taken away, snatched from her and stolen.

It was like having her father taken from her all over again and she knew who had done it.

*

Ginger was ringing Jennifer because of Anton; and more particularly because of his jibe.

He remembered the row, one of many. He'd been telling the vicar about Franciscan tertiaries, how they came about. He'd commended St Francis on his humility and Anton had said, 'So what happened to yours?' It was a cheap shot from a cheap man but could a cheap shot be true? The words had lingered like a bad smell, like grit in his shoe, which gave them the ring of truth. And as he thought about these things, the same question returned again and again:

'What happened to you, Ginger?'

He liked the label of tertiary. It set him apart, gave him some mystery but what did it really mean? What did it add up to if the heart of the calling was no longer there? And when exactly had he said goodbye to It? As St Paul said, in some of his more searching lines, 'If I have not love, I am a noisy gong or a clanging bell; if I have no love, I am nothing.' And Ginger had no love.

'This is an unexpected call,' said Jennifer.

Ginger and Jennifer were not close, though they'd once sat together on a local youth committee.

'I've done a bad thing, Jennifer,' he said.

They were words of effort, dredged up with difficulty from the harbour slime of his unconscious.

'I didn't know you did bad things, Ginger,' she said settling back into her chair.

She'd been going through some application forms for maternity cover. Her staff became pregnant with unnerving frequency. But a confession from Ginger would be a welcome distraction.

The phone call finished ten difficult minutes later with Ginger much calmed. The same could not be said of Jennifer, however. After what she'd heard, she was concerned for her life and decided on a walk. She needed to breathe some sea air.

*

Bishop Stephen stood at the back of St John the Baptist, Southover, the posh part of Lewes. He was in meeting and greeting mode, one of his favourite roles. He always enjoyed confirmation services, the chance to be a shepherd to his flock and to pull them up where necessary. And though their faces were happy now, caught up in the post-service excitement of chat and refreshments, they'd not been smiling as he'd delivered his hard-hitting sermon on the crucifixion of Christ. Correcting people was his gift even if they did not wish to be corrected. In his talk, he'd majored on the hateful and ignorant nature of those who had committed the crime: those who had cried out for Jesus' blood, those who had whipped and tormented him, those who had nailed him and swung the cross skywards. Not a Christmas message perhaps but an eternal one.

'Bad people do bad things,' he'd declared, 'bad people do wrong things and we do no one any favours to pretend otherwise. Wrong is not a relative thing, wrong is a killing thing and so, while we speak of forgiveness, let us also honour the gift of correction. Those who are bad, we correct! Those who are wrong, we correct!'

He spoke with many after the service, delighting in their goodwill and his brief sense of prestige. But as he drove home on this longest night of the year, he remembered one conversation above all.

'You confirmed my daughter tonight, Bishop,' said the earnest man, who'd been waiting to speak to him for some time.

'Ah,' said the Bishop, 'and which one was she?'

'Diana.'

'Diana? Splendid girl, you must be very proud.'

'I'm very happy for Diana but perhaps more worried than proud if I'm honest.'

'How so?'

'It was your sermon, Bishop.'

'I don't speak words to please but I hope I always speak the truth.'

'I'm a probation officer by trade '

'I see. A noble and challenging calling.'

'So I'm in contact with people who commit crime, those who you call "bad people".'

'By their fruits shall we know them.'

'I understand. But the more I see of bad people the more I discover they're really rather normal people.'

'Well, my friend, normal people don't commit crimes or our prisons would be rather fuller than they are!'

'I don't find demonising people helpful.'

'Who's demonising?'

'But that isn't why I'm worried tonight.'

There was a pause.

'And so why are you worried?' asked the cleric with polite seething. He adopted a patronising tone, not liking this man's spirit.

'Well I have to say, Bishop, that if you were a client of mine, and let's hope you never are, but if you were, I'd be looking at the way your own self-punishing psyche finds relief in the punishment of others.'

Sixty Seven

Abbot Peter felt the chill as he made the grassy climb. It was 9.00 p.m. Falling away to his right were the white cliffs, a perpendicular drop that had been Christopher Thornton's final journey. The leap had caused shock in Stormhaven as suicides do. Those who give noisy warning rarely commit the act; it is the quiet ones who jump, those who just walk out the door in silence.

'I can't believe it! I mean, why didn't he tell us? I don't understand.'

Abbot Peter knew now why Christopher had felt bad; but the bigger mystery remained: why such a radical solution?

'Life breaks us all but not all break themselves,' he reflected. 'Why is it some of us survive?'

He'd left Tamsin asleep to visit his special place, the place of solitude, before the final act. The Rhodian jigsaw lay shattered in his study but the murder jigsaw was taking shape as he looked back on his home, now lost to view in the winter dark. He didn't know if his niece would wake in peace; he knew only that her disordered soul must rest. Away to his left was the golf course, an empty stage of eighteen holes as his path steepened, taking him to the top of the hill which now flattened. It was here he'd stood with Christopher yesterday but now he continued on, walking a further hundred yards. After a little searching in the damp undergrowth, he found the path, a small and undistinguished affair. To one who didn't know, it appeared the way to oblivion, seemingly taking the walker over the edge of the cliff. But if you trusted it with a first step and then a second, it became a protected if windy route, a sharp, narrow and chalky descent. You walked with care, clinging to the rock face on your left, more a ledge than a path. To your right was a fatal fall, a straight drop down to the watery smack of tide on stone.

Peter made his careful way until arriving at his destination, a small cave in the side of the cliff. And in the doorway of the cave, gazing out across the English Channel, was a large round stone with a natural indent for the human body. Peter called it 'The Seeing Stone' after something his father once said.

'We all need the seeing stone,' he used to say. 'No seeing, no live.'

He'd probably meant 'no life,' his English was not the best, he spoke it like a child. But then again perhaps he'd said exactly what he meant to say. In the desert, Peter would climb up to the Chapel of Grace to contemplate the heavens above and the valley below, his solitary place of decision. In Stormhaven, he'd edge his way carefully towards the cave in the side of the cliff and take his place on the Seeing Stone.

He sat now in the still holding of the rock. Here was a brutal but all-seeing solitude, a mountain seat of freedom which gazed on all that arose, whether wind, wash, gull or distant ship on the altering horizon. All was movement, all was change and all was passing as Peter sat in silence, discerning the shifting textures of the sky. It was good to be free. And then, when the moment seemed right, he put his freedom to work, shining the torch light of consciousness on the band of poor players, currently suspected of murder.

Peter knew and approved the old adage: spiritual people enjoy the flowers along the way but also grasp the nettle. And now was the time for grasping as the inner chemistry of events began to cohere. Uppermost in Peter's mind was the force of the internal fracture expressed in the external savagery of crucifixion. Everyone lives their fracture as best they can, sometimes hiding it, sometimes transcending it. But when the pain is too much we lunge at others and sometimes, with hammer and nails in hand. This was considerable dysfunction, considerable uncaring, but whose? In many ways, he knew the shocking and impossible truth but for clarity, must stay uncertain until all other possibilities fell away.

Nine people had sat down for that fateful meeting in the parish room the night the vicar died. Of those, Anton and Clare had since been murdered and he removed himself from the equation also. This left six probable suspects: Ginger, Sally, Jennifer, Betty, Malcolm and Bishop Stephen. They all had reason to dislike Anton. Anton threatened Ginger's livelihood with his questioning of the youth work; he'd rejected the advances of Sally somewhat cruelly; he'd set the Bishop against Jennifer, his greatest supporter; he'd referred to Betty as Betty Bogbrush within her hearing; he'd removed Malcolm's painting from the church, treated him with disdain and possibly been involved in some minor fiddling of the church accounts; and for Bishop Stephen, he'd been an under-performing clergyman in an under-performing area for which Stephen was responsible.

These were the surface things and none in itself a reason for murder by crucifixion. So what of things buried deeper in the psyche, the secret shapers of life. Peter poured himself coffee from his flask and sipping gratefully, looked out on the black sea. The nine gathered in the room that night had been a particular nine, each representing a different number on the Enneagram circle. And the number of each? Anton had lived from the Seven space and Clare from the Four, but tragically they were now out of the equation. With Peter creating his life from the Five space, that left six numbers to consider.

Sally lived from the Two space, whose tipping point of stress would be feeling they weren't needed or were unappreciated, leading to wounded pride and dangerous resentment. Could such things turn a curate into a murderer? Ginger lived from the Eight space. The eight's point of terror would be the exposure of the weakness they could not admit in themselves and to see their empire threatened. Under extreme stress they would react with avoidant despair which might well include savage vengeance. And then there was Betty, hardly the likeliest candidate but clearly disturbed over these past few weeks by something. Betty lived from the Six space. The Six's tipping point is around a loss of trust. If trust is felt to be abused, any darkness is possible and any madness pursued.

A large gull joined Peter in the cave, so magnificent in the sky but awkward on land, like a god in reduced circumstances. It strutted about in apparent surprise at this unexpected presence, before launching again into the cold night air, swooping down and then up, hollering, screaming, rolling with the battering gusts of wind. Peter was alone once again, still life on stone and considering Malcolm who lived from the Nine space. His psychology was most dangerous when a lack of personal identity encouraged a fantasy ego that could presume anything and do anything. So was Malcolm a lethal fantasist? Or was it in Bishop Stephen that the walls of civility fractured? Stephen lived from the One space, a way of being that is most threatened by a sense of blame, by anyone declaring them wrong in some way. Their self-hate will quickly be transferred onto another. But could that become crucifixion? And then there was Jennifer, Anton's supposed white knight, but his thought was interrupted as a boat appeared on the horizon, faintly lit, a distant thing, chugging its choppy path to somewhere and suddenly Peter was thinking of the cascading jigsaw in his study.

'Of course!' said Abbot Peter who knew he must get back home and do something he'd never done before. He slid slowly from the Seeing Stone, stepped out of the cave and onto the ledge path that would take him back up the cliff. He felt the minutes pressing, danger walking towards his door. He moved as quickly as he could but time was draining away, as in an anxious dream when you want to get there but you can't and you don't and you know you never will.

Sixty Eight

It proved to be the final entry in the murder diary, the diary of a seaside murderer and one rather hastily written, because since the whole CD business at the Christmas Fayre, the killer had been in a slight panic, feeling that things could not always be controlled as was appropriate. And it felt like less of a game now, felt nastier, more anxious, which was a shame, because it was better if it was a game.

'I must deal with the murder tools because I don't think they're safe anymore. I will go back tonight and deal with them. It's been a good place until now but they can't stay there.

This is ridiculous. I keep forgetting that I'm the murderer. But less of that word, I don't like the word, it's not a good word, too separating, so let's all just stop using it. It's not helping anyone.

But I'll get the murder tools and put them somewhere, throw them somewhere, easily done, offer them up to the sea in a weighted bag. That sounds interesting.

And then I'm free which is probably what I deserve, no I do, definitely.'

Sixty Nine

Tamsin was woken from her sleep by the phone. It took some while to gather herself, ripped from the first deep hour of slumber, with no idea where she was or time of day.

And then the phone stopped ringing.

'Damn,' she said.

And then it started again.

'Hello?'

'Is that Inspector Shah?'

'DI Shah, speaking, yes.'

'Who's this?'

'I have a confession to make.'

A man's voice.

'Who is this speaking?'

'Can we meet in the church?'

'What do you want to confess?'

'I'll be there for the next half hour if you wish to hear me out.'

'Why the church?'

'It's the place for confessions, isn't it?'

'Is that you Ginger?'

But the phone was dead.

Tamsin sat for a moment, heart beating. For the first time in the investigation, she wished Peter was around. She rang him, only to discover his phone on the kitchen table.

'Damn.'

Remembering earlier events, she pushed open the study door. The room lay still, clock ticking, icons sleeping and the jigsaw pieces restored to the table. She'd go without him. She hadn't needed him so far and didn't need him now. She dressed quickly, pondered her car keys but decided to walk the half mile to St Michael's. The cold would do her good, give her time to think. The identity of the caller remained a mystery. Her first thought was Ginger and sometimes the

225

first thought is your best. If it was Ginger, she was aware that until this point, they'd only experienced uncomfortable conversations, battles for territory with no clear winner.

But tonight there would be a clear winner. And it would be her.

Seventy

Peter was already in a hurry. The discovery that Tamsin was gone from the safety of Sandy View only made him move faster. After collecting his tools, he set off along the sea front. With cold shingle and turbulent wave for company, he made his way towards his destination. He knew the beach hut he wanted. It was there on Betty's mantelpiece and there again in the picture of her father on the beach in Stormhaven. It was hut No.7 from which Betty seemed to emerge on the night of the murder. Then the incident had puzzled him but no more; now it was assuming significance. He stepped off the road, onto the shingle and walked along the line of huts, closed for winter. Soon he was standing outside No.7 and noticed two things. A newly fitted lock on the door and above the door, evidence of a fresh name painted on the hut lintel:

'Rest 'n Peace'.

Darkly ambiguous. More menacing, however, was the word 'JUDAS' written in thick magic marker across the door. Peter took a chisel and hammer from his bag and with a couple of blows the padlock was splintered free. Beach hut security was minimal at best but even so, breaking and entering seemed strangely natural to the Abbot. He was now pulling open the door and letting the darkness out. He stood in the entrance and felt in his bag for a torch. It was the one piece of technology he'd brought back from the desert. A candle would have been more romantic in those dark monastic corners but not nearly so effective as this fat beam of light which now played across the space. It smelt like a cricket pavilion from a long time ago, wood and resin and was unnervingly clear with no chair or kettle, beach towel or discarded bottles of lotion. In fact there was nothing here for a holiday; just a small covered pile in the left hand corner – a small pile which revealed itself as the murder gear.

Seventy One

Tamsin stood in the dark church. The door had been open and she'd walked in. It was dark.

'Hello?' she called out. 'Detective Inspector Shah. I'm here!'

Silence.

'You said something about a confession.'

There was suddenly a hand on her shoulder. Tamsin spun round.

'Malcolm?' said Tamsin.

'Well, don't look so surprised. Who did you think it was?'

Tamsin screamed and Malcolm put his hand over her mouth.

'It's all right,' he said.

Seventy Two

'I think we should tell someone,' said Sally.

'We?'

Ginger was just finishing off some long-postponed paper work for the council. He'd had an uncomfortable call from the youth department on Friday; uncomfortable for them at least.

'Okay. I think *I* should tell someone.'

'Why?' asked Ginger. 'Other people's rules mean nothing.'

'I know,' said Sally and in her pride, she did. Other people's rules were not for her. 'But I don't like lying.'

'You already have.'

'And I was surprised how natural it all was.'

'I don't know why you're surprised.'

'I do have a dog collar round my neck!'

'Hah! You really think that makes a difference? Everyone lies and you're no different.'

'Well, perhaps I want to stop.'

'Brave woman.'

'So shall we go?'

'Where to?'

'It's time for me to take off my dog collar, I think.'

'And you're sure that's what you want?'

'Haven't I spent six months with you deciding?'

Seventy Three

Abbot Peter stood staring at his beach hut find.

One item after another exposed to the light. Yes, here was the murder gear. What struck him most, however, was the normality of it all, the dull essence of the articles laid out before him. It wasn't a house of horrors; no dark tools from the torture chamber. Everything he could see in the torchlight was available at a DIY store, innocent and helpful in a cupboard under the sink. The yellow rubber gloves, several reels of silver grey gaffer tape, the protective plastic over-garment for messy jobs like painting and drainage clearance, the all-purpose cloths, the kitchen knife and the hammer and nails. What possible problem could there be with items such as these? Only on this occasion, intentions and usage had not been pure. The gloves had hidden finger prints, the tape had tied and imprisoned a body, the over-garment had protected against the blood stains of murder, the kitchen knife had spliced a heart rather than carrots while the hammer and nails penetrated wrists.

Only the bottle of chloroform, *'Duncan's Blue Label, London and Edinburgh'*, looked slightly at odds with innocence – unless someone was installing air conditioning in their home, in which case it would be essential. Then Abbot Peter froze. There were footsteps on the shingle, a visitor only a few feet away outside. He switched off the torch and stood in the trapped darkness of this little wooden box. It was hard to tell in the wind, but he'd heard a crunch, another crunch and then nothing. So where was the visitor now? Peter inched his way round, his heart beating fear. He'd closed the door of the hut behind him, but it was a forced door, a fractured entrance no longer sitting true in its place. No one would enter the hut unaware of that revealing truth. And suddenly the door crashed open, the wind rushed in and a silhouetted figure appeared at the entrance and then went. Peter stepped back, jabbing the torch light at the open hole, waiting. He was crouching now, haunches tense, back against the wall, a monk far from prayer, watching and waiting. Or had he imagined it? Had it been mere shadow, a trick of the dark?

With shocking ferocity the door slammed back shut, followed by eerie quiet, the closed-in quiet of a wooden seaside hideaway in winter. It wasn't right, not how it should be … not for Abbot Peter, at least. People here should be making tea and laughing, eating ice cream, reading the summer gossip, preparing for a dip, wiping sand from their toes and anticipating fish and chips in the early-evening sun. Instead, he stood cold and fearful in the solstice dark of the longest night, close to the tools of savage murder.

'Time to get out, to go home,' he thought to himself.

The fear of the footsteps had subsided. Perhaps he'd misheard and seen poorly.

'Fear comes and fear goes and when it goes we are sane again.'

He cast the torch beam over the murder gear one more time. And then stopped. How had he missed that? He was looking at the hammer and nails and something was puzzling him. How could he not have noticed? And what implications followed?

He turned off the torch and remained still and silent in the gloom. He thought of Betty's father who once stood in this exact spot. He thought of the beach hut communities and friendships that had formed down the years. They'd taken photos, laughed, drank, eaten, argued, gone home … and when their time had come, when their race was run, they'd passed on, passed over. But they were forever here on this desolate shore and Peter sensed them. He was not alone, a cloud of witnesses went before him and stood with him now. Peter sensed their imprint on the space, an imprint impossible to erase.

'I need you tonight,' he said. 'Come with me now, my friends. We shall be an army of righteousness against the destroying hordes.'

He stepped out in to the gale and with his habit flying wildly in the wind he made his gusty way back towards Sandy View.

*

The house was quiet. No light shone inside as he turned the key and entered. He listened for Tamsin. Was she back? He thought he heard her upstairs. He removed his shoes and trod the stairs carefully but found no one in either bedroom. He rang her phone but there was no reply. He wrote a simple note and left it on her pillow:

'Come and talk on your return. I know the killer. It was the jigsaw that finally gave them away.'

He stepped out of his wet clothes, dried himself, wrapped his chill nakedness in pyjamas and dressing gown and cleaned his teeth. He went downstairs and into his study. The Colossus remained undone on the table but that could wait. He went over to his desk, switched on his computer and sat still as slowly the screen lit and offered his emails. There were two in his inbox. One was selling Viagra, a doomed sales pitch, while the other one, from council man Mr Robinson, confirmed the identity of the murderer. He read it once and then read it again. He turned off the computer and sat in the dark for a moment because before something, there is nothing.

He left the study and went to the front door. Opening it, he looked down the road for Tamsin. No sign. If she wasn't back within the hour he'd go to the police station. But he'd prefer to speak directly to Tamsin. He owed her that. Or did he?

'Come on, Tamsin,' he found himself saying. 'Let's bring this to an end.'

Seventy Four

'I want to be truthful,' said Malcolm, now sitting opposite Tamsin in the parish room.

The chairs were more comfortable than the climate. She didn't trust Malcolm. She'd never screamed in her life before but something about him had frightened her. She didn't trust anyone, why would she? But this creature of the shadows posed a particular threat.

'I want to come clean,' he continued, with an almost messianic gleam in his eye. 'I want to be clear not opaque, be precise rather than vague.'

'Tell me what you know, Malcolm. That's all the police ask. Save the melodramatics for the theatre.'

'As Sally said, I wasn't with Clare.'

'How do you mean?'

'That was a fantasy.'

'I think I knew that.'

'She reminded me of my mother actually.'

'Is that relevant?'

'She never paid me any attention either.'

'Your mother?'

Malcolm nodded. Tamsin looked him in the eyes.

'I don't want to be harsh, Malcolm but if this is a misery memoir, you're mistaking me for someone who cares.'

She had little time for self-indulgent reflection on the past.

'I was here in the church that night,' he said.

'The night of the murder?'

So Peter had at least been right about that.

'In many ways I stand guilty of the murder of Anton Fontaine.'

' "In many ways?" What's that supposed to mean?'

'It's not that straightforward.'

'You either crucified him or you didn't.'

'I was waiting to speak to him, I wanted to tell him what I thought of him, I was ready to explode.'

'So you felt full of hatred – but that isn't murder.'

'Jesus said a hateful thought is the same as murder.'

'Meanwhile, back on planet earth?'

Talking with Malcolm was like walking through treacle in a fog.

'I watched Abbot Peter leave the church and soon after I heard voices in the vestry.'

'Did you recognise them?'

'Only Anton's. He was talking to someone but the other voice was very quiet.'

'Male? Female.'

'Too quiet to say.'

'So you have no idea as to who might have been in the vestry with the vicar?'

'No.'

Tamsin wondered if she believed him. It mattered.

'And anyway, I was distracted because then Clare came in.'

'Through the main door?'

'Yes, and I was shocked to see her and disappeared back into the shadows.'

'You're good at that.'

'I was. But I'm coming out of them now, believe me. That's why I'm here talking to you.'

'And then?'

'She went to the main altar, lit a candle and stood there, gazing on it. But then there were ripping sounds from the vestry, it must have been the tape.'

Tamsin raised her eyebrows.

'I've heard how he was found,' he continued.

'And you went to the vestry?'

'No. But Clare did.'

'Clare went to the vestry?'

'But then suddenly she was running back into the church. She almost ran straight into my arms which freaked her out, but all she said was, 'Go and get help, go and get help – now!' She was whispering, I don't know why, though people do in church. Respect, I suppose.'

'Or terror,' said Tamsin. 'Perhaps she'd seen something she shouldn't and the murderer was after her. That might make me slightly hushed.'

'Anyway, I left straight away.'

'Quietly I presume.'

'You must remember I don't exist. Or rather, I didn't exist. I'm changing that now. Now I exist.'

'So where did you go for help?'

'I didn't.'

Tamsin again found herself up against the strangeness of Malcolm Flight.

'Why not?'

Malcolm raised his eyebrows in a dismissive manner and then smiled weakly.

'I just thought "Why bother"? Not proud about it, but that's what I thought at the time.'

'You just thought "Why bother?"?'

Malcolm nodded.

'I can think of one or two reasons,' said Tamsin.

'But what did I really owe Anton or Clare? That's what I was thinking. Did they ever bother with me?'

Tamsin did her best to hide the incredulity.

'So whatever was happening in there, you didn't care? Do you care about anything, Malcolm?'

'Why jump just because they command it? I thought. I've been a doormat for too long.'

Outside, a gull's scream penetrated the fourteenth-century walls. 'Nothing changes anything, you see,' he declared. 'Generations come and generations go but the world stays the same, as the book of Ecclesiastes says.'

'The one book in the bible written by an atheist I'm told,' said Tamsin, happy to be away from the holy.

'We get older and wearier but nothing changes anything. That was my thinking that night.'

Tamsin got up to leave; she had heard all she needed to hear.

'You changed things, Malcolm; because you didn't get help, Anton and Clare died.'

Malcolm grimaced. 'They made their choices in everything they did,' he said. 'It wasn't one choice that brought them to the church that night – it was many choices.'

'So that's all right then?'

'And none of those choices had any concern for me.'

'So you say.'

'I was left alone. And then I left them alone.'

'And what about your many choices, Malcolm? Where have they left you?'

'In my life? Sad. Absent. Stubborn. Cynical.'

'And guilty in so many ways?'

He sat in silence and then spoke simply and clearly.

'And that's why I'm here telling you these things. I'm making a choice to speak, a choice to be honest, to be present, to be here, now. I needn't do it but I am doing it, I have to do it. Not for your sake but for my sake. I'm not going back to how I was; I'm saying goodbye to it.'

'Bit late for that.'

'Have you ever been honest with yourself?'

Tamsin didn't reply.

'I'm starting again,' said Malcolm, with unnerving energy. 'I'm out of the shadows and taking my place in the world. Don't you realise how good that is?'

Seventy Five

Abbot Peter was feeling a little light-headed.

He imagined it was the after-effects of the chloroform in the hut. Delayed reaction ... very delayed but no doubt it would soon wear off. He'd find a book to keep him company as he waited for Tamsin, though nothing sprung readily to mind. He cast his eye along the book shelf as the dizziness returned. Was he going down with something? He turned towards his bed but knew the worst before it happened. His first instincts on entering the house had been right. There had been someone upstairs when he returned and their hand came swift and fast from behind to smother his mouth and nose with a cloth. A sweet organic smell filled his nostrils, pleasant enough, strangely pleasant but over-powering, power over, a losing of power, don't breathe in, he strikes out with his elbow, smashing the chest of the assailant, a groan behind him, a groan he knew but still the cloth strongly held and pressing, don't breathe in, keep it out, though now he was falling forward ...

He must have lost consciousness for a moment, for he was lying on his bed, hands and legs taped with a knife held gently against his throat. Leaning over him was a figure in a familiar white protective garment and a face mask. They must have kept a spare at home. Admirable planning and such a shame there wasn't a war to hand where such dark skill could be used against an enemy and then applauded with a VC.

'Oh we do like to be beside the seaside, Abbot.'

'Indeed we do, though a knife at one's throat takes away some of the pleasure.'

'Not for me.'

'I don't believe you.'

'And I'm interested?'

'This isn't pleasure, this is desperation.'

'I don't feel desperate.'

'How would you know what you feel when you said goodbye to feeling so long ago?'

'Spare me the "so-long-ago". It's such self-indulgence.'

It was the strangest of meetings: one eager to kill, one to survive, and both eager to talk.

'You know of course that every murder is a failure,' said Peter, his head clearing.

'From where I sit, your survival would be failure, not your death.'

By their own logic, this was true. There was no way he could live. He'd seen the force at work as she'd lunged forward to destroy the jigsaw at the mention of failure.

'So now it's goodbye, Abbot – or is it uncle, because you were like an uncle to me?'

'They're just labels.'

'And I must go and clear the beach hut.'

'You were a little slow there.'

'There's still time. It's a long night remember, plenty of darkness.'

The knife pressed against his neck, one change of angle from the killing cut.

But before the twist:

'I knew the Special Witness label would tempt you.'

Peter stayed quiet, in a place beyond words.

'What I didn't know was how seriously you'd take it. But to be killed for a beach hut, Peter? Was that really your imagined staircase to glory?'

Peter was thinking of the paraglider flying free over the sea.

'Your mistake is to imagine life means anything,' said the killer. 'It doesn't. And so if you think I'll feel bad as you choke, I won't. I don't have the remorse gene inside me, I'm afraid.'

The trouble with a murderer's hood is the loss of peripheral vision. It also impairs the hearing. You're in your own little world as every murderer must be. But you don't see or hear behind you and suddenly Peter is witness to Tamsin's wild eyes and the knife dislodged, now flying towards the window and then the short struggle on the floor, an unfair contest, before the detective has the assailant's arm forced firmly up her back.

'Jennifer Gold, I'm arresting you for the murders of Anton Fontaine and Clare Magnussen.'

Detective Inspector Tamsin Shah drew a couple of breaths before continuing.

'You do not have to say anything, but it may harm your defence if you do not mention when questioned something which you later rely on in court. Anything you do say may be given in evidence.'

The Abbot's niece was sitting on Jennifer while he remained in taped isolation, staring at the ceiling.

'But you didn't bang in the nails, did you, Jennifer?'

Tamsin looked at Peter aghast.

'What?' she said.

'I mean you did everything else, Jennifer, but I don't think you actually did the nailing. Well, am I right?'

Seventy Six

Sally was surprised at her desire for cleansing. Cleansing? It was not a word she'd ever used in a sermon. It had something of the nineteenth century about it with their revivalist fervour and insistence on sin. But it seemed strangely appropriate now as a very different future beckoned. It was time to take herself seriously and exchange this vanity for something authentic.

She put on her dog collar for the last time, tidied her hair in the hall mirror, stepped out into the rain, opened the car door, took refuge in its dry security, turned on the engine and pulled out into the road. She'd visit the Bishop first and then the police station.

*

'You have to let me in, Mr Micklewhite! Please let me in!'

It was strange to hear such respect on his young lips. The names Tommy usually gave Ginger were more colourfully obscene; but any port in a storm and this was a bad one for the boy.

'He flung me out and I ain't got nowhere else to go!' he pleaded.

Tommy had beaten on his door, a wet rat in the rain, and Ginger had taken him in. The 14-year-old had a large bruise across his face, darkening even as they talked.

''E just came at me and I ain't goin' back. Never.'

'We'll go back together.'

'What, me and you?'

'That's right.'

'But he'll do it again.'

'No he won't, Tommy. Believe me, he won't.'

'Will you smash 'im?'

'I'll do what's necessary.'

'I ain't going.'

'Then I'll go by myself.'

240

'He'll smash you.'

Ginger smiled. No one had ever smashed him, no one had ever got close, he'd always smashed first though now he looked for a better way. Things would be different. He'd be strong on behalf of Tommy rather than vindictive on behalf of himself.

'Do you want some hot chocolate?'

'Yeah.'

'You hungry?'

'Yeah.'

'We'll have something to eat and make our plans. Now go and dry yourself off.'

He'd protect Tommy. But first he must ring Abbot Peter with a confession.

*

Betty took the long way round despite the rain, walking the length of the sea wall, then down by the caravan park and under the railway bridge before turning right onto the main road back into town. She'd left a note for her home help, whom she didn't need anyway, and for the warden Mrs Neeves.

*

Malcolm fingered the small card, remembering the incident. The words of a stranger in the supermarket last week still haunted him, a question he'd never been asked:

'Well, what would you like to do?'

They'd talked while he stacked the eggs. It was one of his preferred tasks on the shop floor: meditative, focusing and precise. Organic medium, organic large, non-organic medium, non-organic large. Unlike the apples which rolled around, each egg box had its place and stayed there, which Malcolm found strangely therapeutic.

The customer had been pleased to find the eggs, having searched for some while.

'They're not easy to find,' she said cheerily and without hostility.

'Which is why I like them,' said Malcolm. 'I tend to be alone here.'

'Well, I'm sorry to interrupt!'

Malcolm smiled.

'I don't know why the shop is quite so keen to hide them,' he said. No one could ever find the eggs.

'The bigger question is: why are you so keen to hide yourself?'

Malcolm breathed deeply as he added to the stack of organic large.

'Oh, well – there's not much of me to put up on display really.'

'I'll have one of those, please.'

Malcolm handed her a box of the organic large. The stranger checked to see none were broken.

'But this isn't what you want to do.'

'Why do you say that?'

'Each body conveys a message. And that's the story yours tells.'

'Whoever got to do what they wanted to do?' he said wearily.

'Well, what would you like to do?'

'Me?'

'I'm not talking to the eggs.'

Malcolm was thrown, unfamiliar with the interest being shown.

'Sorry if I'm a bit direct,' she said. 'But maybe direct is good sometimes.'

'No, well –. '

'I'm a careers adviser by trade and I don't have time now. But if you ever want help, here's my card. I am a business but only because I believe in people.'

'I don't think you'd believe in me.'

'It's you believing in yourself that's more important.'

'I'm just a commodity in the market of life – and sadly, a commodity no one wants.'

'Cop-out.'

Malcolm was suddenly angry.

'You just want my business.'

The woman paused.

'Come for free. I don't want your money. Come for free and for as long as it takes. But before you do, stop hiding, stop accepting some vague unhappiness as your birthright and consider what you want.'

He'd thrown away many things but he'd never thrown away the card. And tomorrow he was going to give her a call. The stranger … who might be an angel in disguise.

*

Sally parked in the road next to the Bishop's home. It was one of those new Bishop's palaces that wasn't a palace at all but a bland fit into well-off suburbia, four bedrooms, dining room, study, wood flooring and the *Daily Mail*; less ostentatious, authority-lite and no swans in the episcopal lake to worry about. She crunched her way towards the front door but paused before ringing. There was the mother of a row going on inside.

'Well, I'm sure God will forgive you!' shouted Margaret. 'But don't wait for me to!'

Sally knew Margaret from dull 'Women in Ministry' days, a slightly distant soul. She seemed trapped by a role she had no desire for, and given the exchange inside, a husband also.

'You bitch!' countered the Bishop.

'I beg your pardon?'

'Don't make me out as the bad one here!'

'Why not?'

'Don't ever do that, I won't have you do that!'

'No, let's crucify someone else, that always helps ease the pain.'

'Bitch!'

'Pharisee!'

'I'm going now.'

'Good! Don't hurry back. I wouldn't want you imagining you're needed here.'

Sally heard the Bishop moving towards the door. She spun round quickly on her heels and made for the car. The conversation with the Bishop could wait, there'd be better moments. And by the time the front door opened and the gaunt figure of the Bishop appeared in silhouette, she was driving past, driving away, another anonymous driver taking a peek at where that Bishop lives.

And now to the police station. It was time to explain why she was the one who discovered Anton's body.

Seventy Seven

Monday, 22 December

'I knew how the meeting would go,' said Jennifer, 'and the thought of it was quite unbearable.'

They were sitting in Lewes police station, overlooking the town. It was a quieter setting at night than the Stormhaven nick, better resourced, more civilised. Lewes boasted classy middle-class gift shops, its own brewery and a police station which was also the regional HQ with its own indoor firing range, an HR department and a more expensive coffee machine.

It was just the three of them in the room. Jennifer had refused a solicitor with the words, 'Why on earth would I want one of those dreary little people.'

'They can be a friend,' said the Abbot, before receiving a killing look from Tamsin.

'Anton had let me down,' said Jennifer neutrally. 'He'd let me down very badly and unfortunately we have a Bishop who rather feeds on that sort of thing. He loves error in others; it makes him feel so much better about himself.'

'And so you made your plans?' said Tamsin, who sat with Peter on the opposite side of the desk in Interview Room 3.

Each had a coffee in front of them, Abbot Peter's with his customary extra shot to give the necessary bite. It was 2.00 a.m. and interesting conversation was anticipated. Despite the hour, no one expected to fall asleep.

'He had to be punished, obviously.'

'His failure was your failure?'

'And quite exciting in a way. People don't realise how practical I am. I've bought two run-down houses and done them up almost single handed. I know how to do things.'

'Of course, we nearly got you at the Christmas Fayre.'

'No, I was way too quick. As soon as I heard the Berlioz, I sensed danger. Who did put that CD on to play?'

'Sally. She just saw the words 'Christmas Music' on the cover and slammed it in.'

'Why do I care? Anyway, I told my mum I was going to the loo, set off in that direction but went instead to the vestry from the outside.'

Peter was momentarily impressed by this smooth operator.

'No one saw me enter and I was quickly out by the same way I came in. I went straight to the toilet on my return and hid the CD there just in case we were searched and then emerged a few minutes later.'

'So give us the killing details, if you don't mind,' said Tamsin.

This was a key moment. Would the murderer clam up in defensive fear or feel the exhilaration of the stage? For Jennifer it was the latter, her vanity seeking the freedom fields of explanation. She was a good teacher, always had been, but now it was like home, all those years ago; like showing mummy a good piece of homework.

'I once told Anton that I found something sexual about the naked figure on the cross,' she said. 'I don't know if that's allowed. Is that allowed, Abbot?'

Peter smiled.

'It was just a game really,' continued Jennifer, 'but I could see he was intrigued. He'd joke about acting it out.'

'And when it suited you, you did.'

'I couldn't believe it. He was a little boy really, just another little fellow who wanted to be mothered.'

'But perhaps not crucified,' said Tamsin.

'He was crucified long ago,' said Peter quietly. 'As Van Gogh said of himself, "A young sapling caught too young in the emotional frost". That was Anton too.'

There was a pause, a few heartbeats of silence.

'I knew what I would do,' continued Jennifer, undeterred by art history. This was her stage, not Vincent's. 'I needed a store cupboard for the equipment that no one would find and on a sea walk the answer rather leapt out at me.'

'A beach hut.'

'I found the council officer responsible for allocation, a rather pliable man called Christopher Thornton.'

'Now dead.'

'Yes, I read. Hardly my fault, though. He was clinically depressed long before my brief dealings with him.'

'And so you jumped the queue.'

'It wasn't that hard. I played the school card and perhaps one or two others. People so want to help the kids, it's rather pathetic. And they want to please me. They always have done, which helps.'

'But it was about to become Betty's beach hut.'

'I didn't realise the queue I was jumping had Betty at the front of it; nor that the hut once belonged to her father.'

'Would it have made any difference?'

Jennifer offered the joyless smile of the narcissist.

'But with that obtained, everything was easy. All that I needed was stored there as the nosy Abbot discovered. I collected them after the meeting and then called Anton. I told him I'd spoken with the Bishop and that he'd had a change of heart.'

'And that you wanted to see him naked in the vestry in ten minutes?'

'I didn't seriously imagine he'd play along. I was quite prepared for a more traditional murder, a simple stabbing, like Clare. '

'We'll get to that.'

'But he did play along, there he was sitting stark naked recording his ridiculous Christmas music. The Naked DJ was naked. And so I just thought "Why not?" '

'And so you persuaded him up onto the cross.'

'It wasn't persuasion, he was as eager as a rabbit. He liked to live close to the edge, Anton, I think it helped him to feel.'

'So he was up on the table and taped without a struggle?'

'He was as happy as Larry, believe me. In fact, he only stopped smiling when I put him to sleep. Or rather a few seconds before.'

'When he saw the chloroform?'

'He was suddenly scared then, yes, as if he knew. But as you once observed Abbot, his eyes were never far from terror.'

Jennifer paused, as though seeing those eyes again, like Macbeth and Banquo's ghost; as if for a moment, she felt something.

'And then?' asked Tamsin.

'Then stupid Clare arrived! How could I have predicted that when the Bishop had whisked her away after the meeting? But she'd come back, come back to light a candle when she saw the light on in the vestry.'

'The best laid plans and all that.'

'As every teacher knows, no lesson goes to plan.'

'Of course.'

'Poor Clare. She pushed open the door, took a look at Anton, screamed and ran out. I'd just climbed down from the table after putting the dog collar round his neck.'

'You're quite cruel, aren't you?'

'It was just for the record, nothing more, just a keeping of the record.'

'Like the record your mum kept?' asked Peter.

'She didn't need to say anything. She kept wordless records.'

'And you carried on the tradition,' said Peter.

'Maybe.'

'You couldn't break the family pattern?'

'He wouldn't have known anything about it.'

'That wasn't my question.'

'I do believe every child should earn their good marks. We don't help young people – or vicars – by applauding inadequacy.'

'So the answer's 'No'.

'He shouldn't have dragged me into his failure; that was his mistake. The Bishop called me "a pretty poor judge of a disaster". That was a bad thing to say because I'm not a failure.'

'Anton spoke of the look you gave him after the vote,' said Peter. 'He called it "the look of a maniac".'

'But now you had Clare to think about,' said Tamsin, eager to get on. Peter had the habit of taking interviews down psychological cul-de-sacs which helped no one.

'Initially, I confess, I was paralysed. I didn't know what to do, in shock I think.'

'You found Clare more shocking than Anton?' said Tamsin.

'She threatened a successful outcome in a way Anton didn't.'

There was a pause.

'And a successful outcome: was that your only thought?' asked Peter.

'What other thought is there?'

'Perhaps a thought about others, a feeling perhaps?'

'Why does everyone insist on feelings?' said Jennifer, dismissively.

'Carry on,' said Tamsin, clearly disturbed.

'I knew Clare couldn't be allowed to live. So I followed her into the church, calling out, saying she'd made a mistake, saying that I'd discovered Anton like that. I needed to sound weak, I just had to stop her leaving. And then the idea of the mad man came to me. It was brilliant.'

Peter and Tamsin sat impassive. It was the murderer's moment, her great monologue, so there must be quiet in the auditorium as the tape recorder immortalised the performance.

'It was quiet for a while and I walked round to the back of the church to make sure she didn't leave. But I kept talking, kept saying that there was a madman in the building and she believed me, thank

God. Eventually she came out from behind a pillar, frightened herself now and approached me, feeling there'd be safety in numbers.'

'A mistaken walk to safety.'

'But a great relief to me.'

'So you talked?'

'Oh yes. In fact we probably enjoyed the longest conversation we'd ever had. She actually felt very close; we could have been friends.'

'But for you killing her,' said Peter.

'She believed in my mad man completely. "This is terrible", she said. "It is," I said. "Where is he?" she asked me. I said "Up in the gallery, I think. I'm so glad you walked in, Clare. But what brings you here?"

'She said "The unwelcome attentions of a Bishop, if you must know. He was driving me home and then he suddenly pulled over. He grabbed me, wouldn't let me go! Said he loved me."

' "My God!" I said. I mean, I had zero opinion of the man already but now we were some way below freezing.

' "I just came to light a candle", Clare said.

She pointed to the altar where a single flame burned. It was rather striking in the darkness.'

'Of which you, in that moment, were perhaps the darkest part.'

'How reassuringly sanctimonious, Abbot, and such a shame your neck remains intact. But strange though it may seem, I meant what I said, you have been like an uncle to me. I'll miss you.'

'I'll miss you, Jennifer.'

'And to think I recommended you as Special Witness.'

'It was you?'

'I thought you'd be kind but, well, not quite so effective. I'm usually very good with staff appointments, knowing exactly what I'll get. The nativity was good, wasn't it?'

'The nativity was wonderful.'

It had been the highlight of Peter's Friday.

'And then?' asked Tamsin.

'I suggested to Clare that we go over to the candle. I said I'd feel safer there which she believed. I mean, sweet in a way. She just said "Good call" and those were her last words.'

'You killed her by the altar?'

'Does the "where" make a difference? We dress things well but everything's a deceit in the end. And I mean, I put her to sleep first. I only killed her when I'd put on the rather unbecoming overalls. But I did have a concern.'

'Social? Aesthetic? Moral? '

'I feared she'd made a phone call while hidden. I couldn't take the chance, I knew I had to get out so I put her behind the altar, went back to the vestry, grabbed all my gear, turned out the lights and left.'

'Without banging in the nails?' It was Peter who asked this.

'That's right. I don't know how you knew but it wasn't me who crucified the vicar. You still have another arrest to make, I'm afraid.'

There was a silence in the room, broken eventually by Tamsin.

'And then?'

'I went out into the car park and from there into the church garden where I hid. Rain pouring down of course which I thought was all to the good: visibility poor, foot prints washed away, all something of a blessing.'

'And you waited there.'

'I'd know soon enough if the alarm had been raised. It didn't seem like it had, no self-important police cars arriving with their big flashing lights. But then as I left, I saw a figure by the vestry door.'

'Who?'

'I'm sure it was someone.'

'That's helpful.'

'I don't know who it was and don't really care. They must have heard the door banging in the wind, I hadn't shut it properly.'

'So they went inside?'

'Presumably, but I didn't stay. I knew I had to get away, get to the beach hut with my luggage and then home to sort out a story. I was quite sure no one would believe Anton if he told the truth. I doubted he would, the shame would be too great and of course I'd deny it completely and people would believe me, because they do.'

'But you hadn't completed the punishment.'

'Strangely, I wasn't too concerned. His humiliation was complete, that was the thing and I was free to be the wonderful church warden again with Anton gone, because he would be. And you must remember, I now had plenty on the Bishop so he wouldn't be troubling me again.'

'How edifying.'

'But when I heard the next day someone had crucified him – well, I was shocked!'

'There are some sick people out there,' said Tamsin, sarcastically.

'But elated as well. It was better. The nails had actually been driven home.'

'All very reminiscent of your Cyril,' said Peter.

'Cyril?'

'Your teddy bear.'

'Oh, you have been busy.'

'Strong sense of deja-vu.'

'Possibly.'

'Who said the past wasn't important, Jennifer? It provided the first big clue.'

'I didn't say the past was unimportant, Abbot. I merely said it was self-indulgent.'

'Not for the detective.'

'And Clare?' asked Tamsin. 'Anything more to say about her? She was an innocent in all this.'

'I never warmed to Clare.'

'Jealous?'

'What does it matter? In those particular circumstances, I would have killed her if she'd been my mother.'

'How touching.'

Jennifer objected to Tamsin's tone. 'Why this whole thing about us having to like our mothers? Not all sacred cows are sacred, you know.'

Abbot Peter and Tamsin sat silent.

'Anyway, Clare was a flirt. She led the Bishop on. He may have groped her in the car, dirty old man, but she led him on. She pulled people towards her and then pushed them away. I watched her. Savage. Nothing was good enough for Clare. No wonder men were confused.'

'Perhaps married Bishops shouldn't get confused,' said Tamsin, unusually drawn into a moral debate. But Jennifer had moved on.

'I was the youngest head teacher in England when appointed.'

'Yes, I heard,' said Peter. 'Your mother seemed proud of your success.'

'Oh, she was always proud of my success. Like throwing meat to a ravenous lion, success was how I kept my mother happy. But she was never proud of me – just my success.'

Seventy Eight

Tamsin parked the car outside Sandy View. It was 3.15 a.m. on the longest night of the year.

On the empty roads between Lewes to Stormhaven, Abbot Peter had explained the significance of the teddy bear.

'It was her mother who told me about it.'

'She shopped her own daughter?'

'No, she didn't see it like that. She told the story with pride, not shame. I couldn't believe she was unable to appreciate the significance of her words. But she thought it was comical if anything.'

'So what did she tell you?'

'When she was at school, Jennifer crucified Cyril, the teddy who didn't win her "The Cutest Bear" competition.'

Tamsin was silent.

'She made a cross in the garden and nailed Cyril to it and then left him out there to rot, just like the Romans did.'

Tamsin looked haunted.

'Seemed a bit extreme to me too,' said Peter, for once misreading the silence. 'But as I say, her mother thought it a huge joke and quite unconnected to the investigation.'

'I don't see it as extreme,' said Tamsin.

'Okay.'

'She was just a child.'

'Indeed and the girl is the mother of the woman.'

'You don't give up, do you?'

'How do you mean?'

'With your psychological rooting around in the past.'

'Why would I? Our psychology is our decision pool. And of course then it all then began to fall into place.'

Tamsin hated it whenever Peter said 'Of course.' He used it like a Professor, trying to make light of his superior knowledge but failing.

'I remembered Mrs Pipe telling me something about Betty's obsession with the beach huts. And so I looked at the picture she gave me of her father on the beach and there he was by beach hut No.7. My guess is, things finally came to a head inside her. She'd accepted the council decision at first but her unspoken anger grew and grew until she spilled all to Ginger. He then undertook an investigation of his own and spoke to a friend in the council who discovered that Jennifer Gold now owned the hut. It was Ginger who then came up with the idea of the brick through the window, and Ginger who threw it.'

' "We know it was you".'

'That's right. But he didn't connect it to the murder; he just wanted to make life difficult for Jennifer, create some public dismay and get the beach hut back for Betty – who of course had just written "JUDAS" on the door when I met her the night of the murder.'

'But how did you know about the beach hut? I don't imagine Ginger told you.'

'He rang me earlier this evening and confirmed one or two things but no, it was Christopher Thornton's boss, Mr Robinson, who told me on Saturday that he thought it was a teacher who owned the hut. He didn't have a name and promised to get back to me. Much was suddenly making sense however. The young Jennifer crucifies teddy bears because she can't cope with failure and a teacher now had a hiding place for the nails, the sweet coincidence of psychology, tools and opportunity.'

Tamsin clapped slowly.

'But let's be honest,' she said, 'it was hardly the Enneagram which solved the case.'

'You're sounding a bit threatened.'

'I'm just stating the obvious.'

'I can agree to an extent. But it did inform it.'

'Well?'

Peter was being asked to explain himself which always made him hesitant. Inner coherence did not always translate well into words.

'Well, the teddy bear was the first breakthrough and that arose from listening; listening to her mother talk about the past. The girl is the mother of the woman.'

'So you keep saying.'

'But it was you and the jigsaw which had most impact. There, just briefly, I saw an explosion of the demonic energy necessary for murder.'

'I look forward to your Christmas card.'

'And of course any student of the Enneagram would know that the same energy would be in Jennifer. Email confirmation that she now owned the beach hut arrived shortly before she attacked me. But in myself, I already knew.'

'So why not act sooner if you were so certain?'

Abbot Peter paused, his cleverness punctured a little.

'The most certain are the most deceived on earth.'

'That's sounding pathetically gutless.'

'It's possible I was a little slow.'

'A little? You'd be dead if it wasn't for me.'

'A humbling truth I must live with.'

Tamsin enjoyed this small victory. It was good to be back on top.

'But Jennifer didn't crucify the vicar?' she said.

'No, she didn't.'

'How did you know?'

'I didn't know. But I was almost sure once I'd been in the beach hut and seen her gear. The thing was, everything there was used – except the hammer and nails. The gloves, the protective clothing, the tape, the knife, the chloroform had all seen action of sorts. But the hammer and nails, they were still in their plastic seals, unopened, unused.'

'So if she didn't crucify the vicar, who did?'

Seventy Nine

It was 3.45 a.m. on the longest night of the year. For the desk sergeant Ron Reiss on night shift, every night was the longest of the year. On the night shift, time could stand still for considerable lengths of time, the clock hands stuck. There was talk of cutbacks, of closing the station between 8.00 p.m. and 8.00 a.m. bringing the police more in line with the commercial sector. After all, who could possibly want a policeman at night when everyone was asleep?

'We'll be like the supermarkets,' as one of his colleagues observed. 'Doing special offers: "Confess two crimes, get one free".'

Reiss, seemingly glued together by dissatisfaction, complained about nights as he complained about everything. But should the cuts come, he'd miss the uninterrupted company of his Jaffa Cakes and fishing magazines. People asked him if he got lonely on his long night vigils, but for Reiss, loneliness was a crowd, loneliness was his family, loneliness was … life.

He took another Jaffa Cake from the box and was starting an article on the best trout rivers in the West Country when he heard someone at the door. The bell rang and reluctantly he pressed the door release. He didn't like his nights disturbed and looked with some hostility at the old lady making her way to the desk.

'Are you the person I should be speaking to?' she asked.

'It depends who you think you should be speaking to,' he replied, irritated already.

'Is Abbot Peter here?'

'Abbot Peter? It's not a monastery, love.'

He had a particular hatred for the Abbot's involvement in police business.

'I've come to report a murder,' said Betty.

She had the sergeant's attention for a moment, before cynicism set in. 'I see. A cat? A goldfish?'

'The vicar.'

'I think we know about that, love.'

'But I have an important message for the woman detective. Will you make sure this reaches her?'

She handed him a brown envelope, used more than once and now resealed with an environmentally-friendly stick-over, encouraging something worthy like recycling or giving generously to persecuted Christians. On the envelope was simply written 'The woman detective'.

'You will make sure this reaches her, won't you.'

'Yes, madam,' said Reiss, taking hold of it. 'I'll make sure she gets it. Now are you going to be all right getting home?'

Something about this fragile woman's demeanour melted him.

'I'm going to sit for a while,' she said. 'It's a favourite place of mine.'

Epilogue

Eighty

Tamsin returned from answering the front door. It was nine in the morning.

They'd managed four hours' sleep but the day was fine, crisp and blue with no hint of the previous night's squall. It had been a brief conversation with the constable at the door and now she held a brown envelope in her hands. She confirmed the news first given in a phone call ten minutes earlier.

'Betty was sitting on a seafront bench just five hundred yards away. She was there all night, found by an early morning dog walker. No obvious injuries.'

Abbot Peter nodded.

'It seems she just sat down and decided to die, looking out across the water.'

Tamsin wanted a reaction but found none in her static uncle. The traditional response would have been a soul-searching 'We were too late!' or 'We could have saved her!' But Peter would not be beating himself with the stick of meaningless and misplaced guilt. It was what it was.

'She left this with the desk sergeant last night.'

Tamsin waved the envelope in the air.

'I am sorry Sergeant Reiss was her last company on earth,' said Abbot Peter as he sipped some coffee.

'Shall we read it?'

The re-usable label was cut with a knife and Tamsin pulled out the letter inside, a proper letter from a time when people wrote letters, spindly writing in fountain pen but very clear:

'It was me who crucified the vicar. Not the taping but the nailing, that was me. I just came to shut the banging door and found him there. He was quite asleep, like he'd been drugged. But he hadn't been nailed there, just taped and I thought I'd put in the nails. We talked about this when you interviewed me and I should have told you then but I didn't.

How did I do it? I went to my secret cleaning cupboard and got everything I needed, overall and gloves, hammer and nails. And then I got up on the table and banged them through his wrists. He didn't move. It wasn't like when Jesus was crucified when there would have been screaming. I didn't seem to hurt him. There was blood of course but no reaction I could see. Perhaps he was already dead. Then I put everything back in my cleaning cupboard which you can go and check. It's not the cleaning cupboard everyone knows in the corridor, by the way. Every cleaner has to have a secret place otherwise everything gets taken. My cleaning cupboard is behind the spare flower stands in the gallery. Abbot Peter has promised to bury me.'

Tamsin put the letter down.

'Is that true?'

'The bit about burial? Yes, it's true. She asked me the other day, quite out of the blue.'

'And that also explains why we never found anything in the church. We were up against the cleaner's secret cupboard.'

Abbot Peter smiled with sadness.

Tamsin spoke: 'She doesn't say why she did it. Did she hate Anton that much?'

'I don't think it was about Anton.'

'Then who was it about?'

'He just happened to be in the wrong place at the wrong time as eighty-six years of rage and disappointment finally made it to the surface. She wasn't crucifying Anton.'

'She *was* crucifying Anton!'

'Look beneath the story, Tamsin.'

'It's not what police do – we nick people. It's up to lawyers and psychologists to explain them.'

'We spend our lives punishing the wrong people and Betty did that night. She walked into St Michael's, fetched her nails, climbed up on the table and crucified her disappointing parents, her disappointing God, seven disappointing vicars and the disappointing faith which had let her down so badly. She'd been as loyal as a dog to external authority, so trusting of it. But when that trust shattered, there was nothing to fall back on inside, no sense of self to reassure her – and suddenly she was dangerous. '

'The revenge of Bogbrush.'

'Quite so.'

'Ten mad minutes and everything changed.'

'And we all have those ten minutes inside us … coffee?'

Eighty One

'Are you a paedo or something?'

'I wouldn't go down that path, Mr Hucknell, or you'll find yourself in serious trouble.'

'Are you threatening me?'

'I'm informing you.'

Ginger stood outside the fourth floor flat with the front door half-open and the owner filling the space, blocking entry. Ginger raged inside, but for now, he held the force in, controlling it, using it, riding on its back.

'You're on the brink of losing your son for good, Mr Hucknell. Is that what you want?'

'What's that to do with you?'

'Enough for me to be standing here now.'

Their eyes wrestled in the silence.

'Get off my property.'

'I'm not on your property, mate, public thoroughfare this. And I'll be gone soon enough – but so might Tommy and that's why I'm here.'

'You're full of it, aren't you?'

'Be careful.'

'Or what?'

'Tommy is a member of my youth club, Mr Hucknell.'

'Paedo.'

'And he came to me last night with bruises on his face and body. He told me he'd had to get away from you. How do you feel about that?'

'How do I feel about what, you tosser?'

'I thought they were strong words from a 14-year-old boy. Obviously this isn't the first time and I informed the social services. They'll be speaking with you today. I'm just giving you the heads-up.'

'Where's Tommy?'

'Safe, which presently means out of your reach.'

'Where is he?'

'I'm here hoping you're going to be a father to him. Would you like to be a father to Tommy, Mr Hucknell? Break the vicious circle, give him what you never received? Takes a big man that, but perhaps you are one.'

The man moved to strike at Ginger but then moved back; something in him cowered.

Ginger's heart beat fast but his fist stayed by his side.

'The thing is, Mr Hucknell, no one's ever told you how good you could be.'

'Get out of here.'

'But if anyone ever does tell you that, remember to believe them.'

Eighty Two

'It's clearly a life-changing decision,' said Bishop Stephen. 'Really, you should have come round to speak about this.'

Instead, Sally and the Bishop were conversing by phone.

'I mean, you know my door is always open to you, Sally.'

'I did come round, Bishop.'

'When?'

'I came round last night but you were … busy with your own issues.'

'I was in all evening.'

'But distracted as I remember, discussing forgiveness with Margaret.'

'Oh, that was nothing!'

'You were a Pharisee and Margaret was a bitch.'

The Bishop was suddenly in sermon mode.

'Marriage is like climbing a mountain, Sally, as I hope one day you'll discover: moments of struggle, of course but then wonderful new views.'

'Well, those views are not for me, Bishop.'

'But how can you say that?'

'I've decided to become a nun.'

'You've what?'

'It isn't a sudden decision. I've applied to a community not far from here. I think I'd be a healthier soul in seclusion. I need to face a competitive spirit inside me which I do not believe is who I am but what I've become. I've been meeting with Ginger at six every Wednesday morning for the last six months to talk it through.'

'You should have come to me.'

'He's a Franciscan tertiary.'

'As we're all aware.'

'And his brother is a monk in Yorkshire. They've been wise counsellors.'

'Well, there's always a first time!'

'But it did mean we were in the church on the morning after Anton's death.'

'Reasons you held back from the police. I know, because they asked me why I thought you might have been there.'

'I decided not to tell them.'

'Well, I'll say one thing, Sally. You're right to be wary of your aggression.'

'Pot and kettle, Bishop?'

'You hide it well and persuade most people to love you. But Margaret saw it there. She sees everything, as I well know. Those skin eruptions you suffer from.'

Sally reddened with rage.

'Do you know what she said to me about them?'

'I'm not particularly interested,' said Sally 'and nor is it any of your business.'

'She said, 'The control and justification of hatred has to go somewhere.'

There was silence on the other end of the phone until Bishop Stephen continued.

'I'm sorry you were never able to warm to Abbot Peter, Sally. He was nothing to do with me, not my choice. He just arrived in Stormhaven in his ridiculous clothes and somehow stayed.'

'Abbot Peter's fine.'

'You don't need to continue with the pretence. Margaret's analysis, should you be interested, is that he was impermeable to your charms, too independent for you and then when he was made Special Witness – .'

'It was a ridiculous appointment!'

'It should have been you?'

'It shouldn't have been him!'

The aggression shocked the Bishop. Sally excused herself, put down the phone on the Bishop and wept.

Eighty Three

'I'm sorry about the jigsaw, Uncle.'

They were standing by Tamsin's car. She was packed and ready to go but leaving new bed linen as a present.

'That's very big of you,' said Abbot Peter, 'but as I've said, it was you and the jigsaw which proved so enlightening.'

'How exactly? I remember you mentioning it but rather switched off when you got onto "demonic energy".'

'It was the mention of failure that triggered your reaction. You accused me of patronising you as a failure and then launched forward with such desperate aggression.'

'So?'

'Well, you're an Enneagram three, just as Jennifer is. Suddenly her acquisition of the beach hut and her disappointment in Anton made sense. He made a very public failure of her and she had to lunge, just as she did with her teddy bear Cyril.'

Tamsin went silent.

'So you know my number?'

'How could I not know it when you've lived under my roof for five days! Not to mention working together on a case. In stressful situations we reveal ourselves like peacocks. And we've both found ourselves rather stressed.'

'But you're saying I'm the same number as a murderer?'

'You are.'

'Then I hope you're the same number as Hitler.'

Abbot Peter laughed.

'The thing is, Tamsin, it's not really about what number you are.'

'It isn't?'

'Only to begin with.'

'So what is it about?'

'It's about whether you're a healthy version of your number. Any number could murder and any number could save the world. An unhealthy Three is a nightmare but a healthy Three is a glory and it's the same for all nine points on the circle. There are no good or bad numbers, just healthy and unhealthy manifestations of them. It's what makes the Enneagram such a dynamic typology, charting the constant movement of creation and destruction within us.'

'I have to say I sensed similarity.'

'How do you mean?'

'With Jennifer.'

'Ah yes, well you would. In one sense, you will know her inside out.'

'I mean, you were shocked by the crucifixion of the teddy, I could see by your face.'

'I was, yes.'

'I wasn't.'

'No?'

'I understood perfectly. I could have done that myself.'

The waves were quiet today, the sea strangely still.

'Our inner fractures are different,' said Abbot Peter, 'which perhaps made us a rather good team.'

'We were, Uncle, though—. '

'Though what?'

Tamsin opened the car door a little.

'You did become a little independent in the final stretch, a rather disobedient special witness.'

'I seem to remember you declaring it a race.'

'Only if I won.'

'And then of course you were drifting somewhat.'

'Me drifting? What about you?! How was I drifting?'

'You became preoccupied with success rather than truth and obviously I couldn't collude. '

'Obviously.'

'But you also saved my life in a daring act of loyalty which makes you my favourite niece and honoured hero.'

'Really?'

'Undoubtedly.'

'And so maybe again?'

'How do you mean?'

'Together we could solve all the world's crimes!'

'There's a thought.'

'I mean it.'

'And my ego is singing loud songs of self-glory. But my time now must be with the community of St Michael's. There's some mending to do; some mending of things presently un-mended.'

'Each to their own.'

'But before that, one thing,' said Peter. 'Something that's been puzzling me.'

'What's that?'

'How was I excluded as a suspect from the murder enquiry quite so soon? Sally asked the question and I've never heard the answer.'

'You have Sergeant Reiss to thank for that.'

'Remind me to change my will.'

'On the night of the murder, he took a call from a member of the public reporting "a strange man out walking in the rain, in an unnatural manner".'

'Unnatural manner?'

'They thought you might have escaped from somewhere.'

'It just gets better and better.'

'So Reiss found a bored patrol car and suggested they tail you which they did, right back to Sandy View. Once here, on a quiet road and with the sea crashing in, they took the opportunity to drink their coffee and eat their sandwiches. So you had a watertight alibi, given that someone else saw the lights go off in the vestry around midnight. It couldn't have been you.'

'I did think I was innocent but it's good to be reassured.'

'I wish you well, Uncle,' said Tamsin, giving him a hug. 'And believe me when I say: you will see me again.'

'I look forward to it.'

The car accelerated away along the sea front, with the Abbot – or the uncle? – waving. She was driving too fast, people didn't drive like that in Stormhaven. Even so, it was good to have a relation in the world.

Peter paused. He took a deep breath as he looked out to sea and contemplated distant lands. Were the Sarmoun community still out there, living their secret life in Afghanistan? It seemed unlikely. Guns, bombs and reconnaissance planes would have flushed them out long ago. Perhaps they'd upped sticks and found another hideout. Or perhaps they went the way of all flesh, nothing lasts forever. The truth was, they'd probably never know that the man they sent to Europe had a son, who learned their teaching which helped solve a murder on the south coast of England. The Abbot liked the unforeseen but spilling continuity of things and felt a momentary and profound sense of pleasure, caught up in a greater outworking than his small and arrogant self.

He returned inside Sandy View. It was good to find a relation but good also when they left. 'Thank you for coming, thank you for going' as the Swedish apparently say. The house was once again his own and he surveyed the empty space with something akin to greed. He went into the study and sat down by the jigsaw ruins. He did like to bring order and he'd just found two of the corner pieces when the phone rang. It was Edwina Pipe, back in church arranging flowers with who knows what colour in her hair?

'Yes, Mrs Pipe, I'll be in the church a little later, around midday ... we can talk about the Christmas flowers then ... I remember last year's poinsettias, we went to the market early ... well the same again is fine by me, they looked wonderful ... am I looking forward to Christmas? Well, of course I am, why ever not? ... because things are hardly "stable" at St Michael's? ... very witty, Mrs Pipe ... oh, it was one of Mr Pipe's amusing asides? ... I might have guessed ... well, pass on my applause ... though I'm not sure things are ever as stable as we imagine them to be ... in my experience, there is just the fragile moment ... I'll explain later, Mrs Pipe ...'

Peter decided on some coffee, 'two spoonfuls and solitary, please'. But the phone rang again while the kettle was boiling.

'Could I come over?' asked Sally.

'Of course,' said Peter, surprised. Sally never came over. She was a most diligent visitor to every home but his. 'You'd be most welcome.'

'I've made a rather big decision.'

'Well, I'm sure you've thought about it.'

'I'd like to talk about it with you. I probably should have spoken with you earlier.'

'I can't imagine I would have been any help at all.'

'And I have a confession as well.'

'Okay.'

'You sound hesitant.'

'No, no, I er –. '

'Perhaps it's more of an apology than a confession.'

'An apology's good, Sally, preferable, I think. I've heard enough confessions for a while.'

It was shortly after he put the phone down, and as he sat with his coffee, that there was a fizzing sound in the corner. Peter looked round concerned, only to witness an outbreak of lights on his Christmas tree. At last!

And as the Abbot sat, it was a kind light.

Eighty Four

○

Afghanistan,
Late twentieth century

'*The Sarkar is dead, long live the Sarkar! The truth is dead, long live the truth!*'

In the Sarmoun Community, the immolation of the dead Sarkar and the installation of their successor takes place within two days. The new Sarkar, elected by the people, is approached by one carrying a cage containing song birds. The Sarkar reaches inside and draws one out, holds it in his hands and then kneels.

The question is asked: 'Is the bird you hold dead or alive?'

'*The bird is alive.*'

'*You have the power to kill and the power to let live. Shall the bird be alive tonight?*'

'*That is my intention.*'

The Sarkar then kisses the bird.

'*Is the truth you hold dead or alive?*'

'*The truth is alive.*'

'*You have the power to kill and the power to let live. Shall the truth be alive tonight?*'

'*That is my intention.*'

The Sarkar kisses the bird again.

'*Then let go of all you hold and let the truth fly.*'

At this point, the Sarkar releases the bird into the sky.

'*The Sarkar is dead, long live the Sarkar! The truth is dead, long live the truth!*'

In the days that follow, the newly elected Sarkar consults with representatives from the community. They also reflect on the last will and testament of their predecessor, seen only by themselves. After the passing of forty days, the new Sarkar addresses the community.

The twentieth century has brought changes. The Sarmoun community is neither the numerical or physical size of old. It has once had to move due to circumstances of gun, bomb and reconnaissance plane and the previous Sarkar lived for five years in captivity after being abducted by local militia while on a rare trip in the outside world. He was returned unharmed, older in the face though maybe truer in heart. But the community itself lives on, still found by those determined to find it, and still honeybees gathering truth from different flowers and planting it in the ashes of their old selves.

The difference on this occasion, as the Sarkar stands to speak, is that she's a woman. It is not considered of great significance, more the quiet working of common sense, Magdalena being the best candidate in most people's eyes. Towards the end of her address, spoken slowly so her words can be repeated and passed round – microphones are regarded as the enemy of community and personal truth – Magdalena says this:

'One hundred years ago, we gave the nine-pointed symbol to the world, the story of destruction and creation lived out through the nine facets of unity that is humankind. We did not offer it carelessly but after a century of consideration and reflection. It was time for the bird to fly, for the truth must always be risked. If sometimes it is abused, so be it; for sometimes it lives with outcomes beautiful beyond our imagining.

'And now, my friends, as the twenty-first century beckons, we must let truth fly again. For the past one hundred years, we have practised silence in this community, learned of its accuracy, depth, stillness and strength. And my understanding, guided by my dear predecessor and by many of you, is that we now seek a new emissary to give it to the world. As George Ivanovitch Gurdjieff, at the beginning of the twentieth century, left this community to live and teach the nine-pointed symbol, so now we seek a new prophet to send, a teacher of silence for a noisy and distracted world. Now is the hour for the world to learn silence.

'Whom shall we send? Maybe that person sits among us today or maybe, as before, they will come from the outside. Later today I travel to Bokhara. We hear of someone there who asks after us with some persistence. We shall arrange a meeting, a drink of lemon perhaps, talk a little and we shall see. Maybe we shall help them to find us. Not easily of course, for we remain a well-hidden open secret. And yes, they will still have to cross the chasm at Hell's Mouth, like young adventurer George Ivanovitch Gurdjieff, all those years ago. May peace be upon him and his family, wherever they are this day ...'

Appendix 1:
Brief Enneagram Descriptions

The One Space: Issues around doing the right thing. They believe they know the right thing to do and will correct others when they don't do it in that way. Self-perception: 'I am right.' Anger is an emotion not considered proper and therefore rejected. Anger with themselves and the world for not being good is expressed as resentment. Can lead to despair, self-hate, sense of estrangement, fear of personal annihilation. Their inner critic does not leave them alone.

The Two Space: Issues around finding an identity by creating external dependency on them. They are proud, not believing they need help themselves. Self-perception: 'I rescue people.' This hides a felt lack of inner worth and anger at those who did not bestow this on them when young. Their ego is damaged if people do not respond with suitable thankfulness. Offence taken, aggression, self-punishing. Fear of being useless.

The Three Space: Issues around achievement and fear of failure. Self-perception: 'I am successful, efficient.' They find activities/attributes that win widest possible approval in order to promote a successful 'self'. It is a false self but activity protects them from facing the deceit. Cut off from feeling. Inner crisis if activity stops, paralysis, numbness. In their background, an adult who valued them for what they achieved.

The Four Space: Issues around a sense of abandonment in their past, grandiose fantasy and rejection of ordinary things. Self-perception: 'I am unique, special.' From childhood, a strategy developed to pre-

271

vent immobilising depression. Desire for the unobtainable, pushing away that which is close. Haunted by sense of inadequate origins. Envy at common happiness.

The Five Space: Issues around the belief that people threaten something essential to their survival. Seek the corners of life, avoidant, unemotional. Self-perception: 'I am wise.' Anger at others who impinge on their privacy or cause them to feel stupid. Stockpile knowledge for security in unsafe world. Isolationist tendencies with constant question: 'When will I next be alone?'

The Six Space: Issues around trust and security. Big question: 'Where does my security come from?' Self-perception: 'I am loyal, obedient.' Scan horizon for danger, fearful people, dominated by internal debates in their head, paranoid version of reality. They don't trust the world but don't trust themselves either, so sometimes seek external authority.

The Seven Space: Issues around keeping moving, keeping options open and avoidance of sadness and pain. Self-perception: 'I'm okay, I'm fine.' Committed planners towards a bright future, they are future people running from experience of abandonment. Keen to sort things out for others with their many ideas. Struggle to express anger, lacking inner emotional substance. Often starting tasks, may struggle to complete.

The Eight Space: Issues around the need to seize control, emotional dominance and the avoidance of weakness. Self-perception: 'I am powerful, I can do.' They avoid weakness and tenderness and are angry at any who challenge their power and authority. Lust for life, unconstrained by others' rules. Relationships are protection/possession more than intimacy.

The Nine Space: Issues around the avoidance of conflict. Calm demeanour hides stubborn streak. Self-perception: 'I am set, nothing can disturb me.' Avoid inner conflict and turmoil. Tendency towards zoning-out and unfocused use of time. With little sense of their own worth, they'll sacrifice their identity to merge with others. In decline, self-fantasists. Anger is the repressed emotion – it may occasionally explode cataclysmically.

Appendix 2:
Enneagram Diagram

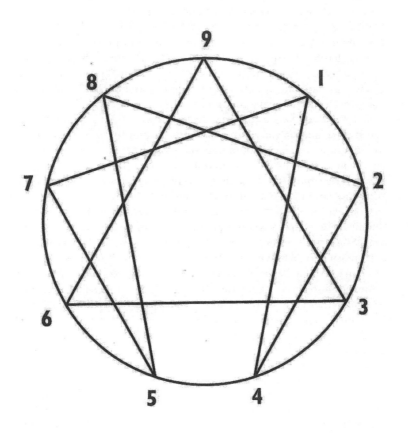

Author's Notes

If planning a day out by the sea, you will not find Stormhaven on the map. But while the name may be fictional, its history and present are rooted firmly in the real town of Seaford, where the cliff walk described is particularly dear to my heart. I hope the town's residents will tolerate the arrival of Abbot Peter. He comes in peace even if he doesn't always find it. And events and personalities at St Michael's are purely fictional, of course, with no basis in fact other than the truth that every community has its secrets.

G. I. Gurdjieff was a real figure and is accurately described here. I've stayed fairly faithful to his own autobiography, weaving in other well-documented facts about him. But while he had a powerful effect on certain women and appears to have had children with some, we have no record of him ever giving away a son for adoption and both Yorii and Abbot Peter are fictional creations.

Concerning the Sarmoun Community, there is mystery. Gurdjieff remains our primary source for their existence but do we believe him? Some are sceptical, suspecting he merely used it as an historical anchor for his teaching. Other voices support him, however. The Chilean psychiatrist Oscar Ichazo – another key figure in bringing the Enneagram to the west and no ally of Gurdjieff – also said he learned of the symbol in a Sufi school in Afghanistan. And in Hisham Kabbani's book, *The Naqshbandi Sufi Way,* he describes a Sufi symbol in which 'each of the nine points is represented by one of the nine saints who are at the highest level in the divine presence'. Meanwhile, in the odd but interesting *The People of the Secret*, Edward Campbell (writing as Ernest Scott), tells of studies in extrasensory perception carried out in the Sarmoun monastery in Afghanistan while the Sufi teacher Idries Shah mentions the Sarmouni several times in his writings, though without ever having had personal contact with them.

Russian philosopher George Ivanovitch Gurdjieff (1877–1949).
(Photo by Keystone/Getty Images; Hulton Collection.)

Reliability of witness remains an issue in all these instances; we tread warily on this historical ice. But allowing for appropriate caution, it seems likely there were Wisdom Schools in the East, teaching, among other things, Enneagram insight in various forms. And the Sarmoun community is often mentioned. In my description of the community, I have drawn heavily on the accounts of Major Desmond Martin, though events described in the final chapter are my invention.

And finally, I have done what Abbot Peter has so far failed to do; that is, get a book on the Enneagram published. *The Enneagram: A Private Session with the World's Greatest Psychologist'* is published by White Crow Books should you be interested to pursue this insightful teaching. As the Sarkar reminds us, we have only scratched the surface here. For myself, I have been both student and beneficiary of it for twenty-five years and a teacher of it for fifteen. Maybe it will become a friend to you.